Julia

EUROPEAN WOMEN WRITERS SERIES
EDITORIAL BOARD

Marion Faber
Swarthmore College

Alice Jardine
Harvard University

Susan Kirkpatrick
University of California, San Diego

Olga Ragusa
Columbia University, emerita

Julia

Ana María Moix

Translated by Sandra Kingery

University of Nebraska Press
Lincoln

© Ana María Moix, 1970.
English-language translation © 2004
by the Board of Regents
of the University of Nebraska
All rights reserved
Manufactured in the
United States of America

Library of Congress
Cataloging-in-Publication Data
Moix, Ana María, 1947–
[Julia. English]
Julia / Ana María Moix;
translated by Sandra Kingery.
p. cm.—(European women
writers series)
ISBN 0-8032-3235-7 (cloth: alk. paper)—
ISBN 0-8032-8291-5 (pbk.: alk. paper)
I. Kingery, Sandra, 1964–
II. Title. III. Series.
PQ6663.O345J813   2004
863'.64—dc22
2004048048

Set in Sabon and VAG Rounded
Printed by Edwards Brothers, Inc.

DEDICATION

For Esther Tusquets
1968

For Esther, once again
1991

Many thanks to Linda and Mom
And for Bobi, always—S. K.

Julia

She covered her head with the corner of the sheet and huddled beneath the blankets, pressing her knees up against her chest, making herself into a little ball. Her mouth was dry. She tried to control the trembling that racked her body. Her heart was pounding in her throat and the throbbing in her ears was too insistent to ignore. She tried to breathe deeply and relax her muscles. She had the impression that she wasn't getting enough air, that she was going to suffocate. Her breath, which she held for a few seconds, created an unbearable pain in her chest, and when she let it come spurting out, it sounded as if some creature other than herself was producing shrieks that would wake the whole house. She imagined, horrified, that they could hear her and would soon come into her room to find out what was going on. She dug her fingernails down into her flesh in order to finally be able to cry. If she could cry, it would undoubtedly calm her down. This had happened before; it wasn't the first time she had gotten scared at night. Her nervousness persisted for a few minutes, until she began to cry and was able to nod off in between the sobs, which became more and more subdued. The nightmares were always the same, with endlessly repeating scenes. No, she didn't want to remember the ones from before, the ones she dreamed when she was little, making her cry out, clinging to her pillow without daring to turn on the light, and scrunching down in bed until someone burst into her room, then throwing her arms around some neck, the neck of whoever it was who approached her bed. Little Julia shouted Mamá, Mamá, even though the arms that hugged her weren't Mamá's and the chest in which she buried herself belonged, at times, to Aurelia and, at other times, to Ernesto, and they would explain to her that Mamá was out at the movies or a play and was sure to be home soon. It's still early, look, there's nothing inside there, silly, don't you see?, they told her, opening the doors of her wardrobe, looking under her bed, and then once again closing up the balcony they had gone out on, to show her that no one could climb up to the fifth floor. Then Julia would fall asleep, grasping a fistful of the pajamas of the person who stayed by her side, promising: When Mamá comes back, she'll lie down with you.

But she wasn't five years old anymore, or ten; back then she could still call out for them. If she admitted her fear as a twenty-year-old, they would laugh at her. No, she didn't want to think about the unsettling scenes she had dreamed. If she were brave enough to stick her arm out from underneath the blankets to press the switch on the table lamp, the light would prove that there weren't any ghosts in her room. Just sticking her head out would suffice. But Julia was afraid that if she uncovered her face, opened her eyes, she might discover there was no light coming in through the balcony the way it should. Maybe she'd only see darkness, everything black, and, at the foot of her bed, gleaming eyes observing her, intently. Julia thought that if the eyes realized she knew about them, she would be lost. No, there was nothing. It was just a nightmare. She would count to twenty and then, suddenly and without further hesitation, open her eyes. She heard a slight noise, right next to her. She wrapped herself into an even smaller ball. Maybe it was her imagination or the shifting of her own limbs in bed. But she heard it again and then felt a weight on her body. She was on the verge of crying out; but couldn't. Her throat was dry. Maybe it was the cat. At times, at night, it climbed stealthily onto her bed. Until realizing that the sounds belonged to the cat, Julia would be frightened. Later she would hug it tightly. She waited a few seconds and moved her legs. She heard nothing. She imagined that the weight could be caused by the blankets. She had become alarmed before but, after jumping with fright, she would realize that she herself had made the covers move. It was impossible for her to breathe underneath there. She had to simply stick her head out once and for all. Maybe there wasn't anyone in the room, and, even if there were, it didn't matter. She had always assumed that she wouldn't mind dying. If they shot her or strangled her, it would be quick. If it wasn't an assassin and she saw something horrible, she would die of shock. Whatever it was, it would be a matter of seconds. Little by little, she stuck her arm out from underneath the blankets and lowered the corner of the sheet. She opened her eyes before lifting her head off the pillow. She didn't have time to close them before she saw it. First one. Then, with her eyes closed, she understood that she had seen more: one, three, then five, in an immense swath that widened toward the back of the room and, even farther back, passed through the wall in a long, endless stream. She had seen them: shapes without form, leathery and fat, their shiny eyes fixated on her. Now they knew she had seen them. She should look at them again, maintain eye contact to make them go away, so that at the very least, they didn't come closer. She should either meet their challenge or forget their presence; otherwise, they would come up to her bed and destroy everything, like in the dream. She heard the movement of their large paws; they were walking, walking. Houses fell, crushed by the monsters. At the foot of her bed, they reached the ceiling, and they were growing, growing even more. She couldn't stop them in their tracks with a look or forget about them. Her nightmare was the end of the world, the strange creatures laid waste to every city in their wake, their disgusting bodies moving slowly and heavily. Now they were in front of her, hounding her, and she wouldn't be able to scare them off. Eva, Eva. She should think about Eva. She made an effort to imagine that Eva was opening the door and running toward her bed. She, Julia, raised her arms toward her, buried her face in her chest, and told her what had happened. Julia didn't dare take a look at the door where, instead of Eva, she might catch a glimpse of one of those repugnant creatures. She closed her eyes and imagined the scene the way she wanted it to be. Eva appeared beside her bed, she believed Julia and met the monsters' persistent gaze until they disappeared completely, beaten at last. But Eva was very far away, and it wasn't possible for her to show up in her bedroom. Julia squeezed herself more tightly against the pillow. She couldn't see anything but Eva, even though she wasn't in the house, or lying in her bed. She found herself next to Eva, who offered her a reasonable explanation for the ghostly apparitions and continued to reassure her that they wouldn't return, and then she, Julia, was finally able to fall asleep.

But she found herself alone, in her bed, and the room was still dark. Nobody had come to banish the monsters, who would stay until Julia found a way to forget about them, to think about something else. Eva wasn't coming, she would never show up at the foot of her bed, not even to say good night. The only thing strong enough to conquer her fear would be the certainty that Eva could be found in the next room, or the neighboring apartment. Julia knew she wouldn't be able to do it. She had been repeating to herself for too long: I'm not afraid, Eva's with me, she's taken my hand, nothing's wrong, too much imagination, that's all, too much imagination.

Too much time had gone by for her to keep Eva's image in her head until drowsiness erased everything else. The image would get blurry as soon as she caught a glimpse of it. She should invent different situations, different words, different rooms, so that what she imagined would seem real and it wouldn't be so obvious that the self-deception was merely a product of her own imagination. For hundreds of nights now, too many nights to be able to believe it was true, Eva had come to calm her and Julia had wrapped her arms around her neck and buried her face in her chest, knowing without a doubt that it was never going to happen. She was too old to be afraid, too old to need Eva. No, she shouldn't even think about Eva. No, she shouldn't, otherwise she would fall into the habit. She already had, she knew that she needed her more every day. It was impossible to get used to sleeping without thinking about anybody, get used to living without thinking about anybody, without waiting for anybody, without needing anybody. She couldn't do it. She'd tried a thousand times, but she always needed to think about someone. It was impossible to stop thinking about Eva. She didn't want to stop. She wouldn't be able to survive. Julia thought she would die one of these nights, the unbearable pain stuck so far inside her heart that no hand could reach it, the only thing that could possibly get that far inside was deeply inhaled air. She would die one of these nights, whether or not she imagined that someone was by her side. She wasn't sure whether it was worse to enjoy Eva's imaginary company for a few minutes and then despair, or to try to finally admit that nobody was there, that nobody would ever be there, that nobody ever had been.

If she could at least turn on the light and read . . . but when she began to think about Eva she couldn't stop. Nobody else existed. She decided to imagine something different. Impossible. She only wanted to be close to Eva, she wanted her presence and nothing else. At times, when she thought about Eva, Mamá's image popped into her head. Julia didn't want to see Mamá at those times. She didn't want to. In the past she did, she wanted to see her all the time, she dreamed about her all the time, awake or asleep. She was five, ten years old. Later she hated her. She hated her for a long time with a combination of resentment and devotion. Now she didn't want to see Mamá in her dreams. She didn't hate her anymore, she was indifferent to her. She didn't want to remember how, in the past, when she would wake up at night and shout Mamá, Mamá, Aurelia would come to her room and make her be reasonable: Mamá's asleep, she'll yell at you. Little Julia, when she was five or six, couldn't understand that: Mamá's going to get mad, that's crazy. No, it wasn't crazy. She had dreamed it, she had seen it. Aurelia would pat her head with her rough, clumsy hands, complaining: With the amount of work I have to do in this house, getting up at seven and on top of all that, this little girl here doesn't let us get a wink of sleep at night . . . No, it wasn't "your imagination." She had seen it and was unable to forget it. She didn't want to sleep next to Aurelia. She wanted to see Mamá, get in bed with her and, once she was in her arms, tell her what she had seen so she could hear her say that it would never happen. She had seen a great fire. Enormous flames, the sky had disappeared. Aurelia appeared in her dream and ran with them, dragging her, Rafael, and Ernesto away, to sail off with Papá and reach the island that couldn't be destroyed. The boat passed through the flames. It was the last one that would make it to the island before the fire devoured everything. And Mamá wasn't there. She wouldn't get there in time, she would never get there. And it was the last boat. The flames were growing, growing; they landed on the island, filled with a crowd that, little by little, had left the mainland. Everything looked red, Papá's face was red, and Aurelia's too. Mamá wasn't there. Little Julia turned around in the boat, hoping to see Mamá appear. The world was going to be destroyed, and the only ones who would be saved were the ones who made it to the island. Finally Mamá appeared with her arm up in the air, waving good-bye.

She made an effort to suppress the memory of the terrified scream that woke her up. Aurelia tried to hold her back. She, little Julia, struggled to free herself from her grasp and run, between the flames, to Mamá, who was saying good-bye to her from the shore of the mainland. She needed to have Mamá reassure her that that was never going to happen. But Mamá didn't come to her room, and she, she recalled, maintained the sense of anguish from her dream until the next morning, until lunchtime, because Mamá didn't appear in the dining room at breakfast. She went off to school without telling Mamá what had happened during the night. At school, they discussed the end of the world and Judgment Day. At the end of time, the good people would be separated from the bad ones. They would take her away from Mamá, for sure. She, little Julia, was bad: everyone told her so. And she would watch the image of Mamá waving good-bye to her, while she, little Julia, was dragged off to hell. She felt like crying all morning. She held back the tears for as long as she could. Everyone always complained about her crying fits. Aurelia went around muttering in front of Mamá: What an unbearable child, you can't say a single thing to her, she's so spoiled. And Ernesto, leaving the theater: I'm not going to any more movies with little Julia, she's so dumb she cries right off the bat. She controlled herself and didn't cry at school; but on her way home, she realized she had mistaken another girl's school smock for her own; when she got home and saw Mamá, she began to cry. Little Julia remembered perfectly well the few times she had cried in front of Mamá. Mamá would be sitting on the sofa in the living room, right in front of the mirror; while she talked, she would observe herself in it and raise her hand to the nape of her neck to arrange her hair. Little Julia, sitting next to her, would bury her face in her lap to cry, wrapping her arms around her waist. When little Julia raised her head, Mamá would exclaim: Oh, oh, oh, what an ugly face! She didn't dare explain her nightmare. Maybe it would turn out to be true. She stammered. Finally she brought out the smock that belonged to the other girl and Mamá, not at all concerned, said: Tomorrow Aurelia will tell the teacher to look for yours, that's all. Little Julia continued to snivel. Mamá got tired of listening to her and made a phone call, or combed her hair, or talked to Aurelia. Little Julia followed her everywhere with her eyes, without daring to speak, to explain that she wasn't crying about the smock but: Because I dreamed that the world was destroyed by fire and you didn't show up in time to get on the boat, I was going away and you were waving good-bye to me and burning up in the flames. She didn't say anything to Mamá. She could never respond when Mamá asked her: What's your problem?, now why are you crying? She fell silent or gave a ridiculous answer. Ernesto, a few years older than she was, would sometimes remind her: You were so dumb when you were little, right, Mamá? You would cry because you didn't want to turn into a little black girl or a beggar. Julia didn't like it when Ernesto told these stories in front of other people. Ernesto made himself look good at her expense; her brother was constantly on the lookout for opportunities to show off by mocking other people. Mamá praised Ernesto for his friendliness; she glowed with satisfaction when she talked about "my son Ernesto." Julia, on the other hand, thought Ernesto was a kind of moron who had squandered all his energy on being friendly, friendly and nothing else. Deep down, he was nothing but a hypocrite. Julia often came to that conclusion when thinking about her brother Ernesto, but she ended up suppressing these thoughts. She felt queasy when she thought about him. Maybe it was jealousy, or hatred, and that idea scared her. She had hated Rafael, before his death, and Julia sometimes wondered whether Rafael had died precisely because of that hatred.

She refused to think about Rafael. She tried to convince herself that no, she had never hated him, or Ernesto either. But Mamá was always following Ernesto around. The minute she walked in the door, Mamá asked: Where's Ernesto?, Ernesto's been gone so long! Aurelia, did my son say when he's coming home? Julia began to feel indifferent toward Mamá's adoration of Ernesto. Now Julia was pleased by it; she thought that in this way, Mamá wouldn't worry too much about her. A few years ago she only wanted to be close to Mamá, to have the feeling that she aroused enough interest in Mamá that she wouldn't need anything else, an interest similar to what Mamá showed for Ernesto and for Rafael. It was after Rafael's death that Mamá started loving Julia. It hurt her to admit it, but now she would prefer it if Mamá didn't smother her with her affection. Mamá's affection flowed hot and cold. Julia had always felt like Mamá loved her on again off again. When Mamá preferred her to Ernesto, she would worry about her, she insisted on dressing Julia like girls your age, you'll have time enough for dark outfits later on. She took her to the doctor's office so that: Check her over thoroughly, Doctor, I don't know what she has, she's always in a bad mood, dozing off to sleep in her chair. Julia, deep down, was comforted by these visits to the doctor. The doctor would ask her: When does it hurt, before or after you eat? Mamá, without giving her any time, answered for her. When they left the office, Julia would pretend to be angry, but it never went any further than a few mild words of reproach; deep down she adored Mamá when she was impulsive, acting like an animal brimming with vitality. That's how Mamá was, thought Julia, unpredictable. That's how she felt loved by Mamá: on again off again.

Julia remembered perfectly that when she was four or five years old, Mamá, when she woke up in the morning, would call her from her bed. She, little Julia, would have been up a couple of hours and would be wandering around in the rooms close to Mamá's bedroom in case she decided to call her. Sometimes Mamá didn't have anything to do, and halfway through the morning she would yell Julia, little Julia. Then she would run to the bedroom, open the door, and throw herself on the bed. Mamá would help her take off her shoes, and she'd get in bed without getting undressed. Mamá would bite her ears, her nose, tickle her. Little Julia would be suffocating, unable to contain her laughter. She would cover her chest with her arms to protect herself from Mamá's attack and then Mamá would tickle her neck. She would move her arms away from her body to protect her neck with her hands, and then Mamá would tickle her under her arms. Little Julia felt the blood pounding in her head and cheeks, and uncontrollable joy made her laugh and laugh. Until Mamá, exhausted, let her head fall back onto the pillow. Then it was little Julia who would bite Mamá's ears, covering her face with kisses until, panting, she would remain motionless by her side observing her lovely profile up close, her soft eyebrows, wide mouth, thin pink lips. Mamá shut her eyes, and little Julia looked at Mamá's closed eyelids and blonde hair on the pillow, without daring to touch her. She didn't know how it had occurred to her that Mamá could die; but she thought about it a lot and saw her like that: with her eyelids closed and her lips half open; with her hair spread out on the pillow. They put a little pillow in the top part of coffins when they locked the dead people up. She knew that. Years later, Julia wondered how she had been able to imagine Mamá dead and locked in a coffin with so much detail back then. She had never seen a dead person. She didn't see one until she was six. Her paternal grandmother got sick, and the trip they took to visit her was the first one Julia could remember. Her grandparents' house was off in the mountains. Her grandmother died in the middle of winter, and, the day after they got to the mountains, the river overflowed its banks. The house was enormous, and at night you could hear the windows creaking and the noise from the river that, during the day, you could see flowing by the bedroom. She got scared. She called out. Papá told her: Mamá can't come now, she's busy. Little Julia had heard Mamá cry, she was sure of it. She didn't dare ask Papá. I'll stay, Rafael said. Rafael was nice to her, Julia believed that Rafael loved her then. She never forgot that night. Julia had been scared in that house where things that she couldn't understand took place. Maybe it wasn't the river that made the noise, but Rafael reassured her: I saw it a few minutes ago, it's coming down fast and heavy and dragging pumpkins, wood . . . , everything. They could hear crying and the roaring of the wind against the windowpanes. Little Julia didn't want to ask —but it came out without thinking— if it was Mamá who was crying. No, Rafael answered, it's Aunt Elena, God how she's carrying on, I guess Grandma died already. He got into bed, with his clothes on, and began to sing a song that you heard on the radio all the time back then: Along the green path, green path that goes to the monastery, ever since you went away, the daisies cry out in sorrow, the fountain has dried up, the lilies have lost their blooms.

Julia still remembered the print on her pajama top, the cold room which only had a white wooden wardrobe, the bed, and a chair, and the creaking of the window. The next day they made her go see her grandmother, who was already in the coffin; she was dressed in black, her face very white, her feet covered with a piece of black cloth. For a long time, every time she was cold or heard the word *river* or was afraid at night, Julia remembered the print on her pajamas, Rafael's song, the sound of the wind against the windows, and Aunt Elena crying with desperation next to her dead grandmother. Little Julia had seen her grandmother on three occasions: two at home, in Barcelona, just a few months before. Her grandmother told them the typical story and, on her final trip to the city, she claimed that a little bird had told her: They send you to do the shopping and you spend the money on candy, is that true? Little Julia shook her head very quickly and blushed. The last time, it was the day they arrived at the house in the mountains. Her grandmother was lying in bed, small and affectionate, and little Julia liked her words: You're going to be as pretty as your mother.

But, before she saw her grandmother in the coffin, little Julia was able to imagine Mamá dead. She couldn't stand it. She would panic when Mamá, playing the tickling game like the other morning, would lie very stiff in bed and she, little Julia, would call her without getting any response. Wake up, wake up. When little Julia gave up, leaning back, on her knees, Mamá would spring up all of a sudden and shout: Ohhhhh, where's that ugly little girl of mine? And the flood of kisses, bites, tickles, and little Julia's uncontrollable laughter would begin again. But it was unusual for Mamá to call her when she woke up. She only did it when she felt sick, or tired, when she didn't feel like going out. Julia remembered very well the mornings she wasted at home, without going to school. Nobody forced her to go to school if she didn't want to; even so, she searched for excuses to stay home. It was Aurelia who would wake her up in the morning and serve her breakfast. Little Julia was good at finding ways to regurgitate the milk that Aurelia forced her to gulp down: That way you won't taste it. When she felt like going to school, she didn't throw up. But on the contrary, if she knew that Mamá would stay home in the morning, she would manage to throw up or she'd waste so much time at breakfast that she'd be late for the bus that would pick her up at the front door to take her to school. The vomiting would take place when Aurelia put Julia's coat on and she went into Mamá's room to pick up her satchel. When Papá went to bed, he would take little Julia's, Rafael's, and Ernesto's satchels to his room: To see how you're doing. It didn't take Julia long to discover that Papá didn't open them except on the nights that Ernesto or Rafael, during dinner, said: Papá, we had drawing class today. Papá was only interested in how the three of them drew. Little Julia almost always drew Mamá: Mamá at the beach, Mamá and the moon. Mamá and the gypsies. She remembered two drawings that Papá ripped out of the notebook and saved in his office, saying: Little Julia has a lot of imagination, she's a real artist. Little Julia told Papá the titles of her drawings, and he wrote the letters at the bottom of the page. One of the drawings was called: *Mamá, Switzerland, and the Railroad*; the other one, which depicted a woodcutter chopping trees in front of a witch's house, didn't have a title. Papá insisted that it needed one, and little Julia dictated: *Mamá's Not Here*. Papá was like that with her: he took care of her drawings, made sure Mamá didn't make her cut her hair, and recited poetry to her. But back then, little Julia didn't pay any attention to Papá; only to Mamá. And when Aurelia got her into her coat and held out her satchel, she would decide not to go to school and throw up her breakfast. Aurelia would yell at her, make her lie down in bed for a while, and then she would leave: I don't need to be given any more damn work in this house. Little

Julia would spend the rest of the morning waiting for Mamá to get out of bed. Her sense of smell never misled her —Mamá said to her: You sniff me like a dog— and by midmorning, she knew whether Mamá would play with her or not. She would wander down the hallway, walking back and forth in front of Mamá's bedroom door, open it a little bit, without making any noise — she knew how angry Mamá got if she woke her up—, and check whether the room was still dark. She'd go to the kitchen, where half the time Aurelia was fighting with the laundrywoman who came to the house in the morning. Aurelia shouted at her: What are you doing here?, you've gotten over your tummy ache already? Go on, go play out on the veranda, get a little sun, you sure need it, see, Francisca?, it looks like they never feed this kid. After a while little Julia would go to the laundry room with Francisca, who didn't yell at her for touching the bleach. Little Julia liked to wet a finger in bleach and watch how it became soft and white and feel how it stung. Also, Francisca took the radio to the laundry room with her. Julia knew Mamá's schedule according to the order of the radio programs. At eleven she would hear: This is the end of our broadcast *Singing While You Work*. Julia would run down the hallway and wait a few minutes. On the days when Mamá went out in the morning, she usually got up when she heard that part about: This is the end of our broadcast *Singing While You Work*. Mamá would get up and, on her way out of her bedroom, would run into Julia, who would pretend she was playing in the hallway and who would get nervous when Mamá asked: So you threw up your milk again? Aurelia would start to explain, and Mamá would cut her off: Fine, fine, so give her something else for breakfast. And she would close herself in the bathroom until Francisca's radio announced: What do you know, Josefina? For great blankets and mattresses, visit our store: La Mallorquina. And do you know where to find it? In Galerías Maldá. Little Julia would count to thirty and plant herself by the bathroom door; Mamá, when she was done with everything except combing her hair and putting on her makeup, would open it and let her in. Little Julia would ask: Can I go with you?, out of force of habit. She could predict the no before it left Mamá's lips, because when Mamá decided to take her along, she would tell Aurelia to get her ready before little Julia even asked if she could go. Little Julia sat on the edge of the tub and watched how Mamá followed her eyebrows with the tip of the pencil while she explained that: I'm going shopping and you'd have to be on your feet for a long time, or I'm going to the beauty parlor and you'd get tired of sitting still, then you always get restless and begin to fuss. Julia would count the black tiles on the wall. If she finished counting before Mamá finished getting ready, she'd talk back and insist on going with her; if she didn't finish by the time Mamá left the bathroom, she'd stay home. And she counted, slowly, very slowly, because she knew that when Mamá said no, nothing could make her change her mind and she became infuriated when Julia insisted. Mamá promised to bring her a surprise when she came back, a surprise that she usually forgot, because: Time just flew by . . . She would follow Mamá to the door and, then, go out on the balcony, standing there until Mamá disappeared around the corner. Then Julia would regret staying home from school. The wait until lunchtime would seem endless; on the radio they still had to play two soap operas, the program with listeners' questions, and the ad for Cascabel. Mamá usually returned home when the radio was playing prelunch appetizer music or *Motor on Wheels*. She regretted not going to school, but at school she would have spent the morning imagining that: maybe Mamá didn't go out today and I would have been able to be with her.

If Mamá wasn't up at eleven after *Singing While You Work* had ended, Julia would wait calmly for quite a while; she knew that Mamá wouldn't wake up until Francisca's radio said: This is EAJ Radio One Barcelona, the time is exactly twelve o'clock noon. And when Aurelia and Francisca insisted: Now be quiet, the soap opera's about to start, she went leaping down the hallway, full of joy, because she knew that it wouldn't be long until Mamá woke up, that Aurelia would respond to her call muttering: Great, she always has to go and wake up when the soap opera's starting, and Aurelia would explain to her about the milk, and Mamá would yell Julia, little Julia, and the two of them would play in bed.

Sometimes, on the other hand, she didn't want to stay home for anything in the world. It was when Rafael was sick and Mamá didn't leave his side. There were days when Aurelia would announce: You're not going to school today, Rafael's sick. And Julia would get upset. She was familiar with those endless mornings when Mamá would yell at her for nothing: Don't make any noise,

Rafael's asleep, get out of the bedroom, leave me alone right now, I have enough problems as it is. Aurelia, take her to the store with you, she's just getting in the way at home. And while they were shopping, Aurelia would explain to the clerks and the ladies who asked how the señora's boy was, that the poor angel suffers from horrible fevers, and he's such a little darling. Whenever she could, little Julia would go into Rafael's room and stand right by his bed so she would catch his disease. Rafael stayed in bed, playing or listening to Mamá sweet-talk him, trying to get him to have some food. Julia remembered how hungry she'd get when, in an attempt to get Mamá's attention, she would refuse to eat. But in the end she gave up. Mamá would tell Aurelia: Let her be, this way she'll eat more at night. Or she'd slap her a couple of times, screaming: I'm tired of all your foolishness. Aurelia diagnosed: Jealousy, when they found her sniveling in the corners or spying on Mamá, who was lying next to the sick boy, or when little Julia didn't want to give Rafael her toys. Rafael liked fooling around with some of little Julia's toys and, when he was sick, he would take advantage of the power he acquired at home, in comparison to Julia, and demand her colored pencils, her storybooks, her paper dolls . . .

She noticed the wet pillow stuck to her cheek. The same thing always happened: it started when she became frightened, she would calm herself down by thinking about Eva, and then, she would be unable to curb her thoughts. She turned on the lamp on her nightstand. She didn't like the light that came from small lamps: half the room remained in shadow, and she was afraid she would discover strange images in the corners. It reminded her of churches, of wakes, of the interior of Romeo and Juliet's tomb that scared her so much when she saw the movie. She had gone to see *Romeo and Juliet* with Rafael, Ernesto, and Aurelia in a theater near their house where they let them in even if the show was for adults only. The movie, back then, really frightened her: it had dead people and coffins in it. Aurelia had the habit of singing while she bustled about the kitchen. After seeing that movie, Julia would cover her ears every time Aurelia began to sing: "Did You Ever Hear That Coughing Sound?" . . . Every time Aurelia belted out "Did You Ever Hear That Coughing Sound?," little Julia heard *coffin*, without being able to help it. At night, when she went to bed, she tried not to think about dead people or cemeteries; but "Did You Ever Hear That Coughing Sound?" would pop into her head, and she would immediately see a coffin. And Mamá would be inside the coffin, she was sure of it. She imagined her inside the coffin with four candles burning around it. She would never see her again. She would always be alone with Papá, who was never at home, and with Ernesto and Rafael, who were constantly chasing after her, untying the bows on her braids and telling her horrible things under their breath to make her cry: You'll turn into a little black girl and Mamá'll sell you off to a circus. Mamá would laugh when little Julia told her: The boys say you're going to sell me to a circus and they'll make me pass the hat there. Julia would get mad when Mamá made fun of her, but she thought it would be even worse when Mamá was dead: she would never be with her again. Then she remembered Bambi, alone in the woods after his mama was hunted down, and other movies like *The Martian Invasion* and *When Worlds Collide*, in which thousands of people died and you saw cities flooded with water. From time to time a child would appear all by himself, crying from the rooftop of one of the houses that remained standing. Thinking about Mamá's death caused her immense pain, she could barely breathe. That's why she didn't want to think about Romeo and Juliet, or remember "Did You Ever Hear That Coughing Sound?," because she immediately saw the coffin and then Mamá, dead. She stretched out her arm and turned on the light switch, afraid that she would discover something horrible. The next morning Aurelia would find the light on, but she wouldn't yell at her. Mamá had come to the conclusion that it was better if Julia slept with the light on rather than bothering her at night.

Julia got used to sleeping with the light on and did so until she was sixteen. She even turned it on now, when she woke up in the middle of the night and couldn't get back to sleep.

She lit a cigarette. She worried that if she smoked she wouldn't get back to sleep for the rest of the night; tobacco woke her up even more. She didn't like to read that early in the morning. She could only think, think. She didn't want to. For Julia these moments of insomnia were like pulling on an endless thread that got tangled up little by little until it turned into such a knotted mess that sleep was the only thing that could free her.

It began when she woke up, startled, in the middle of a nightmare. She was afraid. She took refuge in Eva's image, in the strange passion she felt for Eva. It was impossible to break the chain of images that formed in her head. In order to flee from one image she would turn to another one, which would lead to another, and then to another, and to another, and to another. She made an effort to remain motionless in bed, frozen, to close her eyes and not think about anything. Then scenes, words, observations gathered during the day would burst into her head. Nothing special had happened in the last few hours, nothing out of the ordinary, nothing important that could create the tension that prevented her from resting peacefully. Although it was true that it was never anything out of the ordinary that kept her awake. She often woke up around one or two in the morning and found it impossible to fall back asleep.

She had been with Andrés that morning. Now, with her eyes closed, she saw herself, in class, observed by Andrés. She saw herself in the university courtyard, strolling or chatting with some classmate, beneath Andrés's gaze; having breakfast in the cafeteria next to Andrés. Always Andrés. Andrés suddenly calling her name when she was on her way out of class; Andrés leaving the library when she, tired of wasting time talking with different people, was going out to take a walk in the garden. Andrés would say, in his gentle way: Oh, well, I'll go with you for a while, I just took some notes for tomorrow's class and . . . She was sick of running into Andrés five or six times almost every morning at school. He would pick her up at home in his car: If you don't mind, of course. He would wait for her after her first class and: Let's have breakfast together, we still have half an hour until they open the seminar room. They would get together halfway through the morning, out of force of habit, before

Andrés began to teach his class, and then an hour of class with Andrés. As well as the times when Andrés would leave the seminar room or the library to smoke a cigarette and would inevitably run into her in the courtyard, sitting on a bench. Andrés would sit next to her: Just for a minute, long enough to have a cigarette and find out what you're thinking about. She wasn't thinking about anything. That was the truth. But Andrés always asked: What are you thinking about? And she had to respond: Nothing. She wasn't thinking about anything that she could explain to Andrés.

She was irritated by Andrés's curious pursuit. At lunchtime he took her home again. They would head straight up Balmes Street, and he wouldn't stop talking about his work, how incredibly stupid some of the students were and: Listen to the nonsense So-and-so said to me, I asked . . . and he replied nothing more and nothing less than . . . When he had to stop at a traffic light, Andrés would take advantage of the opportunity to look at her and smile. How're things going for you, Julia? She would turn, facing the street, and pretend to pay attention to Andrés's words: Look at this traffic, God! The trip with Andrés was always the same, the same things always happened. At Balmes-Provenza he would say: Wait just a second, Julia, I'm going to grab the magazines. Andrés would get out of the car and then come running back with two or three magazines that he would put in the backseat. I'm parked illegally, he would always apologize. But the next day he would park in the same spot. Julia had enough time to see the two entrances to the metro on the two street corners. The metro and the people who came up the stairs and stopped next to the traffic light disgusted her. Andrés pushed the frame of his glasses up with his index finger and smiled at her, as if apologizing, while working the steering wheel clumsily to escape the illegal parking space. He would tell another humorous anecdote about the work his students did. He didn't stop talking until they got to Diagonal, where he said good-bye: See you later, Julia. I'll call you this afternoon.

Julia knew that she could tell Andrés: Don't call me again, I don't want to see you anymore, leave me alone. And Andrés would respect her wishes, he would get out of her life in the same way he had brought himself into it, without excessive words, discreetly. He exhausted her. Even when Andrés wasn't next to her, she felt his presence. It irritated her to walk out of class, find him in the doorway, and hear: Let's go, let's get something to drink. Or later, around two: Come on, I'll take you home if you want. In the university cafeteria, courtyard, or hallways, their classmates watched them, her and Andrés, with little giggles and whispered commentaries. When Andrés left, they would say to her: Wow, you're hanging around with the Language Assistant! Deep down, Julia didn't care. The whole gang of idiots who swarmed about in the university got on her nerves. Over the course of the morning they showed up in the courtyard, scattered, or in little groups. It seemed to Julia that they all had the same face, horrible mouths that would open and close and from time to time smile sarcastically. They seemed ugly and dirty to her. Although she admitted that taken individually they weren't bad. She observed them from the second floor and forgot about the shouting, the continuous movement through the hallways, at rush hour, as Andrés called it. Andrés would tap her on the back, asking, What're you thinking about, while she imagined stones raining down on the hundreds of students who wandered from place to place, or how much fun it would be to nail one of their feet down and douse them with gasoline from the building's top floor. Andrés's What're you thinking about brought her back to reality. And once again she would hear the murmur of voices, stumble against someone or other, realize that every morning she lost two or three hours on mere trifles and that after a few minutes she should go into the classroom, copy some notes, and return the original to its owner. But she had gotten used to Andrés's company in the morning, sharing their first coffee of the day (Let's see if this wakes me up, last night I worked really late, I had to prepare an assignment and . . .), breakfast in the university cafeteria next to Andrés, walks in the garden with Andrés. She had gotten used to it, and she felt absurdly lonely and bored on the days Andrés didn't come to school, when she had to take her walk alone, have breakfast alone in the cafeteria crammed full of students, and wait alone in the courtyard, among the couples and groups of students, for another class to begin.

But she didn't love Andrés. He took the liberty of asking her What're you thinking about, and she told him Nothing. Well it must have been something very lovely or very sad, he would say, looking into her eyes and pushing his glasses up with his index finger; he lowered his head and Julia noticed the beginnings of a bald spot.

She felt some affection for Andrés then, although she still hated him for everything, for sticking his nose into her business, for asking her What're you thinking, what're you doing this afternoon, what'd you do this morning, did you like the movie? For being nice to her, worrying about her, because she, Julia, knew that in a way Andrés understood her and was aware of the fact that by lavishing her with his affection and protection, without pressure, without words, without pacts, without promises, without asking anything of her, she would never send him away. It irritated her: he knew how to treat her and get what he wanted. It irritated her because he was good, intelligent, and he could come to understand her; also, she might begin to want and allow herself to be understood. Andrés, when the clock tower struck one o'clock, would say: Well, I'm going to go see if I can find Doctor So-and-so; I'll wait for you over there. It was a lie. Andrés always said I'm going to go see if I can find Doctor So-and-so because he knew that she, at that time, liked to look for Eva. Eva had just taught the literature class and, when she managed to get away from the students who grabbed any opportunity to ask pedantic questions in order to suck up to the professor, she would get together with Julia. Let's have a drink, but not here, Eva would say, and they would leave the building. Hearing Eva pronounce those words made spending the morning in the gray building that smelled like mildew worthwhile. Julia couldn't care less about the major she had picked. She didn't care about anything. Her studies bored her; in fact, she barely studied. Only for Eva's class, nothing else. She ignored the other subjects until final exams.

She wondered how it had been possible to tolerate five or six hours of studying a day in her recent high-school years. Now boredom prevented her from paying attention. She would open her books and close them after a few minutes. The movies she decided to see from time to time didn't distract her. She would often make an effort to become interested in something, to follow the plot of a novel or the explanations in a book attentively; she didn't get any further than the first few pages. For the same reason, she would have left the movie theater if she hadn't been there with someone and if she hadn't thought that it didn't make any difference to her whether she spent two or three hours sitting and thinking about her things in the darkness of the theater or in the patio of a café or at home waiting for an appropriate moment to leap like an enraged lion at the slightest observation, by Mamá or Ernesto, that she considered impertinent or out of place.

Going out with Andrés, going to class in the morning, going to movies, reading, or listening to records bored her as much as staying home. But the last option also depressed her. She couldn't stand Mamá or Ernesto. Even if they weren't home, the rooms, the furniture, the hallways, everything, absolutely everything, seemed heavily laden with their presence. Julia took advantage of every possible opportunity to lock herself in her room and be alone. But even in there, it smelled like them. As soon as she got home, she closed herself in her room: I've got a headache, I'm going to lie down for a while before lunch. Leave me alone, Mamá, I'm studying. All lies. She would stretch out in bed, that was the only thing that was true. She wasn't sick and she didn't study. She would just lie in bed. She would leave the books on the desk and take a novel from the shelf. She liked to page through books when she was lying around. She hated her room, the flowery wallpaper, the complicated ceiling molding that wound around in the corners and in the middle where the light fixture was; the fitted wardrobe in which, for a long time, she was afraid of finding, as soon as she opened the ostentatiously decorated doors, her brother Rafael's corpse. She detested the terry-cloth dolls scattered about on the shelves of the little library.

Every book, every doll, the walls, the bed, the library, every object in her room smelled like Mamá's perfume. It was an acidic smell, like lemon. Lying in bed, she felt on edge, cornered. The balcony faced Balmes Street, and there were times when she just couldn't bear to hear the thousands of traffic noises that weren't even alleviated at night. The squeal of slammed-on brakes, an engine driving noisily away, the continuous stream of passing buses and cars sapped her energy. And during the day she couldn't stand spending time in the room filled with motifs which weren't feminine, as Mamá and Grandmother Lucía said, but childish.

Mamá got home and Aurelia called Julia: It's time for you to come to the table. Dear Lord, that girl. And Mamá, just in from the street, would start like always: The traffic!, you can't even drive in this city, if I told you that I had to drive all the way down to . . . and on top of that they gave me a fine. And Papá, without putting down his newspaper: Well, don't pay it, they should at least have to go to the trouble of coming here to collect. Hi, Julia. Hi, Papá. And Mamá: Oh, you're here?, it'd be nice to say something to your mother, don't you think? What a sight, with that hair. Don't tell me you went out like that.

In truth, Papá didn't matter to her. She had looked down on him ever since he returned home after nine years away. Invariably she would find him sitting in his armchair, reading the paper all day or sleeping in front of the television set. As soon as Papá returned home, everything was over between him and Julia. Julia thought that maybe her life would have been different if Papá hadn't come back, if he hadn't sold himself again to Mamá and Grandmother Lucía, if he hadn't sold her too, in order to enjoy the damn peace and tranquility that he demanded at all times. Sitting in his armchair, he would wake up or lift his eyes from the newspaper: You can all do whatever you want, but leave me out of it; I don't want to be bothered.

Since Papá's return, since the night that he came home (after continuous arguments on the phone between Mamá and various other people) and locked himself in the living room with Mamá, Grandmother Lucía, and Uncle Ricardo until three in the morning (she stayed awake, alert. Ernesto came into her room around one and told her, pleased: Papá's staying, aren't you glad?), she thought that he, Papá, was aware of her accusation. And what's more: that Papá understood it and, deep down, approved of it.

The next morning when she saw Papá in the dining room, having breakfast with the whole family, smiling, as if nothing out of the ordinary had happened, she had to restrain herself from bursting into tears, from insulting him and spitting in his face, from accusing him of immense weakness, cowardice, poverty of spirit, and a lack of love for her. He had disappointed her. Julia, as soon as she exchanged one look with Papá, believed that he knew her feeling of deception, of shame. She believed it because of Papá's clumsy words during that first breakfast at home, after nine years. You look very pretty, Julia. I've seen your cat, it's huge. Her eyes were full of tears, she pressed her lips tightly together, her chin trembled. Papá smiled weakly at Mamá and, then, at Julia; he stared at the mug of café con leche and looked at Julia again. She was sure. She didn't doubt it for a second. She believed Papá's look was his way of apologizing for being home, having breakfast with Mamá (indifferent, calm; after all, his return meant nothing to her, just as Papá's nine-year absence meant nothing), with Ernesto, chatty and grinning (he had his new suit on and had combed his hair more carefully than normal. He seemed happy, satisfied, not because Papá was there, but because he had returned. That return was Mamá's triumph and Ernesto was celebrating it fully, scandalously), and with Grandmother Lucía, sitting upright in her chair, tall, bony, ordering Julia in a hoarse voice: Put some sugar in your milk, it makes you strong.

For a long time, Julia never doubted her alliance with Papá. She thought it was obvious every time Mamá attacked her and expected Papá to back her up during her lecture. Papá agreed with Mamá, but with a simple: Yes, it's true, but what difference does it make?, leave me out of it. Immediately afterward, Papá would sigh and shake his head; he would smile and hug her. Julia accepted that sign of weakness, of apparent deceit, as one of the many facets of the game that had been established between them since Papá came back. Beneath the apparent collusion with Mamá, Julia tried to find evidence of Papá's link to her. She found it. At times it was slight: a simple movement of his head, a vague gesture with his hands, a look out of the corner of his eye. Julia believed she had found it, which sustained her last hope that Papá still belonged to her in some way, that Papá remained more connected to her by their secret pact than he was to the others by living with them every day.

Because of this, now, seeing him conquered, defeated in his armchair, demanding peace and tranquility, she despised him. She couldn't say anything to him, he wasn't connected to her after all, Papá had never understood their alliance. Julia often wondered whether the ancient pact with Papá had been a mere fantasy or whether, on the contrary, Papá had been sincere when he returned home and his betrayal hadn't begun until days had gone by and Mamá and Grandmother Lucía defeated him little by little in the daily all-absorbing fight. Julia pondered the question, but she never spoke about it with Papá. She only broached the subject once, painfully. One year ago. Julia was lying in the hospital bed. Her whole body ached and she had a strange sensation: as if her head had grown bigger and her stomach was full of holes. She was convinced she was going to die. She was afraid, she needed someone by her side. Someone opened the door. Papá came in. She had no interest in seeing him, but she was grateful that it was him and not Mamá. She remembered vaguely that when Mamá appeared by her side (she wasn't conscious of how much time had gone by), she screamed at her to get out. She didn't feel any desire to see Papá, but his presence didn't irritate her. Such a terrible thing, Julia. Such foolishness . . . She was on the verge of accusing him of it then. It didn't hurt her anymore. It didn't matter to her. But now Papá was feigning understanding and interest. He took the liberty of asking her why. Mamá would, without a doubt, be pacing nervously through the hallways, with Ernesto, Grandmother Lucía, and Uncle Ricardo by her side. Ernesto would console Mamá, he was never at a loss for words. He was a charming son, as Mamá said. She didn't want to look at Papá. The sunlight flooded through the window and intensified the whiteness of the room tiles. All that brightness hurt her eyes. She fixed her gaze on the white sheets. It was impossible for her to control the trembling of her body. She was afraid. She didn't even know if she was going to die, but she didn't want to ask Papá. She bit her lip in a last attempt to remain silent, but in the end she said to him: Why did you come back? What did you say, Julia? You returned home. Papá put his hand on her forehead. Julia heard how he murmured: My God, she's delirious. She felt like laughing at Papá's tragic expression. A nurse came into the room: You should go, it would be better, I'll give her a shot, a tranquilizer. Julia turned toward the window and began to cry, very slowly, silently. The alliance with Papá had never existed.

Seeing Papá at lunchtime had many drawbacks and only one advantage. It made Julia anxious about some confusing stories, passages from another time that brought out contradictory emotions in her. The only advantage was that Papá invariably demanded peace and tranquility when Mamá and Grandmother Lucía began to trap Julia in a ring of accusations.

Little by little her irritation at sitting at the table, next to Ernesto, would turn to anguish. Mamá sat in front of Julia and, on the two ends, Papá and Grandmother Lucía. You didn't come home until after ten yesterday, Mamá would say, looking at herself in the writing-desk mirror. Mamá's pale eyes stared at her, waiting for a response.

Although Mamá was still a beautiful woman, Julia thought that there was no longer even a trace of the beauty she had admired so much in the past. Mamá had cut her hair, her face was practically wrinkle free; she maintained her daring air, cold expression, and the firm voice that could turn suddenly frivolous and flirtatious. But Mamá's earlier beauty had been lost forever. Julia remembered a time in her life when Mamá's presence was a sweet, agreeable presence. There was a brief moment of time (that's how it seemed to Julia) when Mamá brought about a type of craziness in her. She created a party atmosphere, a childhood carnival filled with wild laughter. Anything that little Julia said or did was enough to make Mamá burst out laughing. Little Julia, you ugly thing, come over here. She grabbed her. Little Julia felt herself lifted through the air in Mamá's arms. I'll throw you out the window, you ugly child. Mamá, laughing, would open the window and pretend she was going to throw her out into the street. Julia remembered being filled with elation when Mamá would set her on the windowsill. Little Julia looked down and she was filled with dizziness and the deafening sound of the cars circulating in the streets below. She would shout with joy, unable to contain the screams and laughter that burst intermittently from her throat as Mamá subjected her to constant flights from the window to her chest and from her chest to the window. Her two brothers, Ernesto and Rafael, would come running toward little Julia's screams and laughter, and they would beg Mamá: My turn, my turn. Little Julia first, Mamá insisted. Of course, complained Ernesto, because she's the baby and a girl, right? Little Julia felt like she was Mamá's favorite, almost unique, when Mamá lifted her from the floor once again and swung her from the inside of the house toward the street. Should I really throw her out?, she asked the boys. Ernesto and Rafael would sing out in unison: Yes, yes, throw her out the window, let her go; drop her, drop her. They would laugh, all four of them laughing and screaming nonstop until the blood pounded in their throats and they couldn't stand any more. Later, worn out, Julia and Mamá would throw themselves on the sofa. Little Julia would sit on top of Mamá, biting her ears, her neck, burying her face in Mamá's blonde, tangled hair.

Now when Mamá spoke —except when she was talking to Ernesto— her mouth would be hard and her eyes, cold and penetrating. You didn't come home until after ten yesterday, she repeated. I was . . . studying . . . Her voice would get stuck in her throat when Mamá stared at her. She felt clumsy and furious. With whom?

She was irritated by Mamá's control. She couldn't stand being questioned, having them interfere in her private life. She remained silent so as to infuriate Mamá. She stared at the tablecloth. She felt her cheeks turn red and she didn't want to blush in front of Mamá. Later, Ernesto chided her: Sis, you're such a fool, you chicken out over nothing, look at me. I do whatever I want and nobody dares to open their trap. The room closed in on her: the long table, Mamá, Ernesto, Papá, Grandmother Lucía. She made an effort to keep her eyes on the tablecloth. She knew that if she looked up and caught sight of the wall in front of her or Mamá's gaze, she wouldn't be able to control herself. But even looking down, she saw Mamá, the display case full of figurines, the plates with golden dragons hanging on the wall, the horrible paintings that Grandmother Lucía considered true works of art —six lugubrious landscapes distributed throughout the dining room—, as well as the heavy and oppressive green velvet curtains, the two armchairs —also green—, plus the things that were behind her back —even without seeing them, she felt them, their weight pressing on her body—, the writing desk with the mirror which filled the wall, its counter top seemingly breeding clocks. A small covered veranda finished off the dining room, with more armchairs, a sofa, a table, green curtains framing the large windows, and more plates decorating the walls. The whole house was the same. Julia would bite her fists when she walked through it, not knowing what to do. Three display cases full of figurines along the dark, endless hallway. At the end of the hallway, the living room: three more display cases, with even more of the same figurines and other horrible objects, and her grandfather's valuable collection of clocks —as Grandmother Lucía always said. Four armchairs, the sofa, oil paintings of Mamá after the wedding. Enlarged photographs of Ernesto at his First Communion, of Rafael at his First Communion, of her, Julia, at her First Communion, and a piano that nobody ever played.

The only place in the house where Julia felt comfortable was the library. Grandmother Lucía often told her: One could say that this is where your grandfather lived the last years of his life; he spent hours and hours in there, alone, reading, without letting anybody interrupt him. Julia liked that room. It was the only place in the house where she didn't feel everyone else's presence. In the library she felt alone, pleasantly alone. The dark room had its own particular smell. The balcony looked out over the street. Julia opened the shutters halfway, and the breeze made the long curtains sway gently. She could let whole afternoons go by without doing anything, walking around on the creaky parquet, silently. Books filled three of the walls all the way up to the high ceiling, and on the fourth there was a large portrait of her grandfather. Her grandfather had died when she, Julia, was a baby, and she had no memory of him. In the portrait he was thin, with sideburns, a mustache, and sparkling eyes. She imagined that her grandfather was a unique individual. Most of his books were about medicine, that was his profession; but there were also numerous novels, especially French and Russian novels, a large collection of pornographic literature, German philosophy, Egyptian archaeology, history, and a great number of authors she didn't know, as well as yellowing pamphlets about the lives of some music-hall singers. In the library there was an old gramophone with her grandfather's records. The records were kept inside a small redwood cupboard. Classical music, zarzuelas, old-time variety singers, tangos, and some copies of musical reviews whose librettos had been penned by her grandfather. It was before he met me, explained Grandmother Lucía, childish pursuits.

Julia closed herself up in the library when there was nobody home, otherwise someone often interrupted her. What are you doing here? Why don't you go out? Do you need money?, if it was Papá. If it was Mamá who came in: So, you're upset already, you can't handle even the tiniest commentary, don't you know anybody you can go out with? Then Mamá would begin like always: You don't have any friends because you're odd, no one can put up with you, you're not friendly. And she insisted on calling one of her friends on the phone to: See if your daughter's free this afternoon because, Girl, mine's just impossible. Well, yes, yes, she's fine; no, the doctor saw her not too long ago, oh, thin, but you know, her age and this constant bad mood, she's odd, very odd, when I was her age, well, you know perfectly well, but Julia, I don't know, Girl, I don't understand how . . . Oh!, Ernesto's just fine, wonderful . . .

At other times it was Ernesto who burst into the library and destroyed Julia's quiet refuge with his chatter. Listen, you pain, if you make yourself presentable and get rid of that long face, I'll take you out and then we can meet up with some friends in my studio, I'll show you my latest painting, a masterpiece, what do you say?, what do you think of this shirt?, do you like it?, does it go with my pants?, we've got to take care of our looks, it's important to have some tricks up our sleeves . . .

Ernesto always said we've got to take care of our looks, it's important to have some tricks up our sleeves. In fact he devoted himself to it entirely and in his free time he fooled Papá by studying architecture and Mamá by making paintings, horrible in Julia's opinion, but brilliant according to Mamá. What he really excelled at was dressing elegantly. He was tall, thin, had blond hair like Mamá, and blue eyes. He smiled constantly and complimented everyone, usually at inappropriate times and without any compelling reason. Because of that, Ernesto created the impression of being insincere, from which he escaped in the only way possible: by adopting the innocent air of a large child and smiling one of his best smiles, making his gaze clearer and more luminous.

In spite of the intrusions, the library was the only peaceful place in the house. The rest of it closed in on her, especially the dining room at mealtimes. Mamá would begin by flaunting the control that she wielded over her, most often gratuitously, as if wanting to make her understand that she could still exercise it even more strictly. The argument which would begin between her and Mamá would change course. Papá would take Julia's place, he would be the one on the receiving end of Mamá's hard, cold looks. The rest of the meal would be accompanied, like usual, by the same assertions as always, the eternal accusations on both sides. Why did you return?, nobody asked you to. I'm going to leave again any day now. It won't be the first time, it doesn't matter to me. I know perfectly well that it doesn't matter to you . . . And you shut up, Ernesto, and get that disgusting mop of hair cut. What's the matter with Ernesto's hair?, argued Mamá. It's effeminate, every bit of him is effeminate. Mamá, I won't stand for his insults. Then put some decent clothes on and get your hair cut. The argument got more and more muddled, the nine-year absence was brought up, and you know why I took off. Oh, yeah?, what are you saying? Don't make me talk . . .

In fact, staying at home bored her as much as going out with Andrés, going to class in the morning, watching movies, reading, or listening to records. But, besides boring her, the house and its inhabitants depressed her, irritated her. At least Andrés talked about his own stuff, projects and worries that didn't affect Julia one way or the other: his doctoral thesis, the language classes, his scholarship for the United States, his mother (the poor thing's not well, but she's managing, you have no idea how much I owe her). Julia was touched by the excitement Andrés expressed when he talked about his classes. It was his first year as a teaching assistant for the Spanish Department, and he had taken it so much to heart that he assured her all his students would get a B or better on the final exam, and he added: Well deserved, of course; you have to pound it into them, but if you're a good teacher, the students learn the material. He would smile at Julia, as if to apologize for his naïveté and for the enthusiasm he expressed when he talked about *his* career, *his* classes, and *his* students, since Julia knew the results of the midterm exams: only two of Andrés's students got A's, 10 percent got B's, 20 percent got C's, and the other 70 percent failed, to the young professor's astonishment. Andrés claimed that his major, Spanish Language, was the most thrilling, the most appropriate for doing research, and you know what?, Julia, even with the number of hours I spend studying, I feel like I've only just begun.

Andrés was of average height, rather thin, he almost always wore light colors, his index finger was constantly combating the downward slide of his glasses on his short, straight nose, and he would smile automatically at the end of every sentence. Every three or four days he would say to Julia: I met with Eva about my thesis yesterday, she's a very intelligent woman and she thinks very highly of you. Then Julia, upon hearing those words, would forgive Andrés for everything: she felt great affection toward him, she felt the urge to hug him, to kiss the pronounced receding hairline that announced his future baldness. But she would respond: Oh!, really?

Julia thought that every day was the same, monotonous, boring, irritating. Class in the morning, Andrés, lunch at home, Mamá, Ernesto, Papá, Grandmother Lucía, endless afternoons in the library, and boring walks. Julia's only compensations were certain afternoons with Eva and the drink she would have with lunch.

Julia got out of bed and, barefoot, ran on tiptoe over the cold tiles toward the wardrobe. When she got there, she paused for a moment before opening it. She was always afraid of finding someone inside when she opened a wardrobe. She made an effort to convince herself that it was practically impossible for someone to break into the house without being seen and, on top of that, manage to shut himself in the wardrobe. Besides, even if there were somebody, even if she imagined that he was able to make it all the way to her wardrobe, what reason would he have for getting inside? Julia reasoned: the possible intruder would have come out of his hiding place much earlier, without waiting to be discovered. And, even more importantly, why would he hide in her bedroom? Her room wasn't the best location in the house to find valuable objects to steal. If it was an assassin, why would he kill her? There was no reason to believe anyone wanted her dead. There was still the possibility that it was a sociopath. That thought terrified Julia, but she immediately calmed herself down by reminding herself that not even a sociopath was capable of climbing up to the fifth floor without being seen, and that things like that only happen in novels.

The most frightening possibility popped into her head: maybe she would open the wardrobe and, as expected, nobody would be inside it, but she would see something or someone, nonexistent creatures like the ones she tried to flush from her mind. She used to think she had gotten rid of them, but then they would suddenly appear at the end of the dark hallway or on her bed when she went into her room and turned on the light. Those ghostly images were what terrified Julia the most. She understood that they were merely a figment of her imagination. She should overcome her fear.

She had gotten out of bed to get a blanket out of the wardrobe. She was cold. Maybe if she put another blanket on the bed, she would be able to fall asleep. Standing, barefoot, in front of the wardrobe, her feet felt frozen. She was shaking from cold and fear. She opened the wardrobe doors with her eyes closed so she wouldn't see anything. With outstretched arms, she groped at the clothes placed in one of the interior compartments until she felt the blankets. She opened her eyes. She closed one of the doors and saw herself in the mirror that was hanging on the other one. She looked pale, her eyes too wide open for her to maintain the hope of being able to fall asleep soon. She had bags under her eyes. She moved her hair, long and dark —not too messed up—, away from her face. She didn't like to see herself in mirrors, but every once in a while she would study herself in one for a long time. More than anything, she liked to look at her eyes and hair. She liked her eyes, although they seemed too expressive to her. Ernesto often said to her: You're the woman of the impenetrable face, there's no way of knowing how things affect you by looking at it. But it seemed to her that, on the contrary, when she felt happiness, rage, anguish, sorrow, or any other emotion, it came out through her eyes and other people would know. She thought that everyone could find out everything that was going on inside her by just looking her in the eye. When she was with someone, she would constantly blink and look all around so they wouldn't figure it out. She used other tricks too: rubbing her eyes, as if there was something in them that she was trying to remove, or touching her bangs.

She liked to touch her hair. It was black, long, and fine. Mamá and Grandmother Lucía often advised her: You should do something with your hair. Julia chose not to do anything, in other words: leave it straight and comb it in the direction it fell naturally, hanging down on both sides of her face. She got her bangs cut when they hung over her eyes and blocked her vision, and the back when it seemed too long.

Standing in front of the wardrobe mirror, she saw that her hair was too long. Tomorrow I'll tell Aurelia to cut it for me. Aurelia got furious every time Julia showed up holding the scissors and, without daring to ask openly: Can you cut my hair? —she knew from experience what Aurelia's reaction would be—, said Man!, I went to the beauty parlor and it was packed. You should have waited, Aurelia would reply, aware of Julia's intentions. Why didn't you make an appointment? I lost their phone number . . . anyway, it'll only take you a few minutes . . . Aurelia would lose her temper: Look, I've already told you that being a hairdresser's not part of my job, you all give me enough work as it is. Plus, if I ruin your hair —which wouldn't be a bad idea, then you'd finally get it cut short—, your mother would throw me out on my ear; she's a piece of work. None of you care about my problems, your grandmother with her damn plants and her rosary, why do I have to pray with your grandmother?, people pray when they feel like it, when they need it, not when your grandmother's bored. And that brother of yours changes his clothes two or three times a day, do you think that's right?, it's not like he's going to be on TV. Your father leaves cigarette butts lying around the whole house, and when the newspaper falls out of his hands, there it stays. Your mother wants no part of any of it, take care of the meal, Aurelia; take care of the shopping, Aurelia, and on top of that, she's constantly filling the house up with crowds of people on me. It's just not fair, Lord. Plus they stick me with that Maruja, who's worthless, just worthless; instead of helping me and taking on some of my work, I end up trailing after her for the whole damn day to find out what she's doing and what she's left undone . . . and you, you tell me, why should I know how to cut hair?, why?

But in the end, still grumbling and reciting her list of tasks, Aurelia would take the scissors and cut her hair.

She considered the fact that she would have to put up with Aurelia's endless chatter the following day, but her hair was already down to her shoulders and she didn't like it. In the wardrobe mirror she looked pale and thin. She was afraid of getting sick again. Maruja would say to her: You're too thin, what's going to happen to you?, that's why you don't have any energy, your blood's just water. Maruja's name wasn't Maruja. Her name was Lucía, but Julia's grandmother changed her name as soon as she began working for them. She wouldn't let them call a servant by her own name. Lucía said: Okay, I'll do like the señora wants; but don't call me Andrea, I won't accept that. Call me Maruja, which is my middle name and the name of my mother may she rest in peace (she crossed herself) the poor thing, if the señora doesn't like it I'll leave. Grandmother Lucía complained: It's the name of a cabaret performer, or a loose woman, the type of girls running around nowadays, Good Lord.

Frequently Maruja, if she saw light in Julia's room at night, would come in to chat before she went to bed. Just for a while, I promise, I'm beat, Girl. But she would often go on talking about her problems until one in the morning. Maruja was two or three years older than Julia, but she seemed much older. Grandmother Lucía would follow Mamá around grumbling: I don't like that Maruja, she's hoping to get something here, look at how she acts around Ernesto. In reality, Maruja was always pulling Ernesto's leg, playing tricks on him, and making a fool out of him: Girl, I know your brother's weaknesses, I can tell you because we're friends. He's afraid of women, well, assuming it's nothing worse than that, a thing I won't even mention because God deliver me (and she would cross herself) from adding fuel to the fire in this kind of situation when it's best to keep your eyes and ears open and your mouth closed. Sitting on Julia's bed, Maruja told her things about her village, but more than anything else, she would talk about her boyfriend: That Emilio, he just gives me such headaches, jealous as an Arab but him, he goes after all the girls, men are all just . . . but anyway, what about you and Andrés? Every night Julia would explain to her that Andrés wasn't her boyfriend. But hasn't he asked you?, well, help him out. And every night she would repeat: He's not my boyfriend and I don't want him to be, I don't like him. Well, Girl, he's handsome and he has a car, and since he's a professor, I shouldn't need to say any more, he's got a future, this guy could really be somebody. You can't fool me, I know a few girls who go to the university, you all say it's to study, but I wonder what it is you're all really looking for. Maruja had enormous eyes, a small mouth, almost no lips, she wore her hair very short, and, while she wasn't really fat, she tended to be chubby. In the last house I worked at, they tormented me nearly every day with invasions by the girl's boyfriends. The señora would tell me: Some of my children's classmates are coming over to study today, try not to make any noise and if they want anything, please take care of them. Sure, sure. Instead of coming with books, they would bring guitars, records, and bottles, listen, do you all study with guitars? . . . , and what they were up to, I tell you if they wanted anything it would embarrass me to go into the living room . . . , what do you mean what were they doing?, well, lying on the couch and making out on the floor and God knows what other filthiness, the thing is you have to be discreet and it doesn't matter to me. And you and Andrés, well, you must be old-fashioned.

    Julia remembered the conversation she'd had with Maruja just an hour earlier, more or less the same one as every night. Maruja would start by telling her about her date with her boyfriend and then fly from one topic to another so quickly that it bewildered Julia. One day Emilio wanted to become a sailor, the next he wanted to return to his village, then he wanted to study and get an office job, then he resigned himself to the idea of continuing on as a truck driver and learning about engines over time. What I tell him is to study and get an office job, it's cleaner, and that way there'd be no overnight trips once we're married, because either he marries me or I'm going to kill him after what he's done. Julia knew all about what Emilio and Maruja had done. Maruja had consulted her for more than three months about whether she should or shouldn't. Think about what could happen, where would I go with a baby? Of course, if I knew how to use that antibaby pill; but I don't know, I mean I didn't even go to school, getting an education is so worthwhile, if you . . .

Maruja asked questions that Julia didn't know the answers to. The next day she would have to check with other students at the university, or with Ernesto, or simply pay attention to the conversations her classmates were having, since the subject was in the air. It bothered her to talk about certain things, but Maruja pestered her. So, have you thought about what I told you?, Maruja would ask that evening. Julia nodded her head. Don't tell me to take that pill, because I don't trust it. Well, that's the safest way. Maruja opened her eyes very wide, screwed up her small, nearly lipless mouth. And if they excommunicate me . . . ? even though I don't go to mass, Emilio either, but yes, I believe in God just like anyone who's decent and I pray for people who died. And if the police catch me?, it's illegal, Emilio told me so . . . No, they still haven't made it illegal, I think they sell them in the pharmacy, like aspirin; besides, you can go to a doctor, he'll give you a prescription, and that's it. No way, interrupted Maruja, absolutely not, nobody touches me . . . some doctor, feeling me up . . . anyway, if your grandmother or your mother find out . . . Girl, if you had tried them, then I'd feel safer. You can't fool me, have you tried them? She drove Julia crazy. Their conversations irritated her beyond belief. Do whatever you want, I'm telling you what they told me: It's the safest way and it's cheap. Does it hurt?, asked Maruja. But how's swallowing a pill going to hurt?

Maruja finally managed to get her hands on some. Well, I didn't go myself, you know? The wife of one of Emilio's friends, the one that goes with him in the truck, since she's married, well then it's different. Julia had to explain when she should take them. Good, you figure it out and let me know, I'd forget. Oh Lord!, it's not murder, is it?, moaned Maruja the first day. Do whatever you want, Maruja, it makes no difference to me, it doesn't matter. The next day Maruja was frantic. I'm telling you that my heart just stopped last night, this stuff is poison, it's giving me some weird reaction. No, Girl, it's just the power of suggestion. Rubbish!, my hands are swelling up, my blood's not circulating, I'm going to get gangrene.

After three days, Maruja came into Julia's room, sat on the bed, and said: No way, I'm not going to take them any more. I'd rather join a convent than go through this torture. This concoction just kills you off little by little: I can't hear a thing today, I'm completely deaf. After a couple of months, one night, Maruja announced: That's it. What?, asked Julia. Well, what do you think?, now Emilio doesn't have any choice but to marry me. Maruja burst into tears. Quiet, Girl, everyone'll come. Between sobs, Maruja repeated: He told me he's not that dumb, but I don't believe it, I'm sure I got pregnant. Maruja tried to go into detail, but Julia changed the subject, she was sick of Maruja. I told you not to talk about it. I didn't know you were such a prude.

During the next few days Maruja drove her crazy with: I think I am, I'm sure of it, I told him so, oh my God!, what am I going to do now?, if he doesn't marry me I'll kill him. You can't know yet. Want to bet?, as if a woman doesn't know when she's got a baby inside, I'm telling you I know, it's instinct; swear you won't tell . . . On and on like that for a month, until Maruja found out her instinct had fooled her. I have such bad luck, otherwise Emilio would have married me right away.

Julia found the conversations with Maruja amusing, except when she insisted on telling her what she did with Emilio. Then Julia would lose her temper, it irritated her, she couldn't stand it. That night, more or less an hour ago, Maruja had begun to talk about Emilio. Men are so selfish, he goes and tells me that if I want to wait that doesn't mean he has to, that he can find other girls who're willing, and that what happened that day was nothing, imagine that, that what happened that day . . . Julia didn't think she was going to be able to control herself, she'd throw the pillow in her face or say something rude. She held back. I'm tired, she told her. It was true, but she didn't fall asleep. Maruja's foolishness had woken her up and made her tense. Worrying about it got on Julia's nerves. She tried to think about something else. She was successful. But deep down, everything made her tense. No matter what she was thinking about, she would stop, suddenly, and start to delve deeper into the images, the memories that came to her mind, and no matter what they were, beneath them she would uncover the same tension, the same anguish.

Julia closed the wardrobe, and the noise it made in the silence of the night startled her. Her feet were completely frozen and she was shivering. She got back into bed and hugged her pillow. She heard the front door open and immediately recognized Papá's and Mamá's voices. She looked at the clock and quickly turned off her lamp. It would have bothered her if Papá or Mamá saw the light under her door and came into her room to see what she was doing with her light on at two in the morning. It was dark again, but some light came in through the balcony from an electric sign on the building across the street. From her bed, she heard Mamá's and Papá's footsteps. As they passed the door of her room, Julia heard some words, as if they were arguing. You weren't very friendly. What, did you want me to dance? Your unfriendliness borders on rudeness. And your excessive friendliness is unbearable. Their voices disappeared down the hallway, their steps did too.

In the past, if Mamá didn't stop in her bedroom when she came home at night, little Julia became desperate. She would call out to her. If Mamá was in a good mood, she would spend a little time with her and then go to bed. Otherwise, she shouted at her: You're still awake? Daughter, what a pain, go to sleep right now or go get in bed with Aurelia.

Now she was grateful for Mamá's silence. When she heard her footsteps, she stayed alert, holding her breath. She was afraid that Mamá would come in. But fortunately, Mamá went directly to her room. However, hearing Mamá's footsteps fade into the silence of the night, Julia felt a profound sadness, pain in her throat and chest, the urge to cry for something that had been lost, irretrievably, forever. It wasn't something she wanted to recover —just thinking about its possible existence distressed her—, but its loss caused her immense sadness.

Julia remembered when she began to lose Mamá, the image that she, Julia, had of Mamá, the adoration that she felt for her, the love that tormented her for years and years. At times, when she didn't want to think about it, Julia told herself that it was all too confusing to try to understand now, after so much time. But she knew that wasn't true, she could remember it perfectly. Mamá, a strange and peculiar universe called Mamá, had suffered a gradual but definite degradation; the estrangement had been clearly marked, well defined in specific temporal stages. And Julia could remember those stages and the events that accompanied them. It was absurd to try to search her memory for one day, one unforgettable event, the decisive cause of that loss. It had been a slow process, unconscious back then, a long, drawn-out process that seemed like a film to her, a film that, even though it was choppy, still had an unmistakable continuity in spite of the long, dark, muffled, forgotten sequences. It was a brief story that came to an end when she, Julia, was able to begin remembering it; when, suddenly, she began to feel different, began to feel that everyone else was different too, when she heard herself say Mamá to Mamá and she understood that that wasn't Mamá. She was amazed by Ernesto, tall, very handsome, with a man's deep voice. She looked for Papá and found him sitting in the same armchair as always, sleeping and nearly obese, with wrinkles on his face and gray hair. A name came to her lips and she was on the verge of shouting it: Rafael. Where was Rafael? A photograph in a silver frame reminded her that Rafael was dead. She felt like a stranger among strangers. Confronting both herself and reality, she felt absolutely stunned for a brief instant. She was overcome by a strange dizziness, she didn't known if it was because of the astonishment caused by the reality, recently discovered, that surrounded her, or if, instead, the dizziness was caused by memory, that mental peculiarity, a coiled spring that had been sleeping until then and that was, she suddenly realized, a vehicle that would drive her, inevitably, down a long, endless road, because —and she also realized it in that instant, vaguely but with certainty, without thinking it, without saying it to herself— she, Julia, had erased the end of that trip, buried it outside herself. It was a moment of astonishment, as if she didn't exist, as if even though she didn't exist, she could think, and she called out, in search of herself. She was puzzled by her body. She realized that that precise moment was the culmination of a time she could overcome by putting that unique vehicle, the memory, into gear; that vehicle was, at times, a swift car with a suicidally insane driver, advancing at full speed, colliding with the road's arboreal shadows, and running over every obstacle that got in its way, and at other times, a black hearse, driven by a ghost and guarded by four footman cadavers. The appearance of that unique vehicle, memory, had made reality fictitious. A thousand things were left behind, in time, and she, little Julia, lived there, also forgotten, drowning, struggling among the shadows, waiting for them to open the road so she could reach the real time where another Julia, grown up, unknown, lived.

Julia, even before putting the motor of her memory into gear, knew when and where she would find herself for the first time. By simply closing her eyes and trying to be aware of her body, she would find little Julia. With her eyes closed, without being able to see her body, she felt smaller. Lying in bed, it seemed to her that her legs had shrunk in half and her arms were shortened, and she noticed her little hands down where her elbows would really be. And even though she tried to avoid it, it was little Julia, small, thin, quick, and elusive, who always passed her by, seizing control of memory's motor, steering her down windy, confusing roads, changing directions abruptly as if she wanted to play in an exitless maze and, at the same time, amuse herself by fooling Julia, telling her, when she spotted the way out off in the distance: Come on, that's not the right way. And little Julia would again drive her down dark tunnels, decrepit bridges, with old planks that threatened to break under her feet, to collapse completely, sending her to her death, devoured by the disgusting reptiles that were fighting under the bridge, waiting for a victim.

Little Julia, through time, dragged her to where she lived, as if she blamed her for abandoning her in childhood and then allowing herself to go on living without her. That's why little Julia returned, in shorts and a navy blue sweater with an anchor on the chest. Little Julia would appear at the front door of their house, with her braids undone, barefoot, her summer tan and big, lively eyes, staring at the end of the unpaved street, bathed in August sunshine. Little Julia, sitting in the doorway of their house, with her bare feet on the hot ground which was burned by the sun, waiting. It was three or four in the afternoon, the hottest time of day. Inside, everyone was asleep. Aurelia, when she woke her up in the morning, had told her: Mamá's coming today. When? Before lunchtime. That morning, Aurelia had taken them —Julia, Rafael, and Ernesto— to the beach. Going to the beach with Aurelia was unbearable: she didn't get in the water, and she observed the three children from the shore, only letting them go in up to their knees. But they managed to escape easily. Little Julia was six then. Mamá would tell Aurelia: Don't worry, she swims like a fish. Besides, Cousin Arturo was spending the summer with them, and he would propose races out to the buoy. Master Arturo, shouted Aurelia, enraged, my señora will be informed about how you get the children all riled up, you can be sure of that.

Aurelia didn't like going down to the beach, she complained about getting sunburned: I have to take care of all the housework, and on top of that, this torture. Little Julia didn't like the beach either, and even less if Mamá wasn't there. She would enjoy herself for a while when Ernesto and his friends organized battles in the water, but Cousin Arturo and his friend Víctor (both much older than Ernesto) always spoiled their games. Hey, you guys, come over here, we'll buy you a snack at the Chiringuito. The Chiringuito was a bar located right on the beach where Arturo and Víctor would sit and sunbathe instead of lying on the sand like everyone else. In the Chiringuito your skin tans more quickly and you get darker faster, they would say. Ernesto and a couple of guys his age would go with Arturo, and the game would be over. Ernesto, before he followed Arturo, would look at Rafael and little Julia, raising a finger to his lips and telling them: Ssshhhh, so they wouldn't go tell Papá. Papá yelled at him when he saw him with Víctor and Arturo. I've told you a thousand times, I don't want to see you with those two. Why not?, asked Ernesto. Because I don't like them. And Papá wouldn't give any further explanation about why he didn't like Arturo and Víctor and why he didn't want Ernesto to spend any time with them.

Little Julia didn't like Arturo and Víctor either. They would show up when they, the boys, began their games and spoil everything. They would take Ernesto and the other boys his age, the ones who organized everything, away; they were the ones who, when she or Rafael asked: Where are we going?, what are we doing this afternoon?, would decide for everyone and announce: A bike race from the Plaza Mayor to Vinyet. Or from the church to Terramar, and then we'll go to the miniature golf course. Or: They're showing a good movie at such and such a theater, outside.

The bike races excited little Julia, even though she didn't have a bike. Ernesto or Rafael would take her on the back of theirs. More than anything, she liked the rides to Vinyet, a church located on the outskirts of town. To get there, they had to go down a long avenue with pine trees, cactuses, and homes that Julia found beautiful, with carefully tended gardens and flowers that peeked out over the iron gates. During the ride, she smelled the jasmines and the pine trees which gave them shade from the sun. She didn't like the ride to Terramar. Going from the Plaza Mayor to Paseo Marítimo, they had to go down a poorly paved incline, and little Julia would get scared. The street did turn out to be dangerous: the day of the town festival, when the parade went down that very street, the giant tripped and fell, she rolled down the hill, and, after her, another giant and the people wearing the big-headed masks. Going down it on their bikes, the boys would yell: Last one down's a rotten egg. Also, almost all the summer vacationers got together on Paseo Marítimo in the afternoon and, going by there on their bikes, they would always run into someone they knew —parents of Ernesto's friends— who would call them: Where're you going to?, careful with the cars, there's a lot of traffic, do you want something to drink? If she saw Mamá, sitting in the patio of some bar or strolling with the other ladies, little Julia would get off the bike, abandoning the trip. Then she'd be sorry, because Mamá wasn't pleased by that decision: You'll be bored to tears if you stay with me; go on, go with them, here, go buy yourself an ice cream. But little Julia clung to the idea of staying. Later on she would indeed get bored during Mamá's endless walk down the avenue with the palm trees to the church and from the church to the avenue with the palm trees. Mamá, without paying any attention to her, never stopped talking with her companions: The town is packed this year, way more than last summer. Yes, it's true, and it's affecting the prices.

If she didn't find Mamá on Paseo Marítimo or at the church plaza, she continued the trip to Terramar. She didn't like that road. On one side of the avenue, you could see the sea, and, on the other side, an endless row of whitewashed houses. After a while on the bike, the palm trees would disappear. Halfway through the afternoon the sun would still be beating down; and the sea, the houses, and the very pavement which the bicycles glided over seemed to blend into a single, intense shimmer. Rafael explained to her: That's why they call the town White Suburb, Dummy. She had to furrow her brow and wrinkle up her nose, the excessive whiteness making it hard to see and hurting her eyes. When they rode their bikes to Terramar, she would end up with a headache and in a bad mood.

Arriving at Terramar Point, they would often find Víctor and Arturo, who would spoil their fun.

Little Julia didn't like running into them. The truth is that they acted friendly, especially with her and Ernesto: they invited them to have ice cream, to play miniature golf, to go to the movies and on walks. Arturo sang Italian songs which were in vogue that summer: Tourist, when you get to Roma, you soak up art and history, you go to Trevi fountain to test its power. And then he'd get louder: Arrivederchi Roma, good-bye, adiós, au revoir. When he finished his serenade he would exclaim: Nilla Pizzi is such a great singer. Víctor didn't sing, but he laughed at everything Arturo said. They were similar to each other, even physically: dark complexions and light eyes, wearing white pants and T-shirts, speaking to each other slowly —in soft voices, intoning their particular song—, in Italian. Julia, remembering them, figured they were approximately thirty years old, although it was difficult to be precise after so much time.

At night, after having dinner, Víctor would go to their house to chat with Arturo (who was spending part of the summer with them) and with Mamá. They would go out in the yard until very late at night, except on Fridays, Saturdays, and Sundays. On Friday night, Papá would arrive from Barcelona and stay with them until Monday. At night, he and Mamá would go out with their friends. But when Papá was gone, they would relax in the yard after dinner. They would sit under the linden trees, and the geraniums and carnations would smell good.

Víctor would show up with a pile of comic books, *Florita*, *Porky*, *Superman*, *Hazañas de Guerra*, *The Puma* . . . He divided them among the three children and insisted on putting little Julia on his lap and showing her how bears kill their victims. They approach them very slowly, acting like they're good friends, and when the victim's no longer afraid, when she feels safe, powww, they hug her, they squeeze her very, very tight in their huge arms until she suffocates.

While giving this explanation, he would hug little Julia tightly. Little Julia felt bad with Víctor. The heat was suffocating, it made her feel sick to be sitting on Víctor's lap while he hugged her to show her how bears devour their victims. Leave me alone, shouted little Julia. Víctor would laugh, but he wouldn't let her go. He'd say: Yummmmm, now I'll eat you up (and he'd open his mouth very wide), I'm a bear, a terrible bear. With her face pressed against Víctor's chest, she saw only darkness, she felt the unpleasant contact of his hot, sweaty skin, and she heard the conversation Mamá was having with her friends like a distant murmur, as if they weren't in the yard. Let me go, she shouted. Víctor would laugh: Don't be afraid, it's just a joke. Rafael would help her out: Don't frighten her, you bully. Little Julia's just a kid and she gets scared. Later on she'll drive us crazy all night.

She would escape from Víctor and run to Mamá, who was talking and laughing nonstop, ignoring her. Little Julia would tap her on the arm, and Mamá would ask: Do you want a Coke? No. And she would keep on touching Mamá until, irritated, she would yell at her or slap her, and little Julia burst into tears. Aurelia — Mamá called— put her to bed, she's unbearable.

Mamá liked Víctor, having him around the house. He's a fine young man, polite, agreeable, and distinguished. And another thing that I won't say, Papá would respond. In your opinion, just because a man's attentive, elegant, and sensitive, he's a . . . Mamá would counter, agitated.

The presence of little Julia in her mind dragged Julia toward a past time that, at first, appeared clear, complete, uncontrollably forceful, and whose clarity later dissipated with the same abruptness with which it had been reborn in her memory, leaving her in pain, full of resentment. An agonizing feeling of heat, a morning on the beach, the sun beating down, burning the sand. Arturo had rented a paddle boat. Víctor, Rafael, Ernesto, and Julia got in it. We'll go to Terramar, Arturo said. But he got tired of rowing just before reaching Terramar Point. Someone said: Let's race to The Point to whet our appetites. Little Julia began to swim, and Víctor did too. Everyone else stayed close to the paddle boat. Only a few meters separated them from The Point, but little Julia was worn out when she got there. She liked being in the water, looking toward the bottom, and seeing her body, much longer than it really was; she moved her legs and they looked like they were broken. Víctor laughed: Let's go up on shore to rest. Little Julia moved toward shore, holding onto the rocks. Víctor helped her, saying: There's a lot of sea urchins on these rocks. Sometimes Ernesto and Rafael would catch sea urchins. They would take them home and let them dry in the sun for two or three days until they died. Then they'd pull out their spines and stick them in a bucket of bleach. Once they were clean, the shells would be hemispheric, with beautiful drawings formed by tiny holes. Víctor got hold of a sea urchin. They reached the shore. Little Julia, tired out from the race, sat down to rest. These creatures are very dangerous, if they sting you, you can die, Víctor said. He brought the sea urchin up to little Julia's arm and then to her neck, looking at her in a strange way.

Little Julia noticed suddenly that the sun was beating down, the sand was burning hot, and The Point was deserted. Víctor brought the sea urchin up to her face. She was scared, and the oppressive heat made it hard for her to breathe. If you're trying to scare me, I'll tell Mamá, she shouted at him, gasping for air. The sea urchin disappeared from sight because she fell to the sand with the force of Víctor's blows. You won't say anything, you idiot. Little Julia rolled on her stomach, her face to the ground. The sand burned. She tried to get up and run, but Víctor caught her legs and she fell again.

She remembered that the sun was falling directly in her eyes, she didn't dare breathe because the smell of Víctor's body made her feel sick, the sand was burning her back and head, and she screamed and hit Víctor, she scratched him until she couldn't any more, and she thought she'd die from the pain. She stretched out her arm and noticed the spines of the sea urchin under her hand. She grabbed it and, while Víctor was breathing very heavily, smashed it against his back. Julia remembered the smell of bad breath, the shout Víctor let out, and the blows she received immediately after that. Víctor, when he felt the sea urchin's spines on his skin, had jumped, and she turned over on her stomach. Rocks were embedded in her skin and her whole body ached. She bent her legs, sat back on her heels and doubled over, placing her forehead on her knees. She didn't remember how long she stayed like that. The sea seemed very far away, far enough that she'd never be able to reach it. She was hot, very hot, as if the sun had hidden itself inside her body. Julia couldn't remember how much time she spent there, doubled over in pain. At times it seemed like only a few minutes and at other times, years, many years from the time when Víctor disappeared until she raised her head and detected Arturo, rowing, his white paddle boat approaching the shore. Little Julia got up, she couldn't walk. What're you doing here?, Arturo asked. We've been looking for you, I thought you went back with Víctor. But . . . did you fall on the rocks? He pulled her onto the paddle boat. Arturo asked her: How did you fall?, did you step on a sea urchin? Little Julia felt sick, dripping with sweat, not understanding what Arturo was asking her and unable to respond. When they got to where the others were waiting and Aurelia began to yell at her and Mamá to slap her, venting in that way the impatience she had suffered (I don't want any of you to go out on the rocks alone, one of these days you'll give us a real scare. You're not to go down to the beach anymore. And Aurelia repeating over and over: Good God, what a fall, she could have cracked her head open), she wasn't able to understand them either.

Little Julia, sitting in the doorway of their house, small and thin, barefoot, her braids halfway undone, the shorts and navy blue sweater with an anchor drawn on the chest, her eyes lowered, staring at two stones that she was pounding together, forced her to remember things like that, confusing, disconnected. Her unique presence spoke to her with images, sensations, memories that popped into her head and that Julia now rejected, as if they weren't hers, attributing them to little Julia, as if she and little Julia were two separate people. Julia, at times, was certain that little Julia still existed, that she was alive and living in an unchangeable, motionless world, outside of time. It was as if little Julia existed with her own life (a life that wasn't hers) and from there, sitting in the doorway of their house (her brow furrowed, pounding two stones together and raising her eyes from time to time with a look that was hard, dark, full of resentment, toward the end of the street that was bathed in the first hours of afternoon sunshine), she bent Julia's will so that she would do, think, and feel whatever she wanted. Little Julia had spent so many years sitting in that doorway that she had gotten old there, she had had time to mature, to realize that she could twist Julia around her little finger. Little Julia had become a persecuting god for Julia, a god who demanded continuous sacrifices to calm her ancient pain.

Little Julia never forgave her for abandoning her there, in a motionless universe, outside of time, within whose shadows she struggled and from which Julia would never be able to rescue her. Little Julia reproached her great weakness, the immense cowardice that prevented her from setting her free forever. That's why little Julia returned, with her shorts and navy blue sweater with the anchor drawn on the chest, and spoke to her through time, without words, always beginning with the same image: her, sitting in the doorway of the house where she spent her summers back then. And she threw in her face the strange sensation she felt that afternoon, while everyone else took their siesta. A sensation that after that day she experienced many times: the need to search inside herself for images, words, fashionable melodies that would produce an immense sadness in her, help her feel anguish, despair, and provide her with enough pain to be able to cry.

Julia had felt the burden of anguish at times, an invisible weight on her body, an anxiety that made it hard for her to breathe, a pain in her chest and throat that she needed to fight in some way. She was able to calm herself down. A very sweet peace came over her. She managed to breathe normally, slowly, profoundly. Then, something in her forced her to return to her earlier state, to look for motives to become sad again, to submerge herself once again in a universe of darkness and fear.

Julia had experienced the need for that kind of torment many times, but she remembered perfectly that it was that afternoon when she first became aware of it. Maybe she had felt it before, but it was precisely then when she discovered, with joy, the strange sensation, saying to herself that she was never going to forget it, forcing herself to remember it always. She engraved the spot where it was found in her memory so that its surroundings would help her remember it, as if the discovery she had just made was a great event, very important.

She focused her attention on the unpaved street; on the reddish ground, the houses on the other side of it, small, white, very white, bathed in sunlight. The clear blue sky with no clouds overhead. A bicycle leaning against the building across the way. She concentrated on the fountain in the little plaza, located at the beginning of the street, and she remembered that at that time, looking at the fountain, a song that Arturo sang came to mind: The girls in the Plaza España are so pretty, so happy that they laugh and sing . . . and she knew that the song's lyrics had popped into her head because the plaza where the fountain was located was called Plaza de España. She noticed the green shutters that were hanging on the windows, the flowerpots on the balconies, and a very wrinkled sheet of paper with an announcement for a movie rolling down the street: *Pennant Twenty-One*. Mamá, three days earlier, had slapped Rafael because she asked him: What movie did you see? And instead of saying *Pennant Twenty-One*, he said: *Pregnant Twenty-One*. She paid a lot of attention to the movie announcement so she wouldn't forget it: a woman's face with a white X-shaped cross on top of it. And, most of all, she remembered the image she had refined in her head in order to cry: Mamá dead. She used this thought to torment herself over and over until she felt satisfied.

Julia remembered that afternoon and the hours preceding it. When she woke up in the morning, she called Mamá, and Aurelia told her: She's in Barcelona, but she'll be back by lunchtime.

Papá had returned from Barcelona the previous night. He came into the house screaming, in a rage. Rafael ran out to meet him and threw his arms around his neck. Hi, Papá. Papá shoved him and Rafael staggered. They were having dinner in the yard. Little Julia saw Mamá get up from the wicker chair. Papá raised his arm and Mamá fell into the chair again. She heard Mamá's cry and, while Aurelia pushed her toward the boys' bedroom, Antonio's name. From the bedroom she —she couldn't remember for how long— heard them shouting at each other: I saw the two of you, this has nothing to do with gossip, with my own eyes. You were in Barcelona and you didn't sleep at home. And Mamá: You're a disgusting animal. And then a silence that seemed eternal to her, and rapid footsteps down the hallway. Aurelia was saying: Good Lord, Good Lord, we've got to call a doctor. The door opened. Papá pushed Rafael into the same room where moments earlier Aurelia had put her. Mamá's dead, said Rafael. Papá had forgotten to lock the door, and little Julia opened it. Mamá's room was across the hall. She saw her lying in bed, motionless. Aurelia was putting something on her nose and her forehead, repeating: Good Lord, Good Lord. Ernesto, go get the doctor. Get in your room, they yelled at Rafael and little Julia. Papá dragged them into the room again, and, this time, he locked the door.

Is she dead?, little Julia asked Rafael. I think so. Little Julia began to cry, kicking and beating on the door. That's enough, shouted Papá from the hallway. But little Julia continued to cry and call

Mamá at the top of her lungs. After a while, Rafael took his handkerchief out of his pocket, blew his nose hard, dried his face; then he helped little Julia blow her nose and wipe her mouth. Boogers aren't for eating, he said. Come on, let's go to bed. Rafael seemed gifted with a strange wisdom. He was dark, like her, not too tall, and very thin. Rafael was ten then, he only had ten years of life left. I want to see Mamá, said little Julia. Me too, but Papá locked us in and we can't get out, they'll open up for us soon. When? When they feel like it. I want out now. They won't let us out now . . . but tomorrow they will, for sure. Aurelia's never made us go without breakfast. Let's go to bed.

The boys' bedroom had a bunk bed, a shiny white wooden nightstand, and a fitted wardrobe. Rafael took off his shoes and little Julia did too. Rafael lay down in the same bunk as little Julia, next to her, and began to sing: *Questa piccollisima serenata,* torero cha cha cha, you and the sea have watched me cry, oh I go crazy if your mouth says love love, remember *Marcelino pan con vino,* Brazilian love, pretty little doll with golden hair pearly teeth ruby lips, I love you so much much much much as much as before forever until the end of time, how lovely you are, how beautiful you are, *Granada tierra soñada,* my song becomes a gypsy when it's meant for you, guide me because the intense light blinds me and like a stranger I'm going to a blue paradise, you owe me a kiss and I'm going to get it even if I have to pay, I have violets for you the same song I learned at your old place remember in Granada at the foot of the Albaicín in the garden together, *ay ay ay ay canta y no llores porque cantando se alegran cielito lindo los corazones* . . . Rafael would finish the repertoire and begin all over again or ask little Julia: Now which one? Until little Julia fell asleep. Half asleep, she heard Ernesto come into the room: Bah, it was a lie, she pretended to faint to scare Papá.

Little Julia woke up in the darkness of the night and noticed that Rafael wasn't by her side. She got up. A very tenuous light came through the window. She saw that she was in her own room. Someone had moved her to her own bed, while she was sleeping, and put her pajamas on. She remembered about Mamá. She didn't think she'd dreamed her death. She was afraid. If Mamá died, she would too. She snuck out of her room. She ran her fingers along the walls with each step. She couldn't reach the light switch. She continued down the hallway to the dining room. The windows were open and she saw the yard, dark. She could vaguely make out the table, the colonial white wooden furniture, and the wicker chairs in the darkness. Standing in the dining room, she heard heavy breathing. Someone was there. She held her breath and trembling, on tiptoe, went toward the table to hide underneath it. But when she was close she saw a shadow moving in the darkness and she heard one of the wicker chairs creak. She closed her eyes. She wanted to scream. She couldn't. She opened her eyes. Someone was there, in the dining room, a large body, very large, like a bear. She crouched down and screamed. She heard rapid movement. She screamed again, two, three times until the dining-room light was switched on and Papá appeared with his hand on the switch, fully dressed and with a sleepy face. Little Julia, what are you doing here? I'm scared, she whispered. And then Aurelia arrived, in her nightgown and with messy hair, and took her to her room. Where's Mamá? Where do you think she is?, sleeping.

The next morning, when she woke up, Aurelia told her: Mamá's in Barcelona, she'll be back at lunchtime. I want to see her. How're you going to see her if she's in Barcelona? Don't give me any grief.

She spent the morning fighting with Ernesto, and when Aurelia took them down to the beach she refused to get in the water. Aurelia didn't stop lecturing her during the two hours they spent on the beach: Your mama's really going to yell at you when I tell her the type of morning you've given me, picking fights with Ernesto, don't you understand that he's bigger and he's always going to win? Just wait and see when your mama finds out . . . My God, the way the beach gets on Saturdays, pretty soon we won't all fit . . .

Julia remembered the onset of a dark and confusing feeling toward Papá. She spent that morning at the beach, after her irrevocable decision to stay out of the water, under the beach umbrella. She got bored when she didn't get in the water, but she didn't want to let them tell her what to do. The thing that irritated Mamá the most was when she, little Julia, misbehaved in her absence. That's why she didn't want to have breakfast, or swim, and she spent the morning fighting with the boys and sniveling behind Aurelia. She got bored under the umbrella, tired of building mountains in the sand, of burying her feet and her legs up to her waist in the sand, of looking for ladybugs in the sand. She was fed up with so much sand. Do you want me to take you to your father?, asked Aurelia. He's fishing on the other beach. How long's he going to fish? How long do you think? Until lunchtime, come on, put something on your back so you don't burn.

Papá was fishing on the other beach, San Sebastián, located behind the church. That beach was smaller than the other one, Oro Beach (the one where the summer vacationers swam). Little Julia liked San Sebastián Beach better: almost nobody went swimming there; moreover, there were a lot of boats along the shore. Papá fished from the breakwater. She could walk down the beach alone, getting into the boats if she wanted. Aurelia told her: Don't ever go swimming at this beach, the water's very dirty and, on top of that, if a boat comes in or out it could hit you; don't leave your father's side, the sand is full of rusty nails and hooks . . . Little Julia liked the fisherman's beach.

When he saw her arrive with Aurelia, Papá signaled to her by waving the fishing cap that protected him from the sun. He quickly turned the lever on the reel that wound up the fishing line. Now you'll see, I'm going to catch a fish for you, he promised her. He baited the hook. Get back a little bit, he told her. Papá threw the fishing rod back, swung it a little from left to right so that the line wouldn't get tangled up, and cast it forcefully out to sea. Little Julia tried to keep an eye on the line so she could see how far out it landed. That morning she observed Papá's movements carefully when he cast and —she remembered it perfectly— she thought that the same energy Papá used to throw the fishing line into the water could drag him in as well. While the sea water gobbled up the hook and line, little Julia imagined that the rod went in after the line and, after that, Papá, holding the rod. First she was scared and opened her mouth to shout at Papá: Careful, you're going to fall in. But she was silent. She waited, staring anxiously at Papá's back, wishing the wind would drag him into the water and the sea would swallow him forever. She closed her eyes, hoping that when she opened them Papá wouldn't be there anymore, that she would only see the fishing basket, the T-shirt, Papá's sandals, the package of cigarettes, and the white cap with the blue visor, and that she, faced with Papá's disappearance, would go running to the other beach to announce to Aurelia and her brothers: Papá drowned.

But she opened her eyes and saw Papá, who had already dug the rod into the sand and was lighting a cigarette. The breeze blew out the match, and he told her: Come here, block the wind with your towel, just wait until you see the fish I'm going to catch. She was overcome by a feeling of deception and bitterness that she quickly forgot about, by focusing her attention on the fishing tackle that Papá kept inside the basket. The advantage of staying with Papá was that he didn't talk a lot, smoking in silence, observing the tip of the fishing rod, and never saying to her: Don't touch that, don't stick your feet in the water, don't go over there, you'll fall. And because of that, she could do what she wanted: walk very slowly along the rocks and touch anything she saw within her grasp.

Suddenly she didn't like this beach, which was relatively solitary compared with the one the summer people went to, this beach where Papá usually fished and where, along the shore, there were some boats that needed to be painted. It seemed sad and dirty to her. Walking along the rocks, as Aurelia said, was dangerous: There's rusty nails and hooks buried in the sand, if you step on one you'll have to get a tetanus shot.

When Papá asked her: Do you want to go or should we wait a while to see if they start biting?, she answered: No, no, let's go home, I'm tired. It wasn't true. She was afraid to see Papá cast and to feel, once again, the incomprehensible but real desire to see him sink into the water. She looked away from the sea and Papá and stared down at the sand or her own feet. But even like that she imagined Papá casting the line toward the horizon and then getting lost at the bottom of the sea.

On the way home she let her thoughts wander. Going through the Plaza Mayor, Papá read a movie announcement that was posted on the wall. Look, he said, *The Great Caruso*, if you behave yourselves, I'll take you tonight.

Little Julia was on the verge of asking him if Mamá would be home. It seemed odd that Papá wanted to take them to a movie at night. But all she said was: Is it technicolor? Yes, and it's a musical. Papá spent the rest of the trip singing: *Una furtiva lacrima . . .* while little Julia calculated the likelihood of finding Mamá home at lunchtime, like Aurelia had said, after Papá's promise to take them to a movie at night.

When they got home, little Julia ran to the dining room. She didn't find anyone. Then to the kitchen, not there either. She went out in the yard. Aurelia was hanging Ernesto's and Rafael's towels and bathing suits in the sun. As soon as she saw her, she said: Don't give me that look, she's not here yet, but she promised me she'd be here by lunch. Little Julia felt herself turn red. Her eyes were brimming over with tears. The same thing always happened: Mamá would promise to come home at a specific time, and she would be endlessly delayed. Ernesto and Rafael got out of the shower, wrapped in towels, dripping water. Rafael shouted: Little Julia, I beat him, I beat him at bocce ball. And Ernesto: By cheating, by cheating, there's no way you'd win except by cheating. Liar, liar. And Aurelia: Come on, get dressed, you're messing up the whole house, what slobs, get dressed before you catch pneumonia.

Little Julia sat in one of the wicker chairs around the table that was shaded by the long branches of one of the two fig trees; the yard also had geraniums, carnations, linden trees, jasmines, and other plants creeping up the wall. That's how Papá found her when he came into the yard with the basket and fishing poles. When's Mamá coming back?, asked little Julia, her gaze fixed on the table, where the wind was blowing some leaves that had fallen off the fig tree. I don't know, but what difference does it make?, you're all right with me, aren't you? I already told you that if she doesn't come back tonight we'll go see a movie. Little Julia's hands tightened into fists on the chair. She didn't want to cry about Mamá's absence in front of Papá. She took a stick and began beating at some weeds. In the center of the yard there was a well. She saw how Papá, with his back to her, was getting ready to draw water for the plants with a bucket. Sometimes, she and Rafael would lean over the well and shout words into it to hear the echo. Aurelia would say to them: You're going to kill yourselves. Good God, it's a miracle you're still alive. While Papá, with his back to her, drew the water, little Julia felt the sense of danger again. Papá could fall into the well. On top of that —and she realized it then, with certainty— she could carefully get up out of her chair, take a few steps without making any noise, and push him. She was small and wasn't strong enough to throw him into the well, but she didn't even think about that; just that she could do it and that she wanted to. She was frightened by her own thoughts. She called Rafael, without knowing why. We're going to go see a movie tonight, she told her brother, without pleasure, as soon as he appeared in the yard. Are we really, Papá?

Are we?, he shouted happily. Maybe, Papá responded. *The Great Caruso?*, asked Ernesto. It's in technicolor. Well, I'd rather see *The Search*, but it doesn't matter. Little Julia knew right away when Rafael and Ernesto were happy because they would tease her. They called her little Julia the Ugly Buggly and they sang to her: Ugly Buggly little Julia, got uglier and uglier, buggier and buggier, crazier and crazier, deader than a doornail. That day, during lunch, happy with the news, they began to sing to her: Here comes the black clown, happily singing the *bayón*, I'm gonna dance the brand-new song, everyone shout when she go round, Girl, where you gonna go down?, I'm gonna dance the *bayón*. They sang that song to her a lot and she didn't usually get mad, but that day little Julia welcomed the slightest pretext to become enraged. Hearing herself called the black clown, she burst into tears.

Mamá didn't arrive at lunchtime. They ate in the yard. Papá yelled at them for no reason. He slapped Ernesto for saying: I already know why Mamá's not back, it's your fault. But little Julia didn't care about anything that Papá said, what he yelled. It was as if that morning's desire next to the well had become a powerful weapon that she could use to defeat Papá at any time; an infallible weapon that she, little Julia, was going to have at her disposal from then on. Now she was no longer afraid of Papá yelling, raising his hand to strike out, threatening Mamá with: I'll take the kids and you'll be stuck here.

After lunch, they went to take a siesta. Little Julia, as soon as she imagined that everyone else would be sleeping, got dressed in the shorts and navy blue sweater with an anchor drawn on the chest, slipped down the hallway, and went outside.

She wasn't allowed to walk around town by herself, and especially not to the train station. But suddenly, she felt an irresistible longing for Mamá. She thought she might never see her again and, although this idea had often made her suffer in the past, only to realize that it was absurd, that day she couldn't get it out of her head. The station was close to home. By going straight to the end of the road and then turning right, she'd find the street. She walked slowly, trying not to be spotted by anyone Mamá knew; later on, they might tell on her for being out alone. It was very sunny. As soon as she crossed the road she began to run toward the station.

She went into the park. At times she went there with Ernesto and Rafael to catch butterflies. The garden was quite big, and the trails wound around in circles in such a way that they ended up forming a real maze. Little Julia sat on a bench, protected by the shade of a palm tree. From there she could see if Mamá appeared on the station platform. She wanted to see her arrive but didn't want Mamá to be able to see her. She thought she could make out the time, four o'clock, on the platform clock, but she wasn't sure: she still didn't know how to tell time very well. At that moment she remembered something that Aurelia had told her a few days before: A woman died on a train. She had a heart attack, great trip, huh? Little Julia thought about Mamá and was horrified. She heard a train whistle. She stood up on the bench and looked at the platform through the bushes in the park. A few people got off, but she didn't see Mamá. She recognized Antonio, one of Mamá's friends. She thought that if Antonio arrived on that train, Mamá would come on the next one, like she had noticed on other occasions. She waited to leave the park until Antonio disappeared from the platform so she could get home without being seen.

Little Julia liked Antonio, Mamá's friend, the one Papá always criticized. At times little Julia would see him at the beach, under an umbrella close to theirs, and on Paseo Marítimo chatting with Mamá. Papá would get annoyed when Antonio had dinner at their house, but little Julia liked it; Mamá was happy and would laugh for no reason. And Antonio was a nice man. Sometimes, she, Ernesto, and Rafael would go play with his son at his house. From the yard she would look, through the window, at the inside of a room where books and pictures covered the walls; she would watch Antonio work. Antonio wore glasses: little round glasses. He typed, facing the window. From time to time he would get up and say to her: Hi, I believe we know each other, don't we? She nodded her head. Oh yes!, you're Carmencita. Little Julia shook her head. No? Oh no, no!, you're . . . Aurora. No?, hmmmmm, Merche. Antonio pretended like he was really trying to guess her name. Let's see, let's see . . . What does your name start with? And she said: It starts with Ju. Oh right!, Ju . . . Ju . . .

Little Julia made an effort again to read the time on the clock and the name of the town on the sign on the platform. She already knew how to read properly, but that name was difficult: Sitges. She read it and repeated it over and over to learn it, commit it to memory. She always said it like: Chiches, and Ernesto and Rafael would laugh.

Julia remembered that it was then, when Antonio disappeared from the platform, that she ran back home. She sat in the doorway, waiting for Mamá to come home, with a couple of stones in her hand. She felt such profound, wild happiness that it hurt. Mamá was going to show up any minute now, and she felt content, happy. She felt like going inside, waking Rafael and Ernesto up, biting, kissing, kicking them, asking them to sing the one about the black clown and little Julia the Ugly Buggly. Suddenly she felt the urgent need to punish herself for that happiness. She didn't deserve it. She had committed a grave offense that morning. She was guilty. Papá appeared in her mind, and then the well, dark, deep, swallowing him up. Julia remembered that it was precisely that afternoon, in the doorway of their house, in the summer, in Sitges, beneath the sunlight that was beating down, when, for the first time, she had felt the need to think about something that would fill her with pain, with fear, with anguish. She imagined Mamá dead, on the train that was going to arrive at any minute, and that she, little Julia, would never ever see her again.

Remembering those years, Julia felt as if a thousand invisible fingers were squeezing her throat, making it difficult for her to breathe freely but not completely suffocating her. Something or someone remained locked up inside her, impudently showing her the indestructible chains of her slavery. At times Julia felt the urgent need to breathe deeply, very deeply, and then release the air from her lungs slowly. At school, she would try to find a seat close to the window, compelled by the absurd obsession that, like many times before, the feeling of suffocation might overwhelm her. At other times, on the street, she would realize she wasn't breathing correctly, she needed more air. Paradoxically, she would quicken her step, begin to run in order to become completely exhausted, forced to stop after a few minutes, leaning against a wall, her need to breathe deeply over and over justified.

It had always been like that: a sensation of anguish, of heaviness, as if a nebulous hot mass was expanding inside her head. It seemed strange to her that other people could talk, walk, read the newspaper, study, without stopping to examine their respiration. She, Julia, couldn't think about anything except her own breathing. Sometimes her preoccupation with it was unbearable, and she tried to avoid it for a few minutes by thinking about something else. Sitting in class, she would observe how the other students breathed. The boy or girl next to her paid attention to the teacher's explanations or took notes or doodled. Julia realized that her classmate's attention was focused on what he or she was doing or hearing. She tried to do the same thing. For a few minutes she would pay attention to the teacher; she made an effort to listen to the explanations, retain the words, understand their importance, and forget about herself. The same thing happened in the movie theater, or talking with Andrés or with anyone else. She had to make an effort to concentrate on what she was doing, otherwise she obsessed about her breathing and the same old anguish and concern as always took hold of her, the eternal dread that invaded her at night, when she couldn't sleep and memories, images would begin to parade through her mind, making her, Julia, tell herself once again that she had lost something, that a peculiar feeling, an incomprehensible law had deprived her of something —unknown— a long time ago and now made her recognize, once and for all, the great emptiness inside herself.

Trying to experience those dead years again, still so close by, meant finding little Julia sitting in the doorway of their house, during the summer when she was six years old, with the shorts and the navy blue sweater with an anchor drawn on the chest. And little Julia (she, Julia, knew it very well) was the ideal guide for people whose spirit of adventure compelled them to take a long trip toward confusion and fear. However, in spite of the contradictory emotions that little Julia inspired in her by making her relive those years, Julia found a glimmer of light, a little space where the air that was blowing was calm and pure, the comforting sense of having at least loved someone and knowing that someone had loved her. It was a wayside on the exhausting trip that little Julia subjected her to. A memory, a heartbreaking sadness that nevertheless didn't hurt. A memory that, in the past, had been called Rafael.

Julia felt sad when she thought about Rafael, as if she was indebted to him: she owed him remorse for her ancient hatred, she needed to fulfill the trust which had been established between the two of them too late, left pending in time as a mere promise, abruptly interrupted by Rafael's death.

Julia remembered Rafael —she was seven years old and he was eleven—, short for his age, extremely thin, with a dark complexion, very lively dark eyes, and hands that never stopped moving.

Rafael began to suffer frequent fainting spells and terrible headaches. Julia would come home from school and Aurelia would say: Shhhh, don't make a racket, Rafael's sick again. They would often bring him home from school, and the person accompanying him would explain to Mamá that Rafael had suddenly fainted and that, when he came to on the ground, he didn't know where he was, didn't recognize his teacher or classmates. Rafael would stay in bed for two or three weeks every time he "got that," as Aurelia said, and then there were the days he was recuperating, when he was unbearable. Mamá went out less often than normal, and it was like putting candy in little Julia's mouth and then quickly snatching it away because, although she was filled with joy when she saw Mamá at home, she would then have to pay the consequences of Mamá's incomprehensible bad mood. Mamá would spend the whole day next to Rafael, lying down with him in bed, reading him books, hugging him, telling him stories, promising him movies, an excursion up the Tibidabo, a boat trip around the port when he got better. She fed him and told him: If you want, you can sleep with me, and Ernesto with Papá. They took Rafael to Mamá's bed and, from there, he ruled the whole house. Lying in bed, Rafael would say: I want this. And Mamá would give it to him, even if it was Ernesto's or little Julia's toy. Little Julia cried every time they snatched her things away from her to give them to Rafael. Give it to him, ordered Papá, can't you see he's sick? Little Julia, during those long days, cried about everything; she was in a bad mood, and Aurelia drove her crazy when she would say: I know a little girl who's jealous. She wasn't jealous. Little Julia repeated it over and over to herself and got enraged when everyone else talked about it. She wasn't jealous. She cried out of powerlessness, humiliation. Rafael would pick any game he felt like and tell her to come play with him — and don't upset him, Mamá warned her— and then, when she was just starting to have fun, Rafael would exclaim: Now go away, I don't want to play with girls. And Mamá would scream at her: Don't you pay any attention? Don't bother Rafael. She cried out of desperation, not jealousy, when after weighing the possibilities, she'd screw up her courage and dare to approach Mamá, wrapping her arms around her waist and putting her head in her lap, and Mamá yelled at her: Again?, come on, let me go, you're such a pest, can't you hear?, Rafael's calling me. She would have given Rafael her toys, colored pencils, coloring books, everything she owned in exchange for being in his place, lying in bed, with Mamá by her side, even if her head really hurt and she had to endure a high fever. At times she thought it was true: she had no reason to be jealous, Mamá loved all three of them equally. But little Julia thought and thought and arrived at the conclusion that, if she was jealous, her jealousy was justified: Mamá never stopped going out when she was sick, nor did she move little Julia to her bed to spend the night by her side. At most, if little Julia had a high fever or insisted on not sleeping alone, they would let her go to bed with Aurelia. And if you keep on crying, not even with Aurelia, Mamá would say.

Julia remembered that Papá, Ernesto, and Rafael would feel sorry for her when she cried at bedtime because she didn't want to sleep alone in her room. Ernesto (who at fifteen was now allowed long pants, was as tall as Mamá, and had gotten a very strange voice: deep and dry, but from time to time a squawk would come out and everyone would laugh) would suggest to Mamá: She can sleep in our room, Rafael'll sleep with me, and little Julia in Rafael's bed. But Mamá would say: No, no, she'll get used to it and there'll be no way to make her sleep alone again, don't even think about it, the other day I swore it was the last time.

The last time, as Mamá said, little Julia, after announcing her steadfast refusal to sleep alone, sat down in her pajamas on the cold tiles in the middle of the hallway. Mamá slapped her and said: Today you're going to get away with it because you've got a cold and I'm not in any mood to deal with a case of pneumonia; plus, I've got to go out; but this is the last time. And that night she slept in the boys' room. When Mamá went out, they were already in bed, but they still hadn't fallen asleep. As soon as they heard Mamá say good-bye to Aurelia (Aurelia, watch the kids, give Rafael his pill and Julia the cough syrup and go to bed early) and close the door, Ernesto and Rafael got up. We're going to put on a play. Ernesto and Rafael put on costumes and acted out *Samson and Delilah* and scenes from other movies from those years. Rafael played Samson and sang to Ernesto (who played the role of Delilah): Delilah, don't cut my hair, because for fifteen pesetas the barber'll cut it for me. They continued with imitations of Carmen Miranda and Bob Hope in the movie *Scared Stiff*, Mario Lanza and Ann Blyth in *The Student Prince*, *Frankenstein*, *The Wolfman*, Stan Laurel and Oliver Hardy, Xavier Cugat, and Abe Lane. Ernesto's and Rafael's imitations were accompanied by famous songs, but they changed the lyrics at will and made little Julia laugh. The last number ("the grand finale," as they said) consisted of producing a three-dimensional movie in the bedroom. To help little Julia understand, Ernesto said: We mean in relief. Imagine that you're sitting in a seat in the theater and you're the audience. The three-dimensional movie that Ernesto and Rafael acted out was *Charge of Feather River*. In order for little Julia to notice the film's relief, Ernesto and Rafael, in their battles, threw weapons (pens, a shoehorn, shoes, socks, combs . . .) at the headboard of little Julia's bed. Rafael organized the game and made up the rules. Julia remembered Rafael's great skill at dominating situations without anyone really noticing his control, the power he wielded over them. Ernesto, the oldest of the three, invariably rebelled as soon as he noticed that anyone placed himself on a higher plane than he was. Listen, you don't boss me around, understand?, I'm the oldest, he would say to Rafael when he told him: Now paint your eyes black and . . . But this rarely happened, because Rafael had a special talent for getting Ernesto to do what he wanted without letting him realize it. Ernesto felt profound admiration for Rafael in spite of being four years older than him. Rafael was one of a kind at coming up with good ideas, organizing games, getting money out of Papá when they spent the amount they were given on Sundays, lying to Mamá if after getting out of school they went out for a walk or to play soccer, and they got home later than normal, finding excuses when they broke something in the living room. Moreover, Rafael brought home better grades. Ernesto was fifteen years old and was repeating his freshman year with three subjects from eighth grade. Rafael was eleven, almost twelve, and he was in the seventh grade. Papá, at the end of the month, when they showed him their report cards, would become enraged with Ernesto and humiliate him in front of Rafael: He's younger than you, he's sick, and look at these grades, you should be ashamed, you good-for-nothing. Mamá defended Ernesto: Leave him alone, he's at a difficult age. Ernesto endured the humiliation with tears in his eyes and pale with envy. He didn't care what Papá might say about him, but the comparisons drove him crazy. Rafael's in seventh grade, he's still okay, we'll see what happens when he gets to high school; plus, they're out to get me, Ernesto said. It's true, Rafael agreed, the headmaster can't stand him, I've seen it, Papá. Of course, shouted Mamá, it has to be something like that. At the end of every month, after seeing their report cards, an argument would break out between Papá and Mamá. If the teachers did their jobs right . . . complained Mamá, and the next day she'd go talk to the headmaster of the school, a Jesuit who, according to Ernesto: Knows absolutely everything, he must be the devil himself.

After Papá's comparisons, the relationship between Rafael and Ernesto would get colder for a few hours; but Rafael, always guided by his rare common sense, would apologize to Ernesto for his good grades: Buddy, they've got it in for you, I sure wish I could draw and play basketball like you do. With those words, Ernesto would begin strutting and assume once again the prerogative of the oldest son, although always dominated by Rafael. His dominance was evident at every moment: choosing the movie to see on Saturday afternoons, dividing up the money that Papá gave them, deciding what classmate they could or couldn't stand to study and play with, and making up the rules for their games.

 The control that Rafael wielded over Ernesto had negative consequences. Whenever something happened that irritated Mamá, he got the blame. They were having so much fun that night putting on plays and three-dimensional movies that they didn't hear the door open when Mamá got back, or her footsteps down the hallway. It's three o'clock in the morning, Mamá exclaimed, bursting into the bedroom. The three of them shouted and froze at the same time. Mamá started to scream like a madwoman when she saw what they'd done to the room. She began to slap all three of them, but it was Rafael who received the brunt of it. Just wait until tomorrow, I'm going to beat you until you feel it. Bah!, I'm not afraid of her, said Rafael as soon as Mamá disappeared, by tomorrow she'll have forgotten all about it.

 That was the last night they let her sleep in the boys' room. When she was sick she slept with Aurelia, but with Mamá, never: not even to keep her company during the day. She didn't understand why they said she was jealous. It wasn't jealousy, it was the obvious injustice that put her in a bad mood. When Rafael was sick, she acted up at school, didn't eat, and constantly went around sniveling in the corners. Little Julia thought she'd get some attention by acting up and then Mamá'd be a little more affectionate with her. But she achieved the opposite: she enraged Mamá. If she doesn't want to eat, let her be —she told Aurelia—, that way she'll have more at dinnertime, and if she cries let her cry, she'll get tired of it, I'm sick of this nonsense, I have enough problems as it is. Little Julia wished that Rafael would just die and get it over with. She only wanted the benefits his disappearance would bring, she didn't understand, back then, the idea that death was linked to "forever." But Rafael "got that" more and more often. Mamá was unbearable, she divided her time between Rafael and mysterious errands that caused arguments between her and Papá, and, if little Julia approached her with some pretext to be able to spend a moment of time with her, she would yell: Aurelia, get her out from underfoot, I can't vouch for my nerves.

Little Julia began to hear vague conversations between Mamá and Grandmother Lucía (who didn't live with them yet and only went to their house on Sundays) about her. They constantly repeated two things: jealousy and Aunt Elena. And Mamá: Anyway, just until Rafael gets totally better. And Grandmother Lucía: So that she misses him, of course it'll only be the first few days, later on . . . she'll get over it. If Papá was with them, he would say: I think it's a bad idea, very bad. And Mamá: Well, what do you want?, she's jealous, she doesn't eat, she cries all day, she's losing weight. If you were a different kind of mother . . . Papá reproached her. What are you trying to say? That people who aren't capable of raising children shouldn't have them. And then they would fight.

They're going to sell you, Ernesto told her. Don't be dumb, he added, in response to little Julia's unhappy expression, they're selling you to Aunt Elena, what I wouldn't give to have them sell me to Aunt Elena, I wouldn't have to study, Papá wouldn't yell at me all the time . . . it's great luck, plus you get to live with Don Julio.

Don Julio was their paternal grandfather. The entire family, even Papá, called him Don Julio. His grandchildren called him Don Julio rather than Grandfather; his nieces and nephews called him Don Julio instead of Uncle; Mamá called him Don Julio; even Aunt Elena, his own daughter, called him Don Julio. Don Julio had been living in the mountains for the past twenty-five years. Little Julia had heard them talk about him, but she couldn't imagine what he was really like. Mamá would say: He's a crazy old man, who would even think of burying themselves alive in that valley? Just because they lost the war, it's not as if he lost it all by himself. Anyway, said Papá, people have their own personalities and ideas; some of them don't know how to handle defeat. Grandmother Lucía was the one who said the worst things about Don Julio: An atheist, dear Lord, an Anarchist, even worse than if he'd been a Communist. Bloodthirsty. You can't know, because you didn't live through the horrors of the Week of Tragedies. Barcelona was a sea of blood, and all because of wicked men like Don Julio. Why take it out on the priests and nuns if the politicians want to come to blows? An anarchist and, on top of that, vulgar.

In spite of the way Grandmother Lucía and Mamá sullied Don Julio's image, he had grown in little Julia's imagination and even more so in Rafael's. Rafael, when he played war games with Ernesto and his friends, proposed: I'll be the bad guy, Don Julio. Little Julia imagined that he was tall and solid, dressed like a general, with a scar across one cheek and one eye covered by a black patch, riding a white horse, with a sword in his hand and killing everyone who got in his path. They didn't meet him until their grandmother died and they went with Papá and Mamá to the house in the mountains. Little Julia remembered Don Julio vaguely. The powerful, fierce, cruel warrior figure that she had imagined had nothing to do with Don Julio. When Ernesto announced: They're going to sell you to Aunt Elena and Don Julio, little Julia remembered her grandfather's tall, hunched figure, dressed in mourning; his beard and hair completely white. During the two days that they stayed at his house because of her grandmother's death, they didn't hear him say a word. He was pacing through the dark, cold room with his hands clasped behind his back and his head bowed toward his chest. Papá didn't dare interrupt his silent pacing through the dark room until they were ready to leave. We have to go now. Papá hugged Don Julio. You haven't met the children. For the first time since they'd gotten there, they heard the deep, electrifying voice resonating in the room: That's true, where's my granddaughter? As Don Julio approached her, a dreadful fear came over little Julia. Don Julio took hold of her chin and raised her face toward him. He studied her for a few seconds and kissed her on her cheek. He ran his hand over Ernesto's and Rafael's heads and said to Mamá: I have four children, seven grandsons, and only one granddaughter. And then, looking at the two boys, in his booming voice: Cannon Fodder.

Little Julia, for a few days, lived in doubt about whether the "sale to Aunt Elena and Don Julio" was one of Ernesto's customary jokes or might be true. She continued to hear conversations between Mamá and Grandmother Lucía about her, jealousy, Aunt Elena, and Don Julio. One morning Mamá took her shopping: You're going to spend some days with Aunt Elena, it's very cold there, you'll need warmer clothes.

When they got to the mountains it was getting dark. During the trip, little Julia had fallen asleep watching the continuous motion of the windshield wipers sweeping the raindrops from the glass. Papá parked in a service station to fill up with gas, and they went to the snack bar. We'll be there soon, said Papá. And once again, he repeated the admonitions that Mamá had made before they left Barcelona. You behave yourself, tell Aunt Elena to keep you bundled up, it'll be very cold there, it might snow. Don't make Aunt Elena mad, and if Don Julio yells at you or says anything mean, don't pay any attention, he's very old and doesn't know what he's saying. You're going to stay with Aunt Elena until summer, but we'll come see you all the time. It was very cold, and Papá added: Put your scarf on and don't open your mouth. But little Julia, during the short walk from the snack bar to the car, opened her mouth, letting her breath out slowly, very slowly, observing the cloud that formed in the cold air. They got in the car again and soon drove through a small town with practically deserted streets. The houses were old and low to the ground, their roofs white with snow. The mountains were also covered with snow. The car struggled forward slowly. Is it much further?, asked little Julia from time to time. We're almost there.

Don Julio's house was a bit separated from town. It seemed enormous to little Julia, compared to the ones she had left behind. It was four stories high, and, in front of it, there was a huge yard. While she and Papá were walking up to the house, they saw a man running up to open the gate. Hi, Joaquín, how's everyone doing? Welcome, sir. We expected you sooner. The señora has been worried, the roads must have been very bad in this weather. Julia remembered that the porch seemed spacious, dark, and cold; a feeling of devastation came over her. Joaquín took her suitcase and had them come inside. The room seemed almost empty; riding saddles, leather straps, cords, and baskets were the only things visible. They went up a wooden staircase with steps that creaked beneath their feet. When they got upstairs, Aunt Elena came out to greet them with cries of joy: Finally, I thought you'd never get here. She kissed Papá and hugged little Julia repeatedly, saying over and over: Look at how much you've grown, you're so big. Come in, come in by the fire. Don Julio's out. In this weather?, asked Papá, surprised. Yes, she said to her brother, yes, our father is like that. Martina, Papá exclaimed when he caught sight of a short woman, about sixty years old, with white hair, very heavy set. Martina, how are you? Young Master Julio, what a great joy, dear God.

Aunt Elena brought two armchairs up by the fire, she made

herself comfortable in one of them and sat little Julia on her lap. Papá sat in the other one, and they began to talk about how odd our father is, how are the kids?, and your wife? The room seemed magnificent to little Julia. She figured it was the dining room: in the center of the room there was a long oak table. It reminded her of the tables she had seen in movies with plots that took place during the Middle Ages, like *The Knights of the Round Table*. The chairs that, instead of being around the table like at home in Barcelona, were leaning against the wall, also reminded her of the ones in that movie: they had very high backs and seemed narrower than normal. A tall writing desk occupied one of the walls of the room, and there were pots, ladles, and copper utensils on dark wooden shelves. The fireplace was blazing in one corner. There were two leather armchairs at the far ends of the room. Little Julia, somewhat curious and somewhat frightened, saw animal skins and a deer head hanging on the walls. On the floor, a thick rug of several colors, mostly shades of red over brown and black.

Aunt Elena helped her take off her scarf and coat, while she said to Papá: I got your room ready, how many days are you going to stay? No, no, I have to get back to Barcelona tonight, I've got so much work to do, it's crazy. Little Julia was dozing off. Half asleep, she could hear Papá and Aunt Elena talking, and from time to time she would open her eyes and see Martina and Joaquín. She had the sensation, even though the trip had been relatively short, that she was very far away from Barcelona and that it'd been years since she'd seen Mamá.

When Martina woke her up to serve her dinner, Papá had already left. Come here, Martina said, you and Aunt Elena will have dinner in the kitchen; Don Julio always eats alone. In the kitchen she saw a table that was almost as big as the one in the dining room but made of marble. Martina pulled up a chair for her. Now, Aunt Elena said to her, we'll have dinner and then off to bed. Little Julia remembered the night her grandmother had died, two years before, and her fear in the room upstairs where she could hear the roaring of the wind against the window, the beating of the shutters, and the river. She remembered Rafael singing "Green Path," and she had the sensation that someone had died. In the kitchen, the firewood was being consumed by a brisk, crackling fire that lit up

Martina's and Aunt Elena's faces. She made an effort to hold back her tears, but she couldn't. Oh!, don't cry, exclaimed Aunt Elena, if you want, you can sleep in my bed with me. Little Julia nodded her head but kept on crying, trying to do it silently and focus her attention, in order to distract herself, on the furniture in the kitchen. She was thinking about Mamá, she felt a pain deep down in her chest and the certainty that it had been a long time since she had been abandoned there, at Don Julio's house, far away from Mamá, from Rafael and Ernesto. It made her blood boil to admit that she missed Rafael and Ernesto. During the car trip she had convinced herself that it was Rafael's fault they were throwing her out of the house, and she hated him. But now she thought that at least if the two boys were with her, everything would be different; she would be able to play with them. Ernesto and Rafael always distracted her from Mamá's absences. But there wasn't anyone there, not even Aurelia. Maybe Mamá would never come. The situation seemed strange to her. She had been sitting at the table, waiting for dinner, and she didn't know what to do, how to distract herself, whom to talk to. She didn't know Martina or Aunt Elena or Joaquín, she didn't even know the house well enough to walk around in it. It was as if Mamá had died and that was why she, little Julia, was there. She kept her head down and looked at her feet. She heard Martina and Aunt Elena: Poor little thing, she's breaking my heart. Quiet, Martina, I think it's best to act like we don't even notice, what would we say to her?

Footsteps were heard through the dining room, and then a thunderous voice resonated in the kitchen: Why is my granddaughter crying? Little Julia lifted her head, startled. In the doorway she saw a tall, thin man, dressed in a dark corduroy suit, with white hair and a white beard, large twinkling eyes, which he fixed on Martina and Aunt Elena. I don't want to see my granddaughter cry, what's wrong with her? Well, what do you think's wrong with her?, said Aunt Elena. She wants to see her mother. Bah!, you two are worthless; if you don't know how to comfort a child, what good are you? Don Julio left the kitchen and appeared again, after a few minutes, with a pipe clenched between his teeth. Elena, wipe my granddaughter's face. And then, addressing Martina, he demanded: Who told you to serve dinner here? My granddaughter will eat with her grandfather.

Martina and Aunt Elena exchanged a look of astonishment.

The old man headed toward the dining room and, with his head, signaled little Julia to follow him. In the dining room, Don Julio took a chair and sat at one extreme of the endless table. Little Julia took another one and placed it at a prudent distance from her grandfather: not too close, because Don Julio's voice frightened her, nor so far that Don Julio would realize she was scared of him. Martina, shouted Don Julio, doesn't it even occur to you that my granddaughter won't be able to reach the table from this chair? Yes, Don Julio. You're right as rain, we'll have to give her a cushion. Don Julio was sitting in an unusual position: one foot on the floor and the other one resting on one of the rungs of the chair, a hand on one knee, and his body erect, leaning slightly back. From time to time he observed little Julia closely, staring at her with his intense, twinkling eyes. Little Julia liked to look at his white hair and beard, his tan face, and the distinctive blue veins on his temples and hands. How old is my granddaughter?, Don Julio asked Aunt Elena. Little Julia's seven. Her name's not little Julia, her grandfather said, raising his voice. Her name's Julia, like me. Little Julia furrowed her brow, they had never called her just plain Julia before. She didn't like or dislike the sound of it, but it surprised her. Don Julio must have noticed the impact his words had on the girl and probably believed it was greater than it really was. For the first time since she had arrived at the house, her grandfather, in a friendly tone, laughing, spoke to her: Can you imagine if they called me little Julio? But she's a girl, replied Aunt Elena. Bah!, a girl, a girl . . . Children don't exist, what's a child? Julia's not a child, understood?, he said, staring at Aunt Elena. She's a person who's . . . let's say, small, that's it, and in reality, thinking about it carefully, too small for her mother to leave her —and furrowing his brow he continued, addressing Martina and Aunt Elena—: The two of you will probably show your stupidity and uselessness by not knowing how to treat Julia in a way that will help her forget that she suffers the misfortune of being her mother's daughter. Don Julio, please, don't talk in that tone of voice, you're going to scare little Julia, exclaimed Aunt Elena. I said her name's Julia, Julia, and you, Daughter, get it through your head once and for all that my granddaughter isn't afraid of anything or anyone, isn't that right? Little Julia was frightened, but she wanted to seem brave. Furthermore, even though Don Julio's stern appearance and his booming, electrifying voice silenced her, she wasn't afraid of him. Aunt Elena chided Don Julio for his brusqueness, but Julia thought her grandfather was nice to her, nicer than she would have expected. No, Grandfather, she said in a tiny voice, I'm not afraid. When she uttered the word *Grandfather*, little Julia saw how Aunt Elena covered her mouth with her hand. Martina, who was placing a couple of cushions on the chair so little Julia could reach the table, stopped, rigid, her mouth agape. Don Julio looked at her intently, seriously, and then smiled: Okay, you two, what's the matter? What do you want a granddaughter to call her grandfather? My granddaughter isn't afraid, and she calls things by their name. Her grandfather took a packet of tobacco that smelled like honey out of his coat pocket and filled his pipe.

The dinner was dominated by silence. Little Julia began to think about Mamá again. She kept drinking water to loosen the knot in her throat and avoid crying. The house seemed unreal to her. Maybe she was dreaming and would wake up at any moment, finding herself in Barcelona, in her bed or Aurelia's. When she woke up, she'd see Mamá. But she remembered the trip, Mamá's admonitions, Ernesto and Rafael saying good-bye: You'll see, Don Julio's going to keep you on your toes, he's a monster. Only Don Julio's voice, thunderous, could pull her away from her thoughts. They heard steps on the stairs, and Joaquín appeared in the dining room with a bottle of wine. Let my granddaughter try some of our wine, Joaquín. Wine invigorates your blood and makes you grow. Don Julio's voice cut through the silence as if it were a wall of ice that crumbled beneath the pointed weight of his words and melted away in a flash. Don Julio, when he saw that Julia's lips were trembling, her eyes filling with tears, her face turning red, tapped the table nervously with his fingers and looked at Aunt Elena out of the corner of his eye. He slammed his fist down on the table, making the plates and glasses rattle. He exclaimed: Joaquín, I think my granddaughter likes horses, maybe she'd like to see them before she goes to bed. Why don't you go down to the stable and turn the lights on? He immediately nodded his head as if recognizing that he had had a great idea. Little Julia shouted: Yes, yes, I want to see them, how many do you have? First you have to finish your dinner, Martina said. I don't want any more. No, if you don't eat, no horses for you. Quiet, shouted her grandfather. If she doesn't want any more, she doesn't want any more. And, waving his pipe in the air with one hand, he added: One of the things I'm going to teach my granddaughter is that she can live without having anyone dictate her actions. But . . . Don Julio, implored Aunt Elena, it's so cold out, and so late. My granddaughter isn't cold. It's true, said little Julia in a tiny voice, I'm not cold.

They went down to the stable. Don Julio let her pet the horses as much as she wanted; he sat her on one of them and, with laughter and long explanations, answered her questions: What do they eat?, can they run in the mountains when there's snow?, why do they move their heads so much?, how many teeth do they have?, which one's oldest?, do they sleep standing up?

Julia got cold in the stable, like Martina had predicted; but when they got back, she didn't complain. She got up close to the fireplace and sat in the armchair in front of her grandfather's. She was falling asleep in the chair, she couldn't keep her eyes open, and she tried not to yawn, delaying bedtime as long as possible. Aunt Elena asked her: Shall we go up to bed now? The closer she got to bedtime, the sadder she felt and the more she wanted to cry. Nearly collapsing with exhaustion, she began sobbing. Her grandfather got up and started to pace around the dining room, his hands behind his back and the pipe between his teeth. Damn it, he shouted. My granddaughter's crying, and I said I don't want to see her cry. She's worn out from the trip and she's tired, we're going to bed right now, said Aunt Elena taking her by the hand. Will my mama come tomorrow?, she asked. Little Julia had managed to avoid the question during dinner. She didn't know why, but she had the sense, from the first instant, that her grandfather wasn't going to like it if she cried about Mamá's absence. Your mother! If she walks through that door, she'll be sent right back out through the window, shouted Don Julio. Then, pulling on his white beard, he called Martina: Martina, Martina, where have you gotten to? I'm always tripping over you around every corner, but then when I need you I never know where the hell you are; did the cat have her litter yet? And then, very seriously, looking at little Julia: If you promise not to cry anymore, tomorrow I'll give you a present. It's . . . well, it's a secret. Good night. And he walked out of the dining room.

Aunt Elena took her by the hand and they went upstairs to the bedroom. Little Julia counted seven doors down the long hallway.

The cold penetrated to her bones. Aunt Elena helped her get undressed and put on her pajamas. Aren't you going to bed?, she asked her. Of course, with you, but I have to go downstairs for a minute . . . No, I don't want you to. Aunt Elena stayed and went to bed.

Little Julia fell asleep quickly, but she woke up at midnight. She heard strange sounds at the windows. Aunt Elena was asleep by her side. She was younger than Mamá —she must have been around thirty then—, with very dark hair and eyes, delicate skin, a soft voice, and full rosy lips. Little Julia was frightened. She sat up in bed and Aunt Elena woke up. She was afraid Aunt Elena was going to scold her; instead she turned on the light and asked: Are you thirsty? She wasn't thirsty, but she said: Yes. Aunt Elena handed her a glass that was on the nightstand. What's that noise? The wind. There's no dead people? Dead people? What foolishness! Don't you want to drink any more? Little Julia shook her head. She remembered the night of her grandmother's death: she —little Julia— and Rafael had slept in a room like this one. Mamá was with them. When she thought about Mamá, it seemed like summer would never come and she began to cry. Aunt Elena hugged her and squeezed her to her chest: Little Julia, sweetie. You're not afraid, are you?, I'm right here with you. And tomorrow?, asked little Julia, will I have to sleep alone? No, of course not; come on, lie down, time to go to sleep. Aunt Elena turned the light back off, and little Julia clung to her tightly.

When Aunt Elena woke her up, it was after eleven o'clock in the morning. Hurry, little Julia; Don Julio is waiting for you in the dining room with a lovely present. Aunt Elena was wearing a dark skirt and a thick wool sweater, light blue. She wore her hair down, and little Julia thought she looked prettier than the day before. Martina came into the room with a towel hanging from her arm and said to her: Let's go, into the tub, you really need it. Later Aunt Elena combed out her braids.

In the dining room, Don Julio was pacing and smoking his pipe. Good morning, Julia. Did you cry last night? She blushed and shook her head. Well, look what I brought you. And he held out a shoe box. Little Julia opened it, and inside she discovered two hairy balls, each the size of her hand, squashed up against each other. She touched them and heard some mews: it was two newborn cats.

They're yours, said her grandfather. And waving his pipe in the air, he added, in a voice that tried to be severe: You're responsible for taking care of them and making sure the dogs don't get them. Don Julio noticed little Julia's feet and shouted: Elena, Martina, just how far does your stupidity go? Little Julia, startled, raised her eyes from the shoe box and looked at her grandfather. He seemed gigantic, violent like the warrior she had imagined before meeting him. Don't tell me you didn't notice Julia's shoes! They're made out of cardboard. My granddaughter needs some boots. After breakfast, we'll go buy some. I'll go with her myself, you two are worthless. And he began to pace around the dining room again, with his hands behind his back, smoking silently and glaring furiously at Aunt Elena and Martina.

Between going to town, buying the boots, and taking care of the newborn cats, the morning went by in a flash. They drove to town. Because with those toy shoes you're not going to be able to take a single step. Coming home, they walked. The branches of the trees were white with snow and the mud was frozen. Little Julia, at her grandfather's insistence, paid attention to the beauty of the landscape and the color of the sky. Breathe deep, Julia, the mountain air will kill off the microbes of that stench you breathe in Barcelona. Barcelona doesn't stink, protested little Julia. Bah!, tell me about it, I was born there, everyone's going to die of cancer, so much smoke, so much noise . . . I don't like cities, too much stupidity. With the pipe in his hand he motioned toward the distance, toward the immense, thick forests and then the mountains, completely white with snow. The sky seemed very blue, with cottony clouds, and the sunlight was nearly blinding as it reflected off the snow. The town was small and the houses old. They came to a plaza where several streets met. Don Julio bought her a pair of leather boots and a fur-lined coat that was a little bit big on her. She struggled to walk with her feet stuck in the heavy boots, but she didn't complain. Little Julia had quickly intuited two things that bothered her grandfather: stupidity and weakness. Later she realized that many other things irritated Don Julio, like injustice, unreasonableness, and talking just for talking's sake. Her grandfather accepted only one truth, essential, unquestionable: freedom. For him, everything else was stupidity. There are more wise men in this town than in the rest of Spain put together: here, at least, they are what they are.

Back then little Julia didn't understand Don Julio's words, but they were engraved in her memory forever. Her grandfather said: You don't understand right now, but someday you will. Little Julia wondered why her grandfather kept talking to her if he already assumed she couldn't understand him. For now, I want you to try to learn just one thing: you're free, just that. Just that we are free. In the name of that freedom, one has the right, even the obligation, to kill if necessary.

Julia remembered the time spent at Don Julio's house with pleasure, in spite of the suffocating anguish that she had felt in the beginning when she thought about Mamá. Mamá would come to mind after lunch, when Don Julio and Aunt Elena were lying down for their siesta, and at nighttime. Then little Julia would think that Mamá could die and she wouldn't see her anymore. And the thing that Mamá sometimes told Papá could come true: I'll leave and you won't see hide nor hair of me again. Little Julia felt the urge to scream, cry, beg her grandfather to take her to Barcelona to see the paved streets, long and wide, with trees and streetcars, the tall, pretty houses. The urge to arrive home, take the elevator, knock on the door, and surprise Aurelia; then run to the living room and find Mamá, Ernesto, Rafael. When she thought about them she would feel desperate and throw herself on Aunt Elena, hugging her, covering her forehead, her cheeks, her neck with kisses, burying her hands in her black hair and caressing it. Aunt Elena, without waking up completely, would hug her and return her kisses and call her my darling.

She would go with Don Julio to the sawmill every morning. Her grandfather yelled and fought with the employees, especially the foreman, named Llop, whom they called Corporal Llop the Red. At night, after supper, two or three times a week, some of Don Julio's friends would come up to the house to have coffee and talk. Her grandfather's friends were Don Raimundo, the town doctor; Don Alfredo, the teacher; Corporal Llop the Red, foreman of the sawmill; and Matías, the pharmacist. By the end of the evening, Don Julio would have fought with all of them and would be in a bad mood. They would sit at the table and, after coffee, drink a very sweet liqueur that her grandfather produced. Corporal Llop would accuse Don Julio of being an Anarchist; Don Julio, in turn, called him a Communist. So what? At least we knew what we wanted. Your group wasn't even organized. Corporal Llop and Don Julio would band together against Matías and Don Raimundo, calling them fascists and corrosive old hermits. Don Alfredo, the teacher, claimed he had become disillusioned. When the Republic fell, everything stopped and my world ended. Yes sir, it's over, I don't care about anything anymore.

Aunt Elena, while Don Julio let off steam at these reunions, would read in a little sitting room next to the dining room. Little Julia divided her evening between the dining room and the sitting room, with the two cats in her arms. She named the male Porky and the female Petunia, after two characters in a comic book that Rafael had bought. She liked to see her grandfather at the precise moment when he turned red with rage and slapped his hand down on the table. Stupidity, stupidity, stupidity. Damn human stupidity. When I was a representative and I directed . . . When you were a representative, Matías interrupted, our country was going through its worst time ever; you couldn't take a peaceful stroll through Barcelona without a bomb exploding on every corner. The Anarchist terrorists like you . . .

Little Julia had heard Grandmother Lucía say that Don Julio was an Anarchist (of the worst kind, a bandit). Both of them, Grandmother Lucía and Don Julio, had declared war on each other before Mamá and Papá got married. The worst thing Grandmother Lucía charged Don Julio with was his refusal to go to the church on Mamá's wedding day; he was vulgar, rude, and heartless and, during the war, he killed all the priests and nuns he could get his hands on.

Don Julio also heaped abuse on Grandmother Lucía and Mamá. Sometimes her grandfather and Aunt Elena had arguments about it. Don Julio claimed that Papá should never have married the daughter of that old witch: an unbearably sanctimonious hypocrite, a disgusting moneybags, and her daughter, a stupid fool. Aunt Elena excused them: People are the way they are, what's to be done about it? Kill them, that's what's to be done, shouted her grandfather in a scathing tone of voice, kill them. My son's an idiot, a weakling. Abandoning his career in order to manage a sock and underwear factory . . . It's shirts, protested little Julia. Same difference, my son's a weakling, an idiot . . . he should have married Eva, that girl, yes . . .

Christmas arrived and, instead of going to get her like she had promised, Mamá sent her a letter and some presents. At first little Julia was annoyed, but when she found out in the letter that Rafael was still sick, she resigned herself to the fact that she would be staying at Don Julio's house. From time to time, she felt like she was just dying to see Mamá; but when she thought about Rafael's illness, she convinced herself that she preferred to stay with Aunt Elena and her grandfather rather than relive the last days she had spent at home.

On January 6th, she got some Epiphany presents from Mamá and another letter admonishing her to be good. Ernesto and Rafael also sent one wishing Don Julio a Happy New Year, with a separate note for her. Little Julia turned red with rage when she read the words they sent her. She spent half an hour with the paper in her hands reading over and over: Ever since they sold you, things are very peaceful here; having a sister is always a pain. We bought you a Crazy Bird doll with our own money; it looks just like you. You've probably gotten very fat and your face must be as red as a farm girl's. We hope you make a New Year's resolution to stop being so ugly.

Am I fat?, is my face all red?, she asked Martina. You?, you're a sack of bones, you're just made up of bone and nerves. She read the boys' letter one more time. Her grandfather remained in his chair at the end of the table, observing little Julia. She was red with rage and biting her lips. I want to go to Barcelona, shouted little Julia suddenly. Is it really true that my granddaughter can't live without clinging to her mother's skirts? What do you need your mother for?, Don Julio asked in a mocking tone. No, exclaimed little Julia, slamming her fist down on the table. I want to kill those stupid idiots. She shouted so loud that the two cats, sleeping on the armchair next to the fireplace, took off like a shot toward the kitchen. Martina and Aunt Elena came running into the dining room. Don Julio smiled. Little Julia had expressed herself just like him, with identical words and gestures. If it was me I'd answer them in a letter. He raised the pipe to his lips. There was a short silence and he added: If they're stupid, it's not worth the bother to go all the way to Barcelona to see them. Those stupid blabbermouths, little Julia exclaimed again. Give me a piece of paper and a pencil. She was so upset that her words, scrawled on the sheet that Don Julio, full of satisfaction, had handed her, were practically illegible. Very good, said her grandfather when he read it: You two are stupid blabbermouths, you're as bad as priests. Very good, repeated her grandfather, your grandmother Lucía will be thrilled to see that you already know how to write.

Aunt Elena reproached Don Julio: You're teaching her bad manners, she's picking up your gestures and curses. So what? I'm going to make my granddaughter into an intelligent person even if she is a woman . . . , do you want her to be as useless as you or her mother? Come on, get a move on, get back to the kitchen, that's where you belong. I forbid you to stick your nose into things that don't concern you.

Papá and Ernesto came to the mountains in March, on little Julia's birthday. Don Julio burst out laughing when he saw the doll Papá had brought her from Barcelona. He slapped Ernesto on the shoulder, making him stagger. Putting the doll in his arms, he said: Take it, Son, go amuse yourself. Papá and Ernesto stayed one day and one night at the house. Don Julio took advantage of the slightest opportunity to make fun of Ernesto and Papá. When his grandfather stared at him, Ernesto would turn red, not daring to look at him. Cannon Fodder (as Don Julio called him instead of Ernesto), what grade are you in? Ernesto, in a tiny voice, answered: Ninth. Don Julio roared with laughter: Don't be in any hurry, Weakling. When you finish, your grandmother will hire you to sell shirts or to keep the records at her repulsive underwear factory, right, Son?, he asked, addressing Papá. Papá tried to change the subject: How've you been? How's the sawmill going? It doesn't pay as well as underwear, but I don't need to have my sons work for me. Then it was Aunt Elena who screwed up her courage and asked about Rafael. But Don Julio returned to the attack: Is your wife still living? Of course, the sanctimonious Lucía probably spends every penny she earns with underwear paying novenas to all the priests in Barcelona so she can make it to Judgment Day. He hit Ernesto on the back and let out a snort that made the dining-room walls tremble, yelling: Don't made that face, Weakling.

Little Julia liked it when her grandfather criticized Ernesto, her grandmother, and, deep down, she was also pleased that he included Mamá. She remained silent when her grandfather started insulting her whole family, but on the inside she felt a profound happiness.

Say hi to Eva for me, her grandfather said to Papá. You know it's been a long time since I've seen Eva. Papá got irritated when her grandfather mentioned Eva to him. I know, but you'll end up seeing her, and then you can tell her to come see me or write me. You were an idiot.

Papá and Ernesto left. The next day, Don Julio prepared a desk for Julia, notebooks, a fountain pen, colored pencils, paints, and a couple of books, and arranged it all in his office, a library located on the fourth floor of the house. I'm going to teach you how to write properly, your penmanship is atrocious, and we'll begin classes: Latin, geography, history, and drawing. Little Julia was interested in this novelty. She's too little, scolded Aunt Elena during lunch. She turned eight yesterday, didn't she?, so it's high time. Latin's good for developing intelligence and reading the classics, drawing will offer her a sense of harmony and balance, later on we'll paint landscapes outdoors and she'll learn to observe nature, by studying history she'll become aware of mankind's stupidity.

Latin and geography fascinated her. She had often heard Ernesto say that Latin was: A nightmare, they've already failed me at it three times. But she thought it was fun. She confronted mysterious words, looking up their meanings in a dictionary, and then she had to discover the proper order to make them make sense. Her grandfather taught her: A few tricks that the grammarians call rules, but we don't need to pay attention to those know-it-alls; it's just a game. The book her grandfather used for her Latin lessons was called *The Gallic War*. Her grandfather told her: Later on I'll tell you about Caesar, a stupid man. To study geography her grandfather placed a very thick book, illustrated with full-color maps, in her hands. When you read something you don't understand, ask me. They began with Spain. Name upon name of cities on the map. Julia wanted to find the one where she was living. Her grandfather marked a red cross on the map. It's so small . . . It was close to a strip of very dark colors where she read: Pyrenees. It seemed to little Julia that they were almost right next to France and that all the cities were stuck together, which made her reach the conclusion that the world was very small. Her grandfather explained that every millimeter on the map actually corresponded to ten thousand kilometers, but it was difficult for her to understand.

From the day they began classes, time went by more quickly. In the morning she would go to the sawmill with Don Julio or downtown with Aunt Elena, play with the cats, go to the stable to see the horses, and take long walks through the woods with her grandfather. After the midday siesta, they would go up to the library and have class. It seemed like Papá's letter announcing the next summer vacation in Sitges arrived too soon. It filled her with doubt: she wanted to see Mamá, but the desire was buried behind a sensation of fear.

When they got there, Barcelona seemed enormous to her. The streets longer and wider than she remembered and the noise deafening. She and Papá spent the night in a hotel and the next day they left for Sitges, where Mamá and the boys had been waiting for her for a few days. Very vaguely, she remembered that short summer vacation in Sitges as a continuous fight between Papá and Mamá, and long silent walks with Rafael through the outskirts of town. The happiness Mamá displayed when she saw her again seemed sincere. At the beginning of their reunion, Mamá pampered her all the time and yelled at Ernesto and Rafael when they picked on her. But then the arguments which preceded Papá's three- or four-day disappearances began. When Papá returned home, Mamá would leave for Barcelona. And when they were both in Sitges, the arguments would resume.

Ernesto had failed his final exams, and they locked him in to study. When Papá gave him permission to set his books aside, he would go out with friends who were older than him; they didn't let Rafael or little Julia join their group.

That summer, Papá gave her a bicycle. Little Julia, almost every afternoon, followed Rafael when he said: I'm going to Vinyet. Or: I'm going fishing at San Sebastián, if you bait the hook for me, I'll buy you an ice cream. She didn't enjoy spending her afternoons with Rafael, but he or Aurelia were her only escape. In spite of the fact that her relationship with her brother had cooled off because of his illness and the favoritism Mamá obviously showed him, little Julia had to admit that Rafael treated her better than anyone else.

They both had a specific strength, a weapon that gave them mutual superiority: Rafael enjoyed the privilege of converting Mamá into a rag doll with no will of her own as soon as he complained of a headache, and little Julia, in turn, astounded Rafael with her knowledge of Latin. Latin was the only subject Rafael had ever failed. After lunch, he translated *The Gallic War* for an hour. The day Julia arrived, when she told Rafael: I know a lot of Latin, if you want I'll help you, everyone burst out laughing. Little Julia kicked Ernesto in the shin and slammed her fist down on the table: Stupid blabbermouth, she shouted. Mamá slapped her: Your grandfather taught you bad manners. But little Julia, instead of crying in a corner like usual, ripped the Latin book out of Rafael's hands, in an outburst similar to her grandfather's, and began to translate *The Gallic War* out loud. Rafael, startled, exclaimed: It's true, it's true, she knows more Latin than the priest at school. Little Julia read slowly so she wouldn't run out of the pages she knew by heart. She could translate any passage in the book without knowing it cold, but she needed to amaze them all, make them believe that she was capable of translating, without a dictionary, the language that Ernesto had failed three times and Rafael once. The effect was devastating, especially for Rafael and Ernesto. Mamá grumbled: Of course, that's why they sent her back so thin, who would think of teaching Latin to an eight-year-old girl?, Latin and bad manners. Her knowledge of Latin intimidated Ernesto and Rafael, who couldn't understand how it was possible for little Julia to translate with such ease. Don Julio taught me some tricks, said little Julia, mysterious. And every day after lunch, she helped Rafael with his translations: You look up the words in the dictionary for me and I'll put them in order, it's a game, commented little Julia, trying to imitate her grandfather's tone of voice.

The walks with Rafael made her sad. Rafael would walk silently by her side. At times he asked her: Do you know where Ernesto went? Rafael was always worried about figuring out where Ernesto went with his friends. His friends are older, he complained. At home, little Julia heard them: Do you and your friends hang out with girls?, Rafael would ask. Don't you think I have better things to do, better things to think about? Sure, but you can't fool me. Whatever. I found some of your pictures of women in . . . Ernesto would fly into a rage when Rafael told him he'd been digging around in his things. Among Ernesto's books, she and Rafael had seen photos of Liz Taylor, Ava Gardner, Marilyn Monroe, and other movie stars. Often, during their walks, Rafael would suggest to little Julia: Let's go down Paseo Marítimo, maybe we'll find Ernesto. They rarely saw him there, and if they ever bumped into him and his friends, Ernesto would avoid them. Later, at home, he complained to Mamá: I'm sick and tired of them following me around, I'm a bit old to be hanging around with children, don't you think? Ernesto was almost sixteen and Rafael thirteen. It was just a coincidence, right, little Julia?, said Rafael as an excuse. I don't need you, it's better to be alone than to be with someone like you, as if I don't know the kinds of things you and your friends are up to. I'd beat you up if you weren't such a little kid, Ernesto threatened. Go ahead, hit me if you dare, replied Rafael. And Ernesto didn't dare, because he knew from experience that Rafael would win, even though he was three years younger.

During the walks with Rafael, little Julia missed her grandfather's house, the town, the mountains, the snowy winter landscape, and the pure air her grandfather had urged her to breathe deeply. She missed the peacefulness of the house during the day, and Don Julio's violent arguments with Corporal Llop and the others at night. Mamá was constantly going to Barcelona, and the days she stayed in Sitges, little Julia only saw her on the beach in the morning and at lunchtime. She wandered around the house, bored, without knowing what to do. At times it seemed like she could hear her grandfather's heavy footsteps down the hallway. She longed to hear the heavy, electrifying voice that would paralyze them all by calling them: Stupid blabbermouths, without a thought in your heads, if it were up to me, I'd send you off to work on a chain gang. She longed for the presence of that tall, thin figure, wearing dark corduroy. The tan, lean face with the distinctive thick blue veins on the temples, the furrowed brow, the long hair and white beard, the twinkling eyes that stared fixedly and seemed to speak without words, the eternal pipe that smelled like honey hanging from his lips. But more than anything she missed Aunt Elena. At night she struggled to fall asleep and she woke up at the crack of dawn. She was frightened and wanted someone to sleep by her side. But she didn't get up and go to Aurelia's bed, as she would have only a year earlier. She remained perfectly still in bed and tried to fall asleep thinking about

Aunt Elena. She hugged her pillow and imagined that the soft cushy shape was Aunt Elena and that she was sleeping next to her, like she did every night at Don Julio's house. She missed the feeling of having Aunt Elena's body next to hers, her soft, delicate skin, the long black hair that she would caress over and over until falling asleep.

Rafael always walked silently, with his hands in his pockets. From time to time, he took a hand out of his pocket, rested it on little Julia's shoulder, and began to sing: Cabaret performer, don't forget I love you. There're two crosses on the mountain of forgetfulness, they're the two loves that have died, yours and mine . . . Or Tino Rossi's songs, like "Torna a Sorrento" and "Santa Lucía." Or Marino Marini's *Tu sei per me la più bella del mondo e un amore profondo me liga a te, tu sei per me una bella bambina primavera divina per il mio cuor* . . . At times Rafael asked her about their grandfather. Is he really crazy? What's Don Julio like? He says he's free, responded little Julia as her only explanation. Is he bad? No!, he has a sawmill, horses, dogs . . . he smokes a pipe and his beard comes down to here —little Julia pointed to her chest—, he knows lots of things. Mamá says he's crazy and Grandmother Lucía says just terrible things about him, he was an Anarchist representative and instigated the war, he doesn't believe in God and he killed all the priests and nuns in Spain. It's true, but he didn't kill all of them, he says there wasn't enough time. But he's good. He was a Red, wasn't he? No!, he was free, the Reds were Communists; our grandfather only killed people who wanted to take control, and since it seems like everyone wanted control . . . well, of course, he had to kill a lot of them. But the priests, Rafael insisted, they're not to blame, and according to Grandmother Lucía they're the ones they always go after when there's a revolution, and the nuns . . . Our grandfather —little Julia explained, very proud to see Rafael so interested in the subject— always says that the priests wanted control, they wanted to interfere in everything, that's why they killed them, and the nuns do what the priests tell them to . . . so they got them too. Does he have rifles and revolvers in his house? A revolver in the desk drawer in his office . . . and shotguns, but they're for hunting. Can you see his scars? Not on his face, but he says he has two: one on his chest and another one on his leg; he was very brave in the war.

They couldn't talk about Don Julio at home, especially in front of Grandmother Lucía, but there wasn't a single afternoon that summer when Rafael didn't ask her something about him. He doesn't love us boys. Because you're Cannon Fodder . . . —and then little Julia added—, but you, it's possible that our grandfather would like you. Do you think so? Ernesto says that instead of calling him by his name, he called him Weakling. Because that's what he is —replied little Julia, trying to impress Rafael by imitating her grandfather's tone—, but you don't talk much and you're not a coward; Don Julio likes people who're brave and don't blabber on and on. Okay, said Rafael, and he sang again: You only love once in a lifetime, only once, nothing more . . .

The summer vacation in Sitges ended abruptly at the end of August. Papá and Antonio, Mamá's old friend, got in a fight one Saturday afternoon on Paseo Marítimo. They were both taken to the Guardia Civil station, and Monday morning they all moved back to Barcelona.

Papá, Mamá, Grandmother Lucía, and Uncle Ricardo locked themselves in the living room all day. Ernesto was in a bad mood. They ruined our summer vacation, just when I was starting to have fun. Papá always destroys everything. From time to time Grandmother Lucía would come out of the living room and tell Aurelia: Make me an herbal tea. She would go to the dining room, where the three children were playing cards. Rafael had had the idea: Let's do something to distract ourselves while we find out what's going on in there. Grandmother Lucía made them say the Lord's Prayer, and then she hugged them, crying: Poor little angels, the parents' sins are always visited upon the children. She crossed herself and returned to the discussion, at the far end of the apartment. Their voices —Mamá's, Papá's, and Uncle Ricardo's— made it all the way from there to the dining room. Aurelia went in and out of the dining room, muttering: Good God, good God, why does life have to be so complicated? And then we complain about how things are going in the whole country; how can a single man govern an entire country properly if two people can't manage to get along with each other and everybody's just killing everyone else off? Lord, what a difficult life! And suddenly, she grabbed them and smothered them with kisses, saying: Poor little things, to think that I saw you come into this world.

Rafael, from time to time, would send Ernesto to the living

room: Try to listen in, but don't let them see you. Ernesto returned and, in an unpleasant voice, said: Bah!, the same old thing, they're going to get separated. But on the third trip: Well, it seems like it's for real this time. Papá's leaving. Where to?, asked Rafael and little Julia at the same time. How do I know?, he's leaving home, us too. And Mamá? I don't know. Go listen again, Rafael ordered after a while. They're arguing about money and about who gets to stay with Mamá. Me, blurted out little Julia. No way, I'm the oldest. Yeah, but I'm sick, said Rafael. And they began to fight. Little Julia was terrified of the idea of going to live with Papá in another house. Maybe he'd get married again and she'd have a stepmother. Mamá, during the two months they'd spent in Sitges, had constantly scolded her because she, little Julia, was acting up. Mamá said that Don Julio had taught her bad manners and corrupted her with his attitude and rudeness: And you're a little copycat. Every time little Julia got angry and struck the table or insulted Ernesto, Mamá slapped her and called her Doña Julia. She didn't pay any attention to her, even though she, little Julia, hadn't seen her in almost a year. Mamá spent the day fighting with Papá or going out with Antonio. However, little Julia didn't even dare think about the fact that they could force her to go to another house with Papá. She suddenly felt violent hatred toward him, she regretted not having thrown him into the well the year before. If Papá ripped her away from Mamá, she would be capable of sticking a knife into his heart. I don't want to go with Papá, she shouted at the same time as she hit the table with her fist. I don't either, said Rafael. Me either, said Ernesto, and without Rafael telling him to, he added: I'm going to go spy. At that moment Grandmother Lucía appeared in the dining room. What are you doing with the lights off? You're going to ruin your eyesight. And she made them say the Lord's Prayer again: So that this doesn't turn into something irreparable, a scandal. Crying, she kissed the three of them and then made them kiss the gold crucifix that always hung around her neck. She gave them three prints of Saint Rita and insisted: Read the prayer nine times, on your knees. Saint Rita is the patron saint of impossible causes.

They read it just once and stayed on their knees. Grandmother Lucía was capable of coming back to see if they had followed her orders. Don't cry, Rafael told little Julia, maybe nothing will happen, and if it's going to happen, it'll happen whether or not you cry. I don't want to go with Papá, repeated little Julia.

Papá didn't take them to live with him, but they didn't stay with Mamá either. The agreement adopted by Papá, Mamá, Grandmother Lucía, and Uncle Ricardo was acceptable to the three children: little Julia and Rafael would go live with Don Julio and Aunt Elena for a while. Rafael until October, said Grandmother Lucía, he has to start high school and between now and then a lot of things can be resolved. Ernesto would stay with Mamá and Grandmother Lucía, because he had to take his exams in September. Papá took his suitcase, agreed to pick Rafael and little Julia up the next day to take them to Don Julio's house, and left.

Little Julia barely slept that night. She got up with the first rays of morning sunlight and went to Aurelia's room. She was tempted to go to Mamá's room and climb into her bed, but she didn't dare. The next morning, Mamá woke her up to try on the clothes from the previous winter to see what she needed to buy her. All the dresses had gotten too short. Look at how much you've grown, little Julia, you're going to be as tall as your grandfather, but you only grow in one direction. It was true. The clothes were short on her, but their width was the same, and some of her dresses were even baggy.

Mamá's behavior that morning made her nervous. She caressed Julia's hair constantly and kissed her without her asking for it. I'll take you to the beauty parlor to get your hair cut, it's too long; that way it'll be less work for Aunt Elena. Suddenly Mamá hugged her tightly to her chest and held her in her arms for a few minutes while little Julia thought about a lot of different things. Until that moment, she had never seen Mamá cry. She noticed Mamá's clear blue eyes, reddened, and saw how the tears slid slowly down her cheeks, pausing on her long, sharp nose and continuing on to her thin, rosy lips. At that moment little Julia was certain that a long, long time would go by before she would see Mamá again. Even though Mamá and Grandmother Lucía assured her: It'll just be for a little while, just until things get worked out, little Julia was sure that she wouldn't see her for many months, maybe years. She felt a knot in her throat, she was going to drown at any moment. She wished the pain would drown her, kill her. She held back the tears, hoping that her throat would finally just explode. She couldn't stand any more and she began to cry, pushing herself up against Mamá. I don't want to go, she murmured in a faltering voice, kicking at the floor. She had a premonition that she would never again hug Mamá with the love she felt at that instant. Time would elapse, far away from Mamá, and, when she saw her again, many things would have happened: her hair would be as long as it was now, even though it would be cut a few times before it was time to return home; she would be as tall as her grandfather, and the dresses that now reached her knees would barely make it to her waist. Maybe Mamá would have gray hair, wrinkles, and her beauty would have disappeared without a trace.

A shudder passed through her body, as if someone had inserted a block of ice into her spine and was pulling it out, little by little, very slowly. Mamá hugged her and held her just briefly in her arms, but it was long enough for little Julia to know that the change she would undergo during the painful absence would not be merely physical. Many things were going to change, while others would die forever or survive in her mind, converted into a vague memory.

Rafael stayed at the house in the mountains until the middle of October. His presence didn't bother her grandfather. Don Julio didn't treat him with as much deference as he gave little Julia, but he didn't mock him by calling him Weakling or make fun of him like he did with Ernesto the year before. Rafael, for his part, followed his grandfather around all day, watching him intently and with wonder. Shortly after his arrival, Rafael told little Julia: You were right, he's fantastic. He didn't miss any of the reunions that their grandfather organized at home after dinner, attended, like the year before, by Corporal Llop the Red, Don Raimundo the doctor, Don Alfredo the teacher, and Matías the pharmacist. Rafael listened with interest and watched all of them with eyes as big as plates. Later he would tell little Julia: The thing about the bombs is true. I guess Don Julio was really somebody, a leader.

Rafael liked Aunt Elena too. She's so pretty, he said to little Julia. When Aunt Elena kissed Rafael or patted his cheeks, he would turn red down to the soles of his shoes. During the month and a half that he stayed with them in the mountains, Rafael only got one of his headaches. Papá had given Aunt Elena the medicine and instructions in case Rafael got sick. Fortunately for little Julia, Rafael only had to stay in bed two days, but it was enough to make her feel jealous again. During those two days, Aunt Elena spent many hours with Rafael, although that didn't make her neglect little Julia. On the contrary, little Julia realized that Aunt Elena didn't waste a single opportunity to pamper her, paying attention to her like she always did. Also, Aunt Elena would constantly call her from Rafael's bedroom, and, in that way, they kept him company together. In dealing with Rafael's illness, Aunt Elena's behavior, so different from Mamá's, barely gave jealousy a chance to surface in little Julia's mind. Don Julio, however, must have been aware of some resentment, because during the walk they took in the woods in the mornings, he said to her: And speaking of freedom, you need to know that it can never be obtained by people whose souls aren't generous enough to resist the temptation of clinging to things so tightly that they become slaves rather than masters. Little Julia understood the meaning hidden behind her grandfather's words perfectly well because of the tone in which he said them.

Julia remembered the month and a half with her brother, at Don Julio's house, as the start of a friendly collaboration with Rafael, the beginning of a connection that death would eventually destroy. They walked in the woods, went to the sawmill with Don Julio, took the easel and paints outside and tried to create a landscape following their grandfather's instructions: a river flowing through the poplars. Little Julia showed him the horses, their grandfather's dogs, the two little cats, Porky and Petunia, and offered him: Hey, I'll give you Porky if you want.

Their grandfather lost his temper because Rafael had failed Latin and Papá's squabbles had prevented him from taking his exams in September. Bourgeois imbeciles, the most normal thing in the world happens to them and they create a scandal, they should be condemned to work on a chain gang. Sometimes Rafael asked him things about the war, and his grandfather responded: It didn't last very long, that was the problem, they didn't give us enough time. My grandmother Lucía says that you killed lots of priests, Rafael commented one day, summoning up his courage. Their grandfather's voice was terrifying: I thought about her at those moments. Every time I killed someone, I imagined wringing your disgustingly rich old grandmother's neck. When I'm older I'm going to be a writer, Rafael told Don Julio. Bah!, the true artist has to be free, and there aren't many men who can be free in the midst of so much stupidity. If you stayed here . . . you might come to understand; in any case, you're not a weakling like your brother, what a clown!, like his mother! And like his father! Yes sir, repeated their grandfather, like his father.

Papá arrived in the middle of October and took Rafael away. Ernesto had failed his freshman-year exams again, and they sent him off to boarding school. Rafael guessed Papá's plan. He protested, to no avail. Don Julio had a violent argument with Papá because they had chosen a Jesuit school for the boys. I never played a dirty trick like that on you; although by the look of things, it did no good, stupidity's innate.

Rafael, before he left with Papá, asked little Julia for a favor: You sleep in Aunt Elena's room, could you . . . well, find a picture of her for me? Rafael turned red when he asked her for it. Julia never forgot Rafael's shaky voice and the deep gaze, filled with sadness, that he fixed on Aunt Elena when they said good-bye.

From the window of the library she watched the departure of the car that was taking him away. She felt violently irritated with everyone. Not because they left her there, but because they took Rafael. It was as if Mamá and Papá were amusing themselves by playing a never-ending card game and they, little Julia and Rafael, were the cards. They shuffled, dealt, and whoever bet the most won. Don Julio claimed that Mamá had the game in her pocket. Papá was weak and she had money. But before the end of the game, little Julia came to believe that she was a puppet moved by strings that someone was manipulating at will. As she watched Papá's car depart, she was thinking that everyone's actions were controlled by mysterious strings and she would never be free of them. The car disappeared in the distance, approaching the top of the mountains, and she was afraid to see it return some day. That would mean that Papá or Mamá (it didn't make any difference anymore) was coming for her, to take her back to Barcelona again.

It took Papá's car five years to reappear through the mountains. Little Julia was thirteen years old. She spotted it from the same window, the one in her grandfather's library, and she wished that before it got to the house it would crash against a tree and its occupant would be killed, whether it was Papá or Mamá.

She remembered those five years like a long, peaceful stroll through the woods, only interrupted by brief visits to the sawmill, evenings at home after dinner, hours of study in the afternoon, and Aunt Elena's caresses. Time flowed by, neither quickly nor slowly. Suddenly the snow would disappear and little Julia noticed the heat. Summer arrived naturally, without surprising her. One day her grandfather would examine the sky and say: The cold weather will be here soon, we'll have to order firewood. And by the end of the month, when she got up in the morning, she would see, through her window, the mountains covered with snow. Porky and Petunia had grown. Porky, the male, began to rebel when little Julia made him lie still on her lap, and he meowed, anxious, when he found the outside door closed. The only thing that could destroy her peace of mind was the possible arrival of a letter and, in the end, the presence of Félix.

Félix would sometimes show up at their house around six in the evening and, at seven thirty, when Don Julio and little Julia were finishing their classes, would look for any excuse to leave. Félix's visits came at irregular intervals. At times, he would stop by every day for two weeks; then a month would go by without a visit from him.

Little Julia realized that Aunt Elena's behavior had been odd ever since Félix began dropping by. She found her unsettled, nervous. She would pace constantly through the sitting room, go in and out of the dining room as if she were looking for something that had been lost, return to the sitting room, sit down with a book in her hands, set it on the table, pick it back up, look out the window, ask little Julia what time it was. Don Julio made fun of his daughter: You've fallen in love like an idiot and, as expected, with an idiot. Do whatever you want, but try not to make me run into that imbecile in my own home.

Little Julia found Félix annoying from the moment he began pestering Aunt Elena. When she and Aunt Elena went downtown in the morning, they would see Félix watching them from inside the casino in the plaza. He would immediately come flying out of the cafeteria to greet them. Félix was tall and gave off the impression of strength, he was blond, with very fair skin and a carefree and boastful air. After saying hello, he didn't go away, he followed them around everywhere and, if Aunt Elena went into any stores, he would wait in the street, whistling, with his hands buried in his pockets. He insisted over and over that Aunt Elena let him carry their purchases, and he escorted them home. When they arrived, he would say good-bye and tell Aunt Elena: I might stop by this afternoon to pay you a visit.

At first, Aunt Elena seemed to get irritated when Félix waylaid them in town. Little Julia would hear the conversations between Aunt Elena and Martina. He's a bore, a braggart, Aunt Elena complained. He's got lots of money and he's popular with the ladies, said Martina. Well, he bothers me, he's unbearably pedantic, who does he think he is? But the next day they would meet up with him in town again, and Félix would escort them home and promise to come see her around six. After a few weeks, it was Aunt Elena who would look for Félix as soon as they got to the town plaza, and she would ask: Should I expect you at six? Let's see how long it takes me to finish up a couple of things, if I can . . .

Since then, Félix only came out to greet them in the plaza from time to time. Generally, he would stay inside the cafeteria. Aunt Elena would come home furious and tell Martina: If Félix comes, tell him I'm out. Félix would stay out of sight for a few days, at the end of which, and when they were least expecting it, he would go out to greet them and begin to talk naturally, as if nothing had happened. Aunt Elena wouldn't respond to Félix's questions or she'd answer in monosyllables without looking him in the face, but after a while she'd become animated and happy, and she would laugh at whatever nonsense he said.

Félix asked me to marry him, Aunt Elena announced during lunch. Don Julio smashed his fist onto the table and his plate and food flew to the floor. He's an imbecile, he roared, enraged. I was afraid of this; afraid that in the end you'd marry a stupid idiot like Félix.

Her grandfather let a week go by without saying a word to Aunt Elena. He had his meals served in the library and only went out to go to the sawmill. Aunt Elena's mood was terrible. At night she didn't sleep a wink and she rolled around in bed constantly. She would hug little Julia and ask her for: A kiss, you don't love me like you used to anymore. You don't like Félix either, do you? She, little Julia, said: No. And Aunt Elena began to cry.

Her grandfather, closed in the library, persisted in the silence he had imposed. He didn't even mention Aunt Elena to little Julia. During the hours they spent studying, Don Julio would go from one side of the library to the other, with his hands clasped behind his back, smoking a pipe in silence. Keep reading the history book, we'll leave the explanations for another day, insisted Don Julio every afternoon. Until little Julia, watching one of his circuits around the library, stepped into his path, and standing in front of her grandfather with her hands on her hips, exclaimed: Your behavior is stupid. You're a tyrant, isn't she free? Don Julio appeared taller and more enraged than ever and little Julia thought she might be slapped at any moment, but she met her grandfather's penetrating gaze. He's an imbecile, and she's weak and cowardly, he shouted, finally. Let her be, said little Julia. Her grandfather maintained his silence and stumbled over to the desk chair. The floor panels creaked beneath his feet. Little Julia watched him cross the room slowly and then drop into the chair. She suddenly realized that

Don Julio was old. He remained seated, partially hidden by the lamp on the desk. A dark image, whose white beard and hair stood out among the shadows. You called me a tyrant, murmured Don Julio. Little Julia barely recognized him in those words, the weak, almost mournful tone. Let her be, repeated little Julia. But he's an imbecile . . . Félix is stupid, she agreed. Go downstairs, I have work to do, her grandfather ordered her. He leaned over the table to light his pipe, and the brightness illuminated his face. The seriousness of his expression made a strong impression on little Julia. There was no anger in her grandfather's countenance, only a gravity that frightened her. You insulted me, Don Julio reproached her, softly. You called me a tyrant.

That night, Don Julio showed up in the dining room at dinnertime. You can do whatever you want, he told Aunt Elena, it's none of my business. The next day they resumed their walks in the woods and their classes.

Julia acknowledged that her grandfather was right: Félix was stupid. He would stop seeing Aunt Elena for a month and then claim he had taken a short trip to Barcelona: For some stuff that needed to be resolved quickly, and I got delayed between one thing and another . . . At times Félix's excuses would turn out to be true; other times, they weren't. Aunt Elena would find out the truth from Martina, who always came home with stories about Félix. Aunt Elena would argue with Félix, but after a few days they'd make up. One Sunday, Aunt Elena went out with Félix and returned home alone and crying, earlier than her normal hour. Little Julia couldn't make out too much of what she said about Félix's other girlfriend and the scandal at the dance. Félix disappeared for a few days only to reappear again, coming out to greet them in the town plaza. Aunt Elena didn't say hello to him or respond when he spoke to her. Félix whispered something in Aunt Elena's ear, and she said to little Julia: Wait here a minute. Little Julia saw how Félix and Aunt Elena began to walk. Félix wrapped an arm around Aunt Elena's shoulders and didn't stop gesturing with his free hand. They went around the plaza a few times with short, slow steps. Félix talked and talked. After half an hour they called her; Félix escorted them shopping and then home, as if nothing had happened. Around six, Joaquín yelled from the stairway: Don Julio, Señor Félix is asking after your daughter. Her grandfather flew down the stairs in a rage and kicked him out of the house. Little Julia opened her mouth to speak, but Don Julio interrupted her: What, was that bad? Yes, she responded, it wasn't enough. I would have killed him. And it was true. She felt a murderous rage toward Félix, and sometimes toward Aunt Elena too. It drove her crazy to see her nervous and in a bad mood because of Félix. Aunt Elena had turned into a sad and silent person. She often cried at night. Little Julia would hug her and kiss her forehead, her cheeks, her eyes, even her lips. She caressed her hair and covered her mouth with her hands to prevent her from sobbing. At those times, she wanted to kill Félix, take the revolver that Don Julio kept in his office desk drawer, pull the trigger, empty the chamber into his chest. She felt furious with Aunt Elena. Little Julia didn't understand why she had fallen in love with Félix or why she let him make her suffer. She didn't understand how —after breaking up with him and promising Martina: I won't see him anymore, I don't want to have anything to do with him, Don Julio's right, he's a scoundrel— Aunt Elena's anger would fade away as soon as she saw him and he came up to her and threw his arm around her shoulders.

She hated Félix, and sometimes she felt scornful of Aunt Elena too. She agreed with her grandfather when she heard him grumble: Stupid people like Félix and my daughter deserve to be condemned to a chain gang, with a hundred-ton shackle on each foot. He turns love into a weapon of possession because his poverty of spirit ensures that his need to dominate will be thwarted, and she excuses his weakness and cowardice. They're made for each other; weak people and stupid people search each other out and always end up finding each other. That's how the world goes. Let it be a lesson to you.

Little Julia agreed with her grandfather. It made her sick to think that she might feel dominated someday, tied down by something or someone. Simply imagining it gave her a pain in the chest that made it hard for her to breathe. It must be like finding oneself locked in a dark room, with no air, where the walls are closing in and the ceiling is slowly dropping toward the floor.

During their walks in the woods, Don Julio talked about two of his favorite subjects: nature's wisdom and people's stupidity. Little Julia listened to him in silence without understanding his need to beat the subject into the ground, but she enjoyed it. Don Julio expressed himself passionately, as if he were acting out a play and his words were very important: at times little Julia wondered why. Don't ever lose yourself in minor details; that's the mistake stupid people make. They waste their time answering idiotic questions, and they never get to the heart of the matter. Contemplate nature and don't ask questions; someday you'll understand.

They were returning from one of those morning walks when a woman, tall and thin, blocked their path. Don Julio stopped, furrowed his brow, exclaimed: Can it be possible? Eva! The woman ran toward the old man and they hugged and kissed each other, laughing.

Eva stayed at the house two days. Eva and Don Julio talked and talked nonstop. Look, Eva, this is Julia, my granddaughter. Eva had black hair in a ponytail, very big green eyes, and she smiled constantly. Nonsense, Don Julio, I'm already almost forty years old, little Julia heard Eva say, but she didn't look it. Her grandfather and Eva talked about Papá and Mamá: Yes, Eva said, your son has changed a lot. We saw each other a few days ago, when I returned from the United States. Her grandfather began to pepper Mamá and Grandmother Lucía with insults. Little Julia had the sensation that Eva was looking at her compassionately, and she thought she was a very kind woman. Her grandfather ranted about the United States. How could you stand to live among savages for ten years? Eva laughed, she encouraged Don Julio's fits of rage when he was talking about politics. They began by discussing what had happened in Hungary the year before, and at the Suez Canal. As Julia had expected, they ended up talking about the Spanish Civil War. Her grandfather lost his temper. She had never heard him express himself with so much violence. Don Julio insisted several times that Eva stay on a few more days. It's impossible, Don Julio. Classes begin next week at the university, I've become a Spanish literature professor and I start . . .

What an idiot your father was, murmured Don Julio after Eva left. And little Julia, once again, agreed.

Papá's letter arrived at the end of summer. Rafael had to leave the Jesuit school because he had gotten sick again. Ernesto, who was studying in Zaragoza, was going from bad to worse. He was living with some of Lucía's relatives there, a couple in their fifties, with no kids, who had let Ernesto get away with too much, losing all control over him. In the letter, Papá said that both Rafael and Ernesto should live with Mamá. Rafael needed someone to take care of him, and Ernesto, someone to clip his wings and force him to study. After lots of excuses and justifications, Papá talked about a "new arrangement" with Mamá: they had come to the mutual agreement that the three of them should live with her again. I live alone and don't have, at my disposal, the time or means to take care of them. All three of them are going through a difficult stage. Little Julia, furthermore, has missed four years of school. I've reached an agreement with my wife in order to keep up appearances and not carry things to the extreme . . .

Don Julio crumpled the letter in his hands, threw it to the floor, and kicked it over and over, shouting: I will not allow it, I will not allow it. No, a thousand times no. Hypocritical trash, damn pigs . . . And he continued shouting insults about Papá, Mamá, Grandmother Lucía, the Church, and the immorality of bourgeois morality. The next day he was hoarse, he could barely talk.

She and her grandfather saw Papá's car appear through the mountains. I hope it crashes, said little Julia quietly. They're going to sap your strength, Julia. You have to be careful and pay attention. These people are capable of destroying five years in a couple of weeks. Don't let them.

Aunt Elena called her from the dining room: Julia, Julia, your papa is here. You go, her grandfather told her, I'll come down later. Little Julia left the library. Her grandfather remained standing, in front of the window, with his back to her. Little Julia thought about how she would never forget that gigantic figure, his dark clothes, the veined hands clasped behind his slightly curved back, the white hair and beard, the pipe that smelled like honey between his thick lips, the furrowed brow, the clear penetrating eyes, and the powerful voice that electrified, awakening fear or admiration.

When she found herself in front of Papá, she couldn't say a word. He seemed older. He had wrinkles on his face and gray hair at his temples. Papá hugged her and kissed her: You've gotten so tall, little Julia, and so pretty.

She felt uncomfortable in Papá's presence, she didn't know what to say. And Don Julio?, Papá asked. But Don Julio didn't come out of the library until Aunt Elena went to find him to announce

Julia and Papá's departure. When her grandfather came into the dining room, little Julia could see that his eyes were red and his features tense. Papá went to hug him, but Don Julio wouldn't allow it and didn't say a word to him. He made his way to the sitting room next door and after a few minutes returned to the dining room with a wicker basket in his hands. Inside the basket, Petunia was sleeping peacefully and Porky was looking around, his eyes wide open. Porky meowed and leaped to the floor, slipping quickly through little Julia's hands as she struggled in vain to hold on to him. We've got to go now, announced Papá, but Don Julio didn't even look at him.

Aunt Elena hugged her tightly. You can come back every year during your summer vacation. Little Julia couldn't respond. They went down the stairs silently and walked through the central courtyard. Little Julia found Porky again next to the front door, meowing for them to open it for him. Little Julia approached the cat, caught him, and put him back into the basket, where Petunia was still sleeping. Porky meowed beneath the pressure of little Julia's hand.

Before she got into the car, she heard her grandfather's deep, sad, but, until the end, powerful voice for the last time: Julia, even among animals there are those who prefer freedom. She contemplated Petunia, sleeping inside the basket, and Porky, who continued to struggle beneath the weight of her hand. Don Julio's voice let itself be heard once more: Are you a tyrant?

Little Julia caught the rebellious cat, petted his back and head, kissed him between his ears, and set him on the ground. She turned toward her grandfather and contemplated Don Julio's smile as Porky took off running and disappeared in the direction of the mountains.

The days seemed long and boring until classes began. Mamá went out very frequently, and Ernesto only made his presence known at mealtimes. Grandmother Lucía made her say the rosary every morning and every night: Once, for Rafael's recuperation, and the second time, to avoid scandal.

The house was closing in on her, it seemed small and dark. Too much furniture, too many objects, the long, heavy curtains. She would go out on the balcony to breathe more freely and, confronting buildings across the street and the noise of traffic, she missed the landscape that was visible from any window in Don Julio's house, the seemingly infinite space beyond the woods and mountains. She felt captured, caged, she needed more air. She went shopping with Mamá or for walks down Diagonal with Rafael (when he had the energy). But she got tired out right away. The noise, the continuous movement of cars and buses, and the sight of so many people in the streets made her feel dizzy.

Grandmother Lucía and Mamá argued about an appropriate school for little Julia. Her grandmother insisted on a religious one. But Mamá said: No, public school's better, that way she'll pass more quickly, she's really far behind.

When she signed up for school, they gave her a written exam. The headmistress called Mamá to tell her that in June she would be admitted, but she would have classes in four different grades. She's only weak in mathematics, and in religion and sacred history she doesn't know a thing; but regarding the rest of it . . . where did she study Latin? Also, a . . . delicate question: your daughter . . . is she mute?

Mamá returned home furious. You're a savage, a disagreeable child. It was true, but she didn't care. She hadn't gone to school since she was five years old and, suddenly, she found herself forced to stay locked up in a classroom for four hours in the morning and three in the afternoon, sitting behind a desk, among twenty other girls. She didn't talk to anybody. If they asked her something, she answered with the fewest possible words. After a week at school, they called her "the girl who doesn't talk." It made Julia angry. She was bored to tears, especially during her free time, but she didn't know what to say, what to talk about with her classmates. After a few days, the students started to form groups, but Julia was excluded because of her odd behavior. Also, she was studying in four different grades and didn't really belong to any of them. Since she chose a seat far away from everyone else when she went into class the first few days, the other students didn't even try to sit next to her. Helplessly, Julia observed how they would come into class, hang their coats on the coatrack, put on their white smocks, and save seats next to each other. She didn't know how to remedy the isolation that she herself had brought about. Although it bothered her, she made an effort to pretend that the terrible loneliness surrounding her at school didn't matter to her in the slightest, and she even acted proud of having achieved it. At times, without knowing how it happened, she would find herself surrounded by two or three girls who would speak to her. She made an effort to establish contact with them, but she couldn't. It was as if the other students had known each other for a long time and, because of that, they had things to tell each other. They talked about and laughed at things that didn't seem remotely funny to her. They were probably referring to earlier conversations that she hadn't participated in, and they used set phrases among themselves that confused her. It was as if they were speaking in code in her presence. It bothered her, she felt clumsy and powerless to overcome these situations, and every day she isolated herself further.

At seven o'clock in the evening, when she returned home, she would hide in the library, studying until dinnertime. She would eat rapidly and bury her head in her books again. She studied her assignments and did the math problems. She reviewed them over and over again, until she was convinced she understood the lessons from beginning to end. She was terrified that she would forget at the precise moment when they asked her a question in class. She was afraid of making a fool out of herself and that they would think she was an idiot. She didn't want them, on top of calling her "the girl who doesn't talk," to add "the dummy" or "the girl who never knows anything." She studied without taking a break or getting distracted by anything else, until Aurelia came into the library and scolded her: Get to bed already, you're just skin and bones from studying so much. Dear God, the contrasts in this household. Some do so much and others so little, you could share some of your energy with your big brother; that'd save us all a good deal of trouble.

At night, in bed, she couldn't stop thinking about Aunt Elena. She missed feeling her body lying next to her and her caresses. She hugged her pillow, closed her eyes, and imagined that Aunt Elena was there, by her side. A growing resentment was accumulating inside her. She recited the recently learned school lesson to distract herself from these thoughts.

She had written a letter explaining all her frustrations to her grandfather. But Don Julio didn't answer. After a few days, Julia wrote him again, without complaining this time, telling him lies. In the letter, she told Don Julio that she and Lucía were fighting and wouldn't speak to each other: Because my grandmother tried to make me say the rosary and go to mass every day and I refused. She almost died of the attack it gave her. Everyone's afraid of me and respects me. They say I'm your spitting image. The shirt and underwear factory will probably go under; that'll be funny. Since they won't have any money to support me, they'll send me back to your house, and when my grandmother dies they won't be able to have any masses said for her. I enjoy school a lot, I get the best grades in my class, except for in religion. I have a lot of fun with my friends. Maybe this summer I can go see you, whether or not Mamá wants, I'm going to go, nobody tells me what to do . . .

Don Julio answered Julia's letter the very next day. It said only: Bravo, Julia. Aunt Elena added: Don Julio can't write you a long letter because he's sick. He will when he gets better. We miss you a lot. A big hug.

She didn't have any choice but to lie to Don Julio, otherwise she would have disappointed him. Before summer another letter from Aunt Elena arrived, this time addressed to Papá, with the news of Don Julio's death and of her upcoming marriage to Félix. Julia felt like a huge lead weight had fallen on her head and she was slowly sinking into a deep, dark pit where there wasn't enough air. When they were all in the dining room, Grandmother Lucía made them turn off the television and say the Lord's Prayer: One must have compassion, even for one's worst enemy. Your grandfather was a terrible sinner. Julia didn't pray. She needed to restrain herself or she would insult her grandmother, spit in Mamá's face when she said: He was a crazy old man. An immense sadness enveloped her for days, but she didn't cry until a month later. At school they gave her an entrance exam for high school and, when the headmistress congratulated her on the prize she received on the Latin section, Julia began sobbing. The headmistress called Mamá to come see her again. Mamá returned home on the verge of hysteria: Do you mind telling me what your problem is? You're a savage, I'm going to lock you away in a boarding school. They implied that my daughter's abnormal. I'm sick of visiting schools. Your brother doesn't study and you refuse to behave like a normal person.

She got furious when Mamá chided her about her odd behavior and shyness. She made an effort to be like the other students, but she couldn't overcome the feeling of helplessness that prevented her from talking to them. The rumor that she was mute had spread, and everyone respected the story by leaving her alone, in the separateness she had apparently chosen for herself.

She felt strange at home too. Mamá was always out, Grandmother Lucía went to mass every afternoon and then had a bite to eat with her friends, old and devout like her, in a café on Paseo de Gracia, always packed with old people. Only Rafael, on the days he felt some relief from his illness, seemed to be aware of Julia's presence. The doctor had forbidden him to study too much: Just continue with the subjects that come easiest to you. When he was feeling all right, Rafael went to the same school as she did, to the boys' section. Through the ninth grade, boys and girls had separate classes, but after that, classes were mixed. At seventeen years old, Rafael was still a freshman and, although he wasn't concerned about being behind, he sometimes regretted not being able to move up to tenth grade: Then it's going to be something else, there's girls there!

Before they went out for recreation, the boys lined up, silently, single file, from the classroom to the recreation area. In Julia's class the girls would become restless. Some asked to be excused to go to the bathroom, others went up to the teacher's desk with any excuse that came to mind. Just so they could see the boys parade past the half-open door. The boys, for their part, when they walked in front of the girls' classroom, looked through the windows and made gestures, faces, stuck out their tongues to attract attention. Once they were outside, the line broke up. First gym class and then games. During the half hour that the boys' recreation lasted, Julia's classmates did nothing but look out the windows, make comments, and laugh under their breath. Punishments rained down through the classroom, distributed among her classmates, especially if the boys' recreation coincided with the hour when they had religion class, taught by a priest, or literature by a bad-tempered teacher in her forties, the terror of the school. She was a tall, heavy redhead, with very small, pale eyes behind thick glasses. The highest grade she gave out on their exercises was a seven. She assured them that nobody in the school was capable of getting anything higher than that. Ten corresponds to God, the essence of wisdom; nine is for me, your teachers know more than any of you do. Eight belongs to the university students who are finishing up their studies and will know as much about literature as I do someday. Even if you know the literature book from cover to cover, I won't be able to give you anything better than a seven, you must understand, if you're capable of reason, that knowing this little book by heart doesn't mean you understand literature. At school they tagged her with different nicknames: Cerberus, the Unloved One . . .

When the freshman boys went out for recreation, Julia looked for Rafael to see if he had come to school. Rafael, even though he didn't participate in the other students' violent games, was always surrounded by a group of companions whom he would be talking and laughing with, endlessly. Julia wondered how Rafael could have so many friends, since he was almost never in class. But then she reminded herself that Rafael was good and kind. It wasn't hard for him to make friends with anybody. He always had a half smile on his lips, and he knew what to say and how to talk to anyone. Ernesto had the reputation for being the friendliest member of the family, but Julia thought Ernesto's friendliness was impertinence and foolishness. To make everyone laugh, Ernesto would say: Look at little Julia's face, she just figured out that they got her from an orphanage when she was little . . . and they would burst out laughing. He was always trying to make himself seem amusing by making somebody else look foolish or by making vulgar jokes at the expense of his victim of the day. He talked endlessly, he didn't know when to be quiet, and he said one foolishness after another. He was twenty years old and was repeating college preparatory classes. He often picked on her, calling her a grind and saying that getting straight A's meant you were dumb, not smart: Since you grinds don't think, you have more time to cram the material until you can parrot everything back. He claimed that if he failed, it was because the teachers held a grudge against him. According to him, they hated him because he was handsome, young, intelligent, with a brilliant future ahead of him and girls fainting at his feet; the teachers were resentful and envied his excellent qualifications: As soon as those failures bump into a young guy who threatens to move beyond them, bammm, they put out a trap for him. He accused the French teacher, who had failed him four times, of having insinuated her interest in him on various occasions, without success.

Rafael didn't tend to talk much just for talking's sake. When he did talk, he said what needed to be said. Julia observed him from her desk, through the window, and wondered how he could seem so happy in spite of being constantly sick. When he didn't go to school, Rafael would spend the day at home alone, listening to the radio, watching television, reading, or playing the same records as always over and over: Miguel Aceves Mejía, Edith Piaf, Charles Trenet, Tino Rossi, Nella Colombo, Marino Marini, Abe Lane, Nilla Pizzi, Sara Montiel, Lilián de Celis, Elvis Presley, Caterina Valente . . . He complained that they had gone out of style and got Mamá to promise that as soon as he could leave the house she would let him buy records. But when the moment came, the last thing he thought about was buying records; he didn't need them any more. Rafael, in his habitual optimism, didn't bargain on the possibility of a relapse.

When she returned home at one o'clock in the afternoon, Julia would find him in the veranda next to the dining room, sitting in an armchair, listening to the radio. In the veranda the color green predominated: green, white, and black wallpaper; darker green curtains, green shutters too. The rug was green and black; the sofa and two armchairs, green; in the corners, green plants, and the tablecloth was a green-and-white print. The one bit of clashing color came from the dreadful porcelain plates hanging on the walls. At lunchtime, the sunlight came straight into the veranda. Rafael, in his armchair, discussed with Julia the record-industry news from his favorite radio program: *Record Mania*. The national hit parade started off with the fight between Paul Anka and Diana, and then José Luis y su Guitarra with a song that Rafael sang all the time: Pretty little María, graceful girl, you are my love, I'd give my life for you, my soul, my very world. Every station had its hit parade, where the popular songs would go up and down in the rankings according to listeners' votes. Rafael followed all of them, and when he didn't agree with the result, he got as irritated as if Barcelona had lost a soccer match. When his favorite songs won spots on the hit parade, he was happy. That year his favorites were: Green fields in the sunshine, green hope that was your love. And others: "Jailhouse Rock" by Elvis Presley, The Platters's version of "Only You," Nat King Cole's songs, some of Sara Montiel's *cuplés*, like "Nena" and "Sus pícaros ojos," the recordings of Los Cinco Latinos, and the sound tracks of the Caterina Valente movies that they had seen in the theater: *Casino de Paris* and *Melodia d'amore*.

Rafael's conversations almost always dealt with songs and movies. He would say to her: Turn around, let's see if you can guess what album this is in less than ten seconds. And he would place on the turntable: "Una casita en Canadá" or "Don't Break the Heart That Loves You" by Connie Francis. Until Aurelia scolded them: Do you think you might ever come sit down at the table?

Sometimes, when Julia went into the library to study, Rafael would go with her to hide from Grandmother Lucía and her accusations that he was reading pornography. I'm sure it's in the *Index of Prohibited Books*, throw it in the fire. Grandmother Lucía's definition of pornography included any book that contained the words *love, kiss, passion, dear, wedding night*, and phrases like: *he took her hand, she looked into his eyes and saw a strange passion*. Rafael would read the novels he found in the library: *Madame Bovary, The Red and The Black, Crime and Punishment*, as well as others by Pérez Galdós, Palacio Valdés, Unamuno, Baroja. He was constantly reading Bécquer's *Rimas*, Campoamor's *The Express Train*, Góngora's *Letrillas*, and Jorge Manrique's *Coplas on the Death of His Father*. At times, Rafael interrupted her studies: Listen, Julia. And he would read out loud. Julia would set her books aside and look at Rafael, sitting near the balcony, reading in the twilight, and jotting down phrases in a notebook.

Rafael seemed happy, and Julia didn't understand why. She was always in a bad mood. She felt uncomfortable at the gloomy school, locked in a classroom that never saw the sunlight, with windows through which you could only see the high walls that separated the dark recreational area from the street. The windows were so small and the walls so high that, from inside the classroom, you couldn't even catch a glimpse of sky. It annoyed her to spend nearly the entire day at school and be obliged to wear the white smock with her name embroidered on the chest, to wear the school uniform: a gray pearl pleated skirt, white blouse, navy blue sweater, and jacket with black and garnet stripes and a shield embroidered on the upper pocket. She often complained about having to wear the uniform. What difference does it make if you wear one color or another?, Rafael would say. That's not the point, she responded.

Rafael passed his exams that year, and in October both of them became sophomores. The classes were mixed. Rafael had gotten better from his illness: the headaches and fevers were less frequent. Some Saturday afternoons, if Rafael didn't have plans with his friends, they would go see a movie. Rafael could get in, even if the movie was For Adults Only; he was already eighteen. But she was only fifteen. Rafael always picked R-rated movies. They'd take a taxi and go to the theaters located in the Sans or Gracia Districts, where they let her in without asking for an ID card. Rafael took her to see movies like *The Wind Cannot Read, A Time to Love and a Time to Die, The Last Time I Saw Paris, Written on the Wind, Sangaree, Some Came Running, Desiree, East of Eden, On the Waterfront, A Streetcar Named Desire, Cat on a Hot Tin Roof*...

Julia remembered the last months of her brother's life. Sometimes on Sunday mornings, they would go out for a walk. How much money did they give you?, he would ask her, and then add: Okay, well, let's go have a drink in the port. They would get on the bus that stopped in front of their house and went down Balmes Street to Paseo Colón. It was winter; it was cold, but it was a pleasure to stroll down Puerta de la Paz. The sun was a sweet caress, and they inhaled the port's particular smell. Sometimes they would take a walk on Golondrina, and other times they wandered along the breakwater. Rafael liked to study the boats. That one's American, it arrived in Barcelona yesterday, I read about it in the paper.

Someday I'm going to leave, he told her during the last walk they took together. Where to? Paris, responded Rafael. I want to be a writer. And you have to go to Paris? Not necessarily, but look, all the great artists have lived in Paris. And Rafael recited an endless list of writers, musicians, and painters who had resided in Paris. Cervantes didn't, Julia interrupted. Of course, back then, in his time,

Paris didn't exist, I mean Paris's bohemian life-style. Julia imagined "Paris's bohemian life-style" like an awning-covered plaza, decorated with colored lights, Chinese lanterns, paper streamers, full of people dancing to the sound of an accordion and where, when people entered, they handed them ID cards identifying them as artists. And what will you write? Novels, responded Rafael with certainty. Novels about life . . . I compose poetry now, can you believe it?, but later on . . . Julia, a few days earlier, had discovered a bunch of poems written by Rafael. She found them inside a folder. In them, he wrote above love and God and death. Are you afraid of dying? No, why? That's not going to happen for a long time. But I wouldn't be able to stand it if I was always sick; like if I went blind or was paralyzed, I'd kill myself. That's so extreme, even if you were paralyzed, you could still write novels, and if you lost your sight, you could read and write with the Braille method, like Ann Sullivan. No, Rafael responded, it's not the same, I've got to travel, I have to go to Paris. Mamá won't let you. I'm going to go, he assured her with a serious expression, looking toward the horizon, toward the dark line where the sea and sky became one. I have to go.

That was the last walk with Rafael. A few days later, leaving school at seven o'clock, Rafael asked her: Do you have a boyfriend? Me?, exclaimed Julia, surprised. Well, it wouldn't be that strange. And then Rafael added: I have a girlfriend and she's only a year older than you, if you can keep a secret, I'll introduce you.

When they got out to the street, they met a girl Julia recognized from school. Her name was Marga, and she was a junior. Rafael invited them to eat something in a café in Plaza de Cataluña, very close to the school. Marga was small, thin, and she was constantly moving; she wore her blonde hair very long, and you could hardly see her eyes beneath the bangs that she pushed aside with one hand. This is my sister, Julia, Rafael said. She's very smart; when she was eight, she knew Latin. Rafael, when he introduced her to someone, felt the need to say: My sister, when she was eight, knew more Latin than a priest. Rafael and Marga were talking and laughing about everything. They discussed a movie they had seen the day before that Rafael had loved. Julia remembered that Rafael had told Ernesto at dinnertime: I saw a wonderful movie, the best one I've seen my whole life. Which one? *The Girl with the Suitcase*, with Claudia Cardinale. Ernesto exclaimed: Bah!, it's not so great; you must have liked the girl.

They spent a while in the café, talking and laughing. Outside it was rainy and cold. Maybe this winter it'll snow again, Marga said. Do you remember the snow last year? Suddenly Rafael dropped his glass of Coke on the floor, let out a scream, and grabbed his head with his hands, collapsing on the table. Come on, Rafael, don't joke around, Marga exclaimed, grabbing his shirt collar and lifting his head. Rafael's face was pale, his mouth twisted, and his eyes rolled back in his head. He's having an attack, Julia said. Marga got very nervous. A waiter came to the table and also a man who was watching them from the counter. The waiter said: I'm going to go get a taxi. But the man stopped him: No, I have a car. I'll take them.

It took them twenty minutes to get from Plaza de Cataluña to Diagonal. Rafael, half-unconscious between Marga and Julia, was swaying weakly from side to side. The owner of the car kept complaining about the traffic: Of course it had to be rush hour. The car went up Paseo de Gracia and had to stop for a red light at every corner. Rafael jerked hard, vomited, and fainted. The owner of the car pulled a handkerchief out of his pocket, unfolded it, and ordered Julia: Wave the handkerchief out the window, we're going to force our way through this. And he began to honk the horn so they would let him through, and he ran all the red lights until they got home.

Mamá wasn't there. She had left a message that she wasn't coming home for dinner and would be home late. Neither Aurelia nor Grandmother Lucía could find her. Aurelia called the nurse, but he was afraid to give him an injection. I'm afraid to, he said upon examining Rafael, I think it's different from the other times; the best thing to do is to call the doctor.

The next day, when Julia came home from school, Aurelia announced, through tears: Poor child, they've taken him away in an ambulance, the little angel. Grandmother Lucía stayed in bed that day. Whenever there was some misfortune at home, she got into bed because it affected her too much. Julia found Ernesto in the dining room, sitting with his elbows on the table and his blond head in his hands. Mamá called, she wants a robe, slippers, and clothes at the hospital, Ernesto said. You go, I'm scared. He gave her the address and money for the taxi. When she got to the hospital, she asked the doorman what Rafael's room number was and ran up the stairs to the third floor. She crossed a deserted room and followed a long hallway that seemed endless. It smelled like chloroform, and the light that came through the windows accentuated the reflection of the white wall tiles that went up to the ceiling. She was near the end of the long hallway when a door opened and she saw a nurse come out pushing a wheelchair with an invalid in it. Mamá appeared behind the wheelchair. Julia realized then that the patient in the wheelchair was Rafael, wrapped in a robe, with his eyes closed and his hands, raised, grasping at air. She felt like she had been kicked in the stomach. Rafael, pale, thin, crippled, and moving his hands in the air gave her a feeling of helplessness, of being absolutely alone. She heard Mamá and the doctor talk, but the quiet words murmured by her side seemed to be whispers that were coming from very far away. She understood something about radiography and a cerebral exploration. Mamá, the white figure of the nurse pushing the wheelchair, and the two doctors, also in white, moved off down the hallway toward the elevator. Julia thought it seemed like they were going very slowly, as if they were going in slow motion. Wait for me, Mamá told her. The waiting room's at the end of the hall.

She walked in front of a door with a sign: Operating Room. In a small room two nurses were talking while they organized the carts packed with gauze, syringes, small bottles of alcohol, and steel instruments. In front of the operating-room door she read: Silence. At the end of the long hallway she found the waiting room. Two women were chatting on the sofa and a boy was climbing on and off one of the chairs by a low, round table. It was beginning to rain, the wind flinging the raindrops hard against the windowpanes and ripping the leaves off the trees. The day was dark. If someone had told her then that it was seven o'clock at night she would have believed it. The few people who were outside were walking quickly and trying to stay under balconies to protect themselves from the rain. A car pulled up right next to the hospital, and she saw Papá get out quickly and, without closing his car door, take off toward the entrance.

She had a bitter taste in her mouth and her head felt hot. She thought the smell of chloroform was coming out of her own stomach. She felt the urge to go outside, lie down in the middle of the sidewalk, let the rain soak into her, and inhale the wet smell that the streets and trees gave off when it rained. Papá and Mamá came into the waiting room. She heard Mamá explain to Papá what had happened to Rafael the day before, and then she talked about a cerebral tumor. He'll have to have an operation, the doctor can't promise anything, I think it's best . . .

She was sure that Rafael was going to die. The sooner the better. She surprised herself by wanting it so badly. She thought: Let a nurse come running in right now to say that Rafael's dead. She was frightened by her own thoughts and felt overwhelmed with uneasiness, listening to the argument between Papá and Mamá. Papá didn't think the operation was a good idea. Mamá did. Rafael's my son, he lives with me. You abandoned the three of them, this is my decision.

Rafael died the next day. Julia saw him for the last time in the hospital morgue, his head bandaged. Only his closed eyes and the eternal half-smile, petrified now, remained uncovered.

When she got home, Julia picked up Rafael's books and folders from the table in the library where they had studied. Between the pages of a book she found a postcard of Claudia Cardinale and Connie Francis; the classification of the last hit parade Rafael had listened to, topped by two Greek songs that had won the Mediterranean Music Festival that year; and one of Rafael's own poems. The book that had fallen into her hands was Jorge Manrique's *Coplas,* and on one of the pages she saw that Rafael had underlined some verses with a red pencil: Let the soul awaken and contemplate how life passes, how death sneaks up so silently.

She lit another cigarette. The light illuminated the bed, but the rest of her room remained in darkness. Among the shadows, she inferred that the wardrobe, the bookshelves, the desk with its piles of books and folders, the small rocking chair, and the drawings she had made years before, framed and hanging on the walls, were all present. She couldn't see these things, but she believed in their existence; familiarity allowed her to know her room inch by inch. With her eyes closed, she could get out of bed, walk over to the wardrobe, and remove whatever she needed, go to the bookshelves and find, blindly, the desired book. Her room had been the same for years, the objects too. The monotony of her room exasperated her. There were moments when she thought it was time to change some things, to ask Mamá to replace the horrible upholstery that covered the doors of the fitted wardrobe and the ridiculous wallpaper design: bouquets of blue and pink flowers. To ask Mamá to have her bedroom walls painted white, leaving them plain, without the flowery motifs that she, even if Mamá and Grandmother Lucía thought they were feminine and appropriate for her age and "your supposed innocence," found ludicrous. She would also ask her to replace the dark wood bookcase, its shelves enclosed behind thick beveled-glass doors, with three or four metal ones, leaving sufficient space between them so they wouldn't make her feel claustrophobic.

But she didn't dare ask for innovations. Not because she was afraid that Mamá would say no; Mamá was always willing to buy new things for the house and make changes in the bedrooms, especially if it was Julia who asked. She complained, on the contrary, that Julia never took the initiative to buy herself a dress or a pair of shoes, to fix her hair or do any of the things that Mamá considered signs of femininity. When Julia asked her for something, some object to decorate her room or herself, Mamá was pleased and got it without hesitation. A girl should be flirtatious and vain, otherwise she's like a man.

Regarding changes in her room, Julia, although she was tired of it, didn't dare ask for anything. Any innovation, no matter how small and insignificant, scared her. She always left things in the same place: her purse on the rocking chair; the books and folders on the desk, creating a carefully studied and controlled appearance of clutter; at the top of the pile, the Spanish literature book, beneath that, linguistics, finally medieval Latin. In another pile, the books she barely opened during the school year, some sheets of paper sticking a little bit out over the edge of the table, the blue plastic folder on top of the papers, the red plastic folder on top of the blue one; between the plastic folders and the books, three ballpoints, a fountain pen, and a pencil. She organized the small clutter daily, and, before getting into bed, she felt the need to inspect it to see if anything had been left out of place. She did the same thing with her clothes and with some of the terry-cloth dolls that watched her from the bookshelves. It irritated her to find herself dominated by that obsession, but if she didn't follow, to the letter, the rules that she herself had imposed, she became increasingly nervous and couldn't sleep. She told herself it was just eccentricity, just an absurd, useless obsession, but the fear that any change in external order could influence future events drove her to despair. If, when she took off her shoes one night, she happened to set them closer to the headboard than the foot of the bed, and the next day things went better than normal for her, she would say that putting her shoes in that spot brought her luck and would find herself forced to repeat it every night.

She was angry at herself for wasting time by obsessing about her every movement in order to cultivate the ones that seemed to favor her or the opposite: to eliminate the ones she believed harmful, that might scare good luck away. She told herself over and over that if one of her actions coincided with good news, or with being in an excellent mood, it was just a coincidence. She would be reasonable for a while, but after a couple of days she would once again begin to give herself over to her obsession with controlling her fate. She spent her life focused on her own movements, with the certainty that any change, any carelessness could destroy her mental stability. These obsessions often became a lead pipe, as big as she was, that came up to her and, opening from top to bottom like an immense trap, clung to her body until she drowned. Then she would decide to simply ignore her obsession. She would make up her mind that every object, every single thing would just stay wherever she dropped it, without thinking, that the decorations would be renovated, that the horrible terry-cloth dolls would be thrown out. She decided to change her haircut, her style of clothes, tone of voice, movements. For a few days she could do it, but little by little, to improve her luck, she would begin to focus once again on the placement of her clothes in the wardrobe, of her books on the desk, of her personal objects in the space she inhabited.

The monotony she had condemned herself to bored her to tears, but changes horrified her. When she wore new clothes she feared the worst. Until she got used to it, any new object that appeared in the house was enough to make her feel nervous, and she avoided looking at it or thinking about it. She was afraid of anything new. She was afraid, she had always been afraid, of the dark, of objects, of people. She was afraid of staying in a dark room, without being able to see, and at the same time, she was afraid of turning on the light and seeing what surrounded her. She was afraid of everything; even more so at night, when she would wake up from a nightmare and find herself alone in her room. She began to believe that fear could take hold of her at any time and, in the end, that's what was happening. Then she would think about Mamá, about Papá, about Ernesto, about Don Julio, until the presence of Rafael and Eva filled her mind and the fear disappeared. Rafael's memory connected her with a time in the past that she felt was hers, lived by her. Everything else was like watching a movie, half asleep, with a protagonist named Julia who had her face but wasn't really her. The memory of Rafael filled her with peace, and a very sweet sadness surrounded her.

Her eyes filled with tears. It didn't hurt to think about Rafael, five years after his death.

In the beginning, it did. She didn't want to think about Rafael. She was afraid of her dead brother. At times she thought she saw him among the shadows in the darkness of the night, wrapped in a sheet, with his head bandaged, and his marble smile, diabolical after his death. She would leave the room when Mamá, Aurelia, or Grandmother Lucía, crying, talked about Rafael. For three months after his death, Rafael was an inexhaustible subject of conversation. Mamá did nothing during that time but tell the story of Rafael's illness, over and over, to everyone who visited them. She relived his childhood, his convalescence, the supposed cure in which she and the whole family had placed their faith, and finally the tragic relapse, the days in the hospital, the operation, the incomprehensible words and phrases spoken by Rafael before he died. And then, invariably, the comforting words from friends and relatives: God has called him to His glory, another angel in heaven. And even though it's hard on you, it's better that he died if, like you're saying, he would have ended up handicapped and blind, because for as long as you live, fine, but once his parents were no longer with him, then what would have become of poor Rafael? Mamá agreed, and Papá did too.

Papá, playing along with the plan to avoid suspicion and possible scandals, spent more time at home for a while, knowing that friends and relatives would visit them. Ever since he had moved out of the house, Papá and Mamá would go out together when it was a question of fulfilling social obligations. They would have dinner with family friends and acquaintances who knew nothing about the separation; if someone knew their secret, he or she would pretend to be in the dark. They would attend baptisms, weddings, and first communions as a couple; they would accept invitations from common friends jointly; and from time to time, they would appear places together for the express purpose of being seen, to belie possible rumors. Every time they went out to keep up appearances, they would end up fighting. Papá would drop Mamá off at home and go to the apartment he had rented. As for Mamá, on the days when she didn't have to fulfill any obligations at Papá's side, she continued going out with Antonio.

Julia thought that Rafael's death constituted the perfect chance for them to give people a sense of intimacy; an auspicious opportunity for friends and family members to leave the house convinced that the scattered rumors were the product of wagging tongues, nothing more. Three months after Rafael's death, Mamá stopped crying, began going out all afternoon and evening, changed to half-mourning clothes, and her dead son turned into a name accompanied by a sigh. What else is one to do? There are mothers who go insane when one of their children dies, but they already had the propensity for craziness inside themselves. And when Grandmother Lucía criticized her for reorganizing her life so quickly, just like that, Mamá exclaimed: And what do you want me to do?, slam my head against the wall? In a situation as terrible as mine, there are only two possibilities: you either kill yourself on the spot or you don't do anything at all.

Julia agreed with Mamá. It would have depressed her to see her crying and moaning like she did the first days after Rafael's death. But, Daughter, Grandmother Lucía chided her, you give the impression that you waited exactly three months on the dot to shake off the pain. Then Mamá became nearly hysterical and assured her that the pain of Rafael's death would be with her as long as she lived.

Mamá returned to her normal life. Papá stopped coming home and only picked Julia up to spend the weekend with him every other week or once a month.

Julia was afraid of Rafael for almost a year. She didn't shed a single tear the day he died, or during the wake when Grandmother Lucía made the entire family pray the fifteen mysteries of the rosary. Two aunts fainted, and one cousin felt the spark of God's call and decided to join a convent. Julia didn't cry or say a word. Not on the day of the funeral either. Ernesto said he didn't want to go to the cemetery, that it scared him. I wouldn't be able to stand seeing how they bury Rafael and then come home, leaving him there, alone. Julia saw that Ernesto was agitated, nervous. From the day they took Rafael to the hospital until two or three days after the burial, Ernesto went around crying in the corners, cursing the entire universe and shaking like a leaf. Grandmother Lucía told him: You're not only a bad brother, a bad son, and a bad grandson, you're a bad Christian. Ernesto, crying, refused to go to the cemetery. He seemed like a child to Julia, even though he was so tall and had a deep and powerful voice. Papá shouted at him: You're going to come with me, by my side. I can't, I can't, Papá, I'm sorry, I can't, I'll faint. Papá, calm until that moment, even though his hand shook every time he raised his cigarette to his lips, vented on Ernesto the tension that had accumulated during the three previous days. At the very door to the church, he screamed at him: I'm telling you for the last time, get in the car. I can't, Papá, I can't, repeated Ernesto. Papá cornered him against the wall and began to slap him: You damn sissy, so what do you want?, you want to go home and say the rosary with the hired mourners? Get in the car. Blood began to drip from Ernesto's nose. Uncle Ricardo snatched him away from Papá. Okay, I'm going, said Ernesto; pale, wild eyed, his nose bleeding, he staggered toward the car between Papá and Uncle Ricardo. And Julia felt sorrier for him than for the brother who had just died.

During the three months of strict mourning imposed by Grandmother Lucía, the radio wasn't turned on, or the television, or the record player. They were only allowed to talk about Rafael's death, and in a quiet tone of voice. They dressed Julia in black clothes too, and every day, in the afternoon, Grandmother Lucía made her accompany her in her prayers.

She was filled with uneasiness when she saw the armchair in the veranda where Rafael would listen to the radio, when she found one of his books, the magazines he used to buy, or anything else that had belonged to him abandoned throughout the house. Rafael had become a dead person, an unknown being that couldn't be seen or touched, but that made its presence known. The air was Rafael and, breathing it, she thought she was drawing a ghost into her body. Any noises were Rafael's footsteps, Rafael's signs. A ghost followed her everywhere, at all times. But what terrorized her the most were the afternoons spent in Grandmother Lucía's bedroom when they summoned her to prayer. Her grandmother's bedroom reminded Julia of a torture chamber, an ideal room in which to go crazy. The room was overflowing with furniture: a very high bed with two mattresses, the wardrobe, a dresser with drawers that squealed when they were opened and were full of yellowing photos, papers, and souvenirs. Between the dresser and the window, a table, and on the other side of the window, another table; both tables and the dresser were completely covered with statues of virgins and saints. The room smelled of withered flowers. The flowers were, in fact, decaying alongside the statues. Saint Anthony, Saint Pancracio, Saint Nicholas, Saint Lucía with her eyes on a plate she was holding in her hand; the Virgin of Fátima, the Virgin of Lourdes, and others. In front of the bed, a small chapel with a bloodstained Christ completed Grandmother Lucía's sanctuary. The phosphorescent statue of the Virgin of Lourdes would light up in the dark. At that moment her grandmother would ask for things without restraint: that there be enough work in the factory, that Mamá's situation be resolved (a scandal would kill me, she would say), that Ernesto study more, that he finally pass his exams and that he not be led astray, that Rafael rest in peace and that he pray and intercede for the whole family from heaven above, that her rheumatic pains go away, and, especially, that she have a very good death, without suffering. At the end she added: And pardon our enemies, but keep them at a distance.

Julia didn't go to school for a month. When she returned to class, dressed in black, she was taller, skinnier, and paler than before. When she looked at herself in the mirror, she told herself that she looked like a ghost, that she was the one who was dead. The first day of class the other students looked at her with pity. Did someone you know die? My brother. Rafael? She nodded. What'd he die of? He was sick. Oh, right. And they left her alone. The only one who didn't ask her was Carlos, her brother's close friend. But when she was leaving school at lunchtime, he said to her: Do you take the Balmes bus?, me too, I get off a stop before Diagonal, but it doesn't matter, I'll get off on Diagonal and then I'll walk.

It annoyed her that the boys and girls in the class acted nice to her suddenly, as if they felt sorry for her. They looked at her with concern and made an effort to smile at her. She sat, like usual, near the window that looked out over the recreational area. It was raining and the walls were wet and the ground was full of puddles. She realized she would never again see Rafael, chatting, happy, surrounded by a group of boys. She would never see him again anywhere. She felt like crying, finally letting it all out, like Mamá, Ernesto, Grandmother Lucía, Aurelia had done, like all the other people who, without even being family members, had gotten all emotional, saying: What a waste, a nineteen-year-old boy. But she held it in. She didn't want to cry in class and have everyone see her and pity her. She felt enormously alone, completely isolated from everyone else, different. From the very first day she had felt isolated at school. From time to time some classmate would turn around in his or her seat to contemplate her in silence. Julia blushed when she realized it, her head sank to her chest, and she stared at her book, open in front of her, so that no one would realize that her eyes were full of tears; she felt lonely, strange, different from them.

An office assistant came into the room and notified Julia: the headmistress, Señorita Mabel, wanted to speak to her.

It startled her. Her classmates scared her, but the teachers even more so. She didn't like them. She was afraid of them. They always put her in uncomfortable situations. She blamed some of them for giving her special treatment; they rarely chose to quiz her about the assignment. They would call on her, ask her questions, and tell her in a nice tone of voice, excessively nice so as not to fluster her any more than she already was because of the simple fact of being called on in class: Don't be nervous, Julia, if you want we can wait a minute, or you can hand in your written answers. Then she would get more nervous and stutter. Other teachers praised her in front of the other students and made an example out of her. It drove her crazy. She felt different from the others, and everyone, including the teachers, emphasized that difference. Señorita Mabel, the headmistress, didn't indulge her as much as the other teachers did; but at times Julia realized that she observed her very intently, and then, if Julia noticed, she would smile at her. It bothered her that Señorita Mabel spied on her and would then talk with Mamá. However, the headmistress's smile didn't seem forced like everyone else's. She asked Julia questions about the lesson, the same way she asked the other students, and when Julia began to stutter, unable to find the words, she would look away and stare at the back wall, ignoring her nervousness. When they imposed collective punishments, the other teachers excluded Julia from the task of copying a thousand times, I will not talk in class. But Señorita Mabel never made a distinction for her, saying: The whole class, except Julia. It bothered her to have to copy whatever it was for a disturbance she hadn't participated in, but in this way she felt equal to the other students and, deep down, grateful. Participating in the punishment signified having taken part in the disturbance, chatting away while the teacher asked someone else questions about the lesson or taking advantage of the teacher's momentary absence from the room to burst into song.

However, when the assistant told her that the headmistress was waiting for her, she got scared. She didn't want to be a lab specimen, and Señorita Mabel observed her closely. She thought that maybe she would talk to her about Rafael's death and unleash some consoling sermon. She didn't like the idea.

When she got to the office, she knocked on the door. Come in. She opened it. The headmistress, behind the desk, was talking on the phone. She covered the mouthpiece with her hand. Hello, Julia, come in and sit down. She sank into one of the big armchairs and waited. Señorita Mabel, in her office, didn't have the hard, serious appearance that frightened Julia in class. As she was talking on the phone her hands and head moved constantly back and forth, and her medium-length dark hair swayed from side to side. She said only: Yes, yes, you're right, naturally. She covered the mouthpiece with her hand again and murmured in a whisper, addressing Julia: She's a pain. She smiled at her. Julia thought she looked like Aunt Elena. The memory of Aunt Elena made her even sadder. The headmistress hung up the phone and Julia jumped in her chair. Come on, Julia, there's no reason to be frightened, it was just the phone. Señorita Mabel went to sit in the armchair, next to Julia. She thought that, depending on what the headmistress said to her, she would begin to cry.

I wanted to talk with you, began Señorita Mabel. It's possible that you won't pass all your classes this year. I know that you'll do everything possible, but you know that you missed a month and a half of classes . . . you'll pass Latin and Greek for sure, but natural sciences . . . I think I'll pass all of them, whispered Julia. Maybe, but since you're used to getting good grades . . . anyway, if you fail something this year you shouldn't become discouraged, it won't be your fault.

The headmistress smiled at her. Julia felt like a weight had been taken off. Señorita Mabel had spoken to her in a nice tone, but normal, without exaggerated indulgence. Julia thought that she had finished when she heard her say: Julia, I don't think you feel very comfortable at this school, I'd like to know why not. Julia didn't know what to say, what to express on her face, or what to do with her hands. Is there something you don't like? Some teacher? A classmate? Julia moved her head from left to right two or three times and then lowered it, gluing her eyes to the floor. A violent tremor shook her body, and she hid her hands underneath the cushion of the chair. Señorita Mabel took her by the chin, making her raise her face. Is it something you can't tell me?, she asked, while searching her eyes. Julia bit her lips, she tried to hold back the tears but couldn't. She began to cry, without being able to contain herself. The headmistress caressed her head. Come on, Julia, don't cry, I know that Rafael . . . No, it's not that, she murmured. The headmistress must not have heard her, because she continued: It'll get better soon, once they let you change out of these clothes. It's not that, she repeated. Well, everything else will get better too, with time. Julia shook her head in disagreement. Of course it will, Julia, it will get better, you don't want to tell me right now, right? But some other time, whenever you want, come here and tell me. Señorita

Mabel took her face in her hands and kissed her. Julia inhaled a pleasant perfume. The headmistress's face was smiling, very close to her own. A strange feeling of sweetness filled her, and she threw herself into Señorita Mabel's arms, pulling herself to her chest.

From that day Señorita Mabel would often call her to her office, during her free time, so she could help her grade the Latin exercises. At the beginning of every month, she would ask her: Can you help me prepare the envelopes to send the bills? The headmistress would write the students' names on the envelopes, and Julia would fill them with the corresponding receipts. Once a week Señorita Mabel dictated the grades that Julia would write on her classmates' report cards. Señorita Mabel didn't talk a lot, but Julia liked being with her in the office during her free hour in the morning and her half-hour break in the afternoon. On the days she helped the headmistress, Julia would feel happy, in a good mood; it didn't matter to her that her classmates refused to talk to her or looked at her disapprovingly: they didn't matter to her. She anticipated her free time with impatience and, when the other students went outside, she would go to the headmistress's office and wait in the hallway until Señorita Mabel appeared and asked her: Would you like to help me?

When Aurelia opened and then shut the door for her, the house would close in all around her. With a little bit of luck, Mamá would be conspicuous by her absence and Grandmother Lucía would too. She didn't count on Ernesto: he wouldn't come home until at least ten, it was often after midnight. Aurelia would serve her a glass of milk. You're undernourished, she would say. You'll end up worse off than Rafael, the poor thing ate like a bird, and now look, he's been resting in peace for almost a year; so you . . . filling up on books and air . . .

She would wander through the house, up and down the hallway, and go out on the balcony for a while. Aurelia would scold her: With your body's lack of defenses, you'll catch a terrible case of tuberculosis. But she wouldn't pay any attention to her. She'd stay on the balcony, thinking about Señorita Mabel's words, about what she had said. Julia often wished the headmistress would be more affectionate with her, that she would hold her in her arms like the first day of classes after Rafael's death. But at least she felt her presence and the security of sharing something with her. In the balcony she remembered the headmistress's words, her movements, her gestures. Thinking about summer made her panic. She wouldn't have school for three months. On Saturday afternoons and Sundays she was in a bad mood. The hours separating her from Monday always seemed interminable.

If, when she came home, she found Mamá or Grandmother Lucía, she would shut herself in the library with the pretext of studying. They irritated her. Grandmother Lucía would inquire: How's school going? Do you talk yet? Don't even think about it, answered Mamá in Julia's place. Not even if they torture her. It's been days since the headmistress called to talk to me. She must've decided she's hopeless. At times Mamá would say that Señorita Mabel was incapable and pretentious, that she exaggerated and didn't know what she was talking about. Julia would be infuriated, but she wouldn't respond. In the library she studied, read, or got lost in her own thoughts. At ten she would come out for dinner. If Ernesto had dinner at home, the meal would be more enjoyable. Ernesto always had stories to tell even if they weren't true. When Ernesto, bragging, would begin to lie, Julia knew it immediately, but it didn't bother her. In the end, the only thing she wanted was for the half-hour dinner to go by as quickly as possible. If Ernesto felt like saying that during the afternoon three girls had asked him out one after another, that he was sure to pass his college prep classes in June, that he had just started a magnificent painting, or that the previous night he and his friends were in a nightclub and, when he made his entrance in a brand-new outfit, everyone turned around to admire it, she didn't care. The important thing was to have Mamá and Grandmother Lucía talk with Ernesto, otherwise they bombarded Julia with questions, objections, and rude remarks, or they talked to each other, criticizing people right and left. Grandmother Lucía discovered immorality in nearly her entire repertoire of friends and relatives. If someone didn't have a daughter who stayed out after ten at night, then he had a good-for-nothing son who was going astray or an adulterous wife. So-and-so's single daughter had gotten herself pregnant. Her grandmother was scandalized: If that happened to a daughter or granddaughter of mine, I'd either kill her or never talk to her again for the rest of my life. Julia thought that if she wasn't such a coward, she would give her grandmother the pleasure of banishing her from her despicable presence. Mamá agreed with everything Grandmother Lucía said. Of course everyone knows it's best not to criticize, but things should be done discretely; there's no reason to create a scandal and give loose tongues more reasons to wag.

Since Rafael's death, Mamá paid more attention to Julia. But Julia avoided her; she didn't like it anymore when Mamá hugged her or stuck her nose in her business. Julia realized that Mamá missed Rafael and was using her to fill the void. She had stopped loving Mamá, and that thought filled her with bitterness and remorse. She disliked seeing Mamá at home. She preferred having dinner alone with Grandmother Lucía and not having Mamá pester her with the frivolous affection that she suddenly seemed to inspire in her.

In bed at night, before she fell asleep, she would think that she'd like to live with the headmistress, sleep with her, go to school with her in the morning, stay in her office instead of being locked in the classroom with the other students, have lunch with Señorita Mabel, return in the afternoon to Señorita Mabel's office, live with Señorita Mabel. She told herself it was impossible. She wished Mamá, Papá, and Grandmother Lucía would disappear so her dream could come true. But even if they disappeared, she was too old for Señorita Mabel to treat like a child, to pamper and spoil. It hurt her to know that she was grown up on the outside and a child on the inside. She'd be sixteen soon. She lost hope. Her desires didn't correspond with her age, but she gave herself over to them and fell asleep hugging her pillow.

She got sick after her exams. Mamá, in July, left on a trip, supposedly with Uncle Ricardo, although Julia knew it wasn't true. She promised to return in three weeks, but it took her a month and a half. Julia received postcards from Italy, Switzerland, Germany, Holland, Belgium, and France. Ernesto passed his college preparatory classes and Mamá, before undertaking her mysterious journey, rented a studio for him at the end of Balmes Street, right in front of the stop for the blue streetcar which Julia had sometimes ridden with Rafael to go up to the Tibidabo.

For more than a year now, Ernesto had been asking Mamá to rent him a studio where he could concentrate on his painting. A work of art isn't created just like that. I need peace and tranquility, a place where I can find myself. Mamá had promised to get it for him when he was accepted into the university, by the School of Architecture, but in the end Ernesto got it after passing his college prep classes. Grandmother Lucía was pulling out her hair. She claimed that renting the studio for him was equivalent to promoting Ernesto's vocation as a painter, which, according to her, would be a catastrophe. We already know what type of people artists are, undesirables and nothing more. And you, you alone —she growled, addressing Mamá— will be to blame when your son goes bad. Grandmother Lucía said that artists were bohemians, crazy people who chose to do art because they were lazy, incapable of earning a living with a normal and honorable job, and since they could barely earn enough to eat, they found themselves forced to rob, cheat, prostitute themselves, and "God knows what else." They went around dirty and unkempt, they got sick because they didn't get any decent food, and the frustration and bitterness caused by the lack of money made them turn to drugs and alcohol. And they lose all dignity, the world's full of wretches like that. They sell themselves off to smugglers or gangsters who drag them into all sorts of things for a mere pittance, and they wind up in jail. That's how you're going to wind up, she shouted at Ernesto, in the electric chair, and it'll be your mother's fault for getting you the studio. Ernesto laughed at Grandmother Lucía's words, and Mamá didn't pay the slightest attention.

Ernesto's studio was the novelty of the first months of summer. Ernesto would ask her almost every day: Want to come over to help me arrange books and things? The studio consisted of a spacious bedroom, a bathroom, a kitchen, a large patio from which you could see the Tibidabo and most of the city and which let in a good deal of light. Ernesto, when Mamá wasn't present, was easier to put up with. He didn't babble as much, his unnatural tone of voice almost disappeared, and the effeminate gestures, imitations of Mamá's, did too. On top of that, he stopped treating her like a child.

Ever since Papá had left home, Ernesto had taken his role as head of the household very seriously, and he constantly reminded her, by his tone of voice and attitude, that he was the oldest and that she was not only the baby, but also a girl. Ernesto was Mamá's spitting image: blond, very pale eyes, tall and thin, narrow hips and long legs. He talked like Mamá, and as he spoke, he would observe himself in a mirror. And like Mamá, his main concern was his own personal appearance. He would waste an entire afternoon going from store to store to buy himself a tie or some socks and, arriving home with the new acquisition, would show it to her with pride. What do you think about these socks for the pants and shoes I bought the other day? Or: Look carefully and tell me whether this sweater goes with my skin tone. As if that weren't enough, he picked on her: Mamá, this morning I saw Julia out on the street. I almost didn't even dare talk to her. She looks like a scarecrow; you've got to get her to dress better. Mamá would be furious: And what do you want me to do? Even if I spend a fortune on her, she looks like it's all borrowed. True —Mamá and Ernesto ganged up on her—. I know lots of girls her age who, even though they're uglier than her, give a different impression, they wear makeup, they take care of themselves . . . in short, Julia, you have no class.

Ernesto finished his speeches with the thing about *class*, and it drove Julia crazy, but she didn't respond. There are worse things about her —grumbled Grandmother Lucía, very tall and bony—; the fact that she wears no makeup is fine, I don't like paint-daubed faces, femininity is seen through other things —and then she glared at her—, piety toward God, for one. A woman who doesn't go to mass and doesn't pray can't be a decent woman, and that, of course, shows up in her looks.

However, in the studio Ernesto was a different person. While he placed the books on the new shelves and arranged canvases and other painting supplies, he talked to her about his vocation as a genius, about his friends, about the trips that he would take as soon as he became a famous painter, about his desire to triumph and confront Papá with the announcement that he didn't want to study architecture and to confront Grandmother Lucía, letting off steam by telling her that God was just a hoax, that he couldn't care less about going to church, that she was a hysterical old bag, and that, when she died, he would sell the shirt and underwear factory and use up all the money by having orgies and distributing it to the whores in the red-light district.

Julia believed that Ernesto, with his little orphan, young-lord face, would never amount to anything, much less confront Papá by refusing to study. Nor would he be capable of reproaching Grandmother Lucía's sanctimonious hypocrisy. Ernesto shook like a leaf every time Papá called him on the phone to ask about his grades and said: We'll talk face to face next Saturday. Or on Sunday afternoons after lunch, when Grandmother Lucía would ask him what the sermon at the mass that I presume you heard was about. She, Julia, had completely resolved the problem of attending mass. She screwed up her courage and one Sunday, when her grandmother was waiting for her in the foyer, dressed like usual in shades of black, gray, and purple, her white hair pulled up into a high bun, her shawl on her shoulders, her missal in one hand and her cane with the silver handle in the other, Julia approached her in her pajamas. Still not ready? We've only got twenty minutes, and you know I like to find a place in one of the front rows. I'm not going, responded Julia. What did you say? I'm not going, not today or next Sunday or the one after that. I'm not going, not going, and not going. Mamá slapped her: I don't care if you go to church or not, but I forbid you to disrespect your grandmother. Ernesto was dressed impeccably; his eyes flew open and he remained silent. Grandmother Lucía crossed herself, grabbed Ernesto's arm, and went to mass.

When Ernesto's friends showed up at the studio, Julia would leave for home. Ernesto would say: Stay, silly, they're fun. However, when Luis came, Ernesto would pull her aside and say: Julia, Luis and I need to talk, could you . . . Julia would take the hint and say good-bye. If you want, take a book, he would offer, thinking she was offended. Julia tried to come home with the type of book that would infuriate Grandmother Lucía. Her grandmother checked the books that she and Ernesto read. She would remember the title and the author's name and, when Uncle Ricardo came by the house, she would consult with him. Poison for young minds, declared Uncle Ricardo once, when her grandmother asked him about *Nausea*, by some Sartre guy. Her grandmother paged through the book in question and others by the same author that she had found in Ernesto's room. She tore them up and told Aurelia: Burn that trash, Sartre is the reincarnation of Satan. But Ernesto bought the books again, and from time to time Julia would sit in the dining room, in front of Grandmother Lucía, with one of them in her hands. Her grandmother would get up, twisting a lace handkerchief between her fingers, and, while heading to her sanctuary, would exclaim: I'm going to pray for the two of you, may my tears and prayers lead to your salvation.

In reality, more than Sartre or Camus —Grandmother Lucía's two enemies—, Julia liked to read Saroyan's sad, quiet tales, the turbulent stories of the Dickensian heroes, the squabbles that prevented Balzac's characters from ascending to the level of the Parisian aristocracy, the melancholy and appealing atmosphere of Chekovian short stories, and the silent desperation of the adolescent protagonists in Pavese's novels. She would read these books and others that she really liked in the library or alone in her room. But from time to time, she would appear in the dining or living room with a "sinful" book that would boil her grandmother's blood. When she, Julia, was sixteen, Ernesto's library was circulating three or four of the authors that had been condemned by Grandmother Lucía on Uncle Ricardo's recommendation: Sartre, Camus, Tennessee Williams, and Françoise Sagan. Being seen by her grandmother with one of these books was the only vengeance that Julia could aspire to. They were often ripped from her hands. If Ernesto can read them, so can I, she said. Ernesto shouldn't either, but he's a man, answered her grandmother. And because she's a woman you want to condemn her to foolishness and ignorance?, Ernesto defended her at these moments. A woman doesn't need to know as much as a man; it's been that way ever since the world began.

Some afternoons Ernesto would invite her to see a movie, but not very often. Mamá hadn't come back from her mysterious trip, and Julia was bored to tears at home. She was counting the days until October, when she could go to school and see Señorita Mabel again. One morning Carlos, Rafael's friend from school, came by the house with a bag in his hand; he was wearing blue jeans and a sweater with blue and white stripes. Aurelia opened the door for him and then announced to Grandmother Lucía that a boy was asking for Julia. Grandmother Lucía went flying toward the foyer, leaping down the hallway. Carlos explained to her that he was going to the beach with his brother and two girls. I thought that if Julia was in Barcelona maybe she'd like to come with us. Her grandmother told him that Julia, for the moment, assuming the devil had yet to lead her into temptation, was a respectable girl. Carlos got nervous and left. Grandmother Lucía spent days torturing her with questions about Carlos: how she knew him, if she saw him outside of school, if they had ever gone to see a movie, if he had invited or taken her to "one of those indecent parties that kids nowadays organize in their own homes." Julia kept saying no to every question, until finally Grandmother Lucía said: I presume you haven't been to a dance. Julia, fed up by that point, responded: Yes, a few times. It wasn't true; she didn't know why she lied, maybe she thought that it would help end the interrogation. But on the contrary, Grandmother Lucía covered her mouth with the lace handkerchief she was always fingering, and after a few minutes of absolute silence, with a serious expression, she began to corner her once again with questions: Did you dance?, did he kiss you?, did he do anything to you?

She had never for a moment thought about the consequences of her lie. She visualized the scene that Grandmother Lucía, with her questions, had created in her mind. Julia had never been concerned with things like that. Love was something that happened to other people, to the characters in movies, in novels, and to people who lived around her but were so unconnected to her that they belonged to the world of fictional characters. Her grandmother, with her questions and insinuations, had placed her in front of a screen where a disgusting movie, starring her and Carlos, was being projected. She noticed a sickening taste in her mouth and suffocating heat in her head; a shiver ran up her back, her hands and legs trembled. She felt dizzy, sick. She could barely breathe and was unable to say a word in response to her grandmother, who kept on inquiring: Was it dark?, how long were you two shut up in that lair?, did anybody you know see you? The last question, it seemed, was what worried her the most. Julia's skin felt damp and sticky; she was filled with profound disgust. She finally managed to murmur: It was a lie, I wasn't at any dance, I've only seen Carlos at school, he's in my grade and he was Rafael's friend. When Ernesto got home, at lunchtime, Grandmother Lucía made him call Carlos on the phone and ask him if he had taken Julia to a dance. Ernesto said he wouldn't call, but in the end, when his grandmother insisted, he gave in.

After hearing Carlos's answer, Grandmother Lucía calmed down. Julia felt defeated by her grandmother. She should never have recanted, but her grandmother had won through treachery. She felt humiliated by the scene that her grandmother's insinuations had created in her mind, and she wondered why she felt so much fear, disgust, and resentment toward her grandmother and toward Carlos.

If you're bored, call your cousins and go out with them, her grandmother told her. She didn't do it. The oldest cousin, Lucía's favorite granddaughter, had renounced her summer vacations and went to a parish in Paralelo every afternoon to teach catechism to the neighborhood children. She taught them religious doctrine and sacred history. Grandmother Lucía, when her favorite granddaughter stopped by the house, would give her a five-hundred-peseta note and say: Take it, angel of God, for your charitable deeds. One Sunday when her cousin dragged her to the Paralelo parish, Julia saw how she went into a bakery and bought fifty pesetas worth of candy for her unfortunate students: she only gave them candy on Sundays, otherwise they would come to expect it.

As for the other cousins, the oldest one was eighteen and the youngest sixteen, like Julia. She didn't call them up to go out with them. However, Uncle Ricardo stopped by the house one Saturday and her grandmother told him: Tell your daughters to call Julia; since she passed all her classes and doesn't need to study, she's getting bored, it's been a month since her mother left, and that scoundrel of a father gives no signs of life. The next day, Sunday, the two cousins showed up at the house after lunch in white knitwear. We're going to go see a movie, they told Grandmother Lucía. When they were out of the house, they informed Julia that they weren't going to go see a movie. A girl's giving a party at her house, but don't tell Grandmother Lucía because our mother would find out right away. Do you have a boyfriend?, they asked her. Well, I mean casually, do you hang out with somebody. No, Julia responded. Well, you're not bad, maybe today you'll meet a boy you like.

The party at her cousins' friend's house put her in a bad mood. Seven girls and nine boys locked themselves in a room, with a record player, a writing desk full of trays of sandwiches, pastries, Cokes, *horchatas*, and gin, a couch, and throw pillows on the floor. Julia only knew her cousins, and they quickly paired off with two boys and left her alone. Before that, the older cousin had taken an eighteen- or nineteen-year-old boy by the arm and brought him over to Julia. My cousin Julia, she said. I'm Romeo, said the boy, laughing and holding out his hand. The boy who said his name was Romeo asked Julia: Are you free? What? Do you have a boyfriend or partner or something? No. Well, now you do, want to dance? No. Then let's talk, come on, we can sit on the floor, it's more comfortable. On the throw pillows, the boy began to play around, messing up her hair to see "if this beautiful long mane is a wig," and then "let me see what strange earrings you're wearing," so he could brush against her neck and cheek while he touched the earring. The earrings she was wearing were the ones from her first communion, plain gold balls. Julia began to count to twenty, determined to get away from that imbecile if he didn't leave her alone. He moved his hand across her shoulders; Julia, without reaching twenty, got up. Are we going to dance?, asked the boy, not letting go of her hand. No. Julia went up to one of her cousins. I'm going. Aren't you having fun? Yes, but I don't feel good. Okay, whatever you want, but don't tell Grandmother . . .

She said she felt sick, and it was true. Since the end of the semester, she had been getting headaches and stomachaches. She felt nauseated and feverish. She thought that her discomfort was due to boredom and the heat. When Mamá got back from her trip, she noticed that Julia had lost weight and was in poor health. In fact, the drowsiness and headaches that plagued her all day were due to fever. She slept badly; exhausting, confusing nightmares woke her up at night. She thought she could hear strong, heavy breathing close to her bed, as if someone had come into her room, and she saw shadows that moved toward her but never got close enough so she could make them out. She wished that the shadow's owner would just make himself known and then leave her alone. She closed her eyes, the fear seized hold of her, she listened to her heartbeat and the slow, heavy footsteps that were approaching her bed. She jumped and hit the light switch; there was nobody in the room.

The doctor made her stay in bed until the fevers disappeared. They lasted until September. What do you think's gotten into Julia now?, she would hear Mamá and Grandmother Lucía wonder. Since Rafael's death, if she or Ernesto got sick, it drove them crazy. They did analyses and explorations of her stomach. I haven't found anything abnormal, explained the doctor. A slight anemia that we'll keep an eye on and nervous upsets that'll disappear as soon as she's better.

In October, when she started her junior year, her problems with Lidia, a classmate, began.

Lidia, new to the school, was two years older than Julia. Two weeks after the beginning of the semester, Lidia planted herself in front of Julia. Are you the one who always gets prizes in Latin? Sometimes only Outstanding, she responded. Well, it doesn't matter, you'll do. You do the Latin translation for me every day and I'll let you be my friend.

Julia was going to tell her that her friendship meant nothing to her and that she had already demonstrated her lack of manners, but the other girl's tone of voice left her speechless. Why do you sit all alone? Are you a leper? Julia blushed. Lidia looked at her and smiled mockingly. Don't get mad, kid, it was just a joke. Okay, so we've agreed you're going to do the translation for me and give it to me before class starts . . . don't do it really good or really bad, just acceptable. And she left. The next morning, as soon as she got to class, Lidia asked her for the translation. Señorita Mabel gave the translation that Julia did for Lidia a B. At the end of class, Lidia said to her: You did a good job, you're pretty smart.

At times Lidia antagonized Julia, she took her books, notebooks, and folder and placed them on the desk right next to the one she sat in, close to the other students. If you want to take notes or follow along in your book next period, you have to sit where I want you to. It irritated Julia that Lidia could change her seat on a whim and that she thought she could control her, but suddenly Lidia would smile at her in a strange way and act affectionate. While they were waiting for the next teacher to come into the classroom, Lidia would say: You have such pretty long hair, let me comb it for you. Or she would suddenly hug her: You're as silly as a goose. And she would laugh. In a few days Lidia had become friends with all the juniors and she could twist them around her little finger. The other students were amazed to see somebody talking to Julia, but then they ended up talking to her too. Suddenly, Lidia would get mad, take Julia's books and notebooks, and move them back to her old desk, next to the window: You're ungrateful, Lidia chided. You're no fun, you don't have any blood flowing in your veins.

It didn't make sense to Julia when Lidia returned her to the exile from which she had removed her against her will, and she began to understand that Lidia got angry over trifles: not laughing at her jokes, or not chatting with her while the teacher was explaining something in class, or not letting her comb her hair. Lidia invited her over some Sundays. We're having a party at the house of one of the girls from class, are you coming? They won't let me, she said, as an excuse. You're an idiot, you don't have to tell them. It was true, but she remembered her cousins' party and didn't like the idea. On Monday, Lidia didn't say a word to her. On Tuesday, she said: You're a strange one, but I like you; come on, I'm going to comb your hair. It annoyed her when people touched her hair, but she didn't dare contradict Lidia.

During her free time, Julia, like the year before, would go to Señorita Mabel's office to help her fill out report cards and mail the student bills. Julia noticed that when she returned to class after going to the headmistress's office, Lidia had returned her books to her old desk. Walking into the classroom, she heard Lidia and a few of her disciples. They were exclaiming: I'm so hungry!, so hungry! Where's that apple polisher keep her apples? The part about the apple polisher was directed at Julia. Lidia was accusing her of "apple polishing" and of being the headmistress's "favorite."

Every time Julia spent her free hour in Señorita Mabel's company, she suffered the consequences. Someone was getting revenge on her, and she didn't know why. In Greek class, the teacher would ask the students to read out loud the translation assigned the day before. At the beginning of class, Julia was looking through her things for her translation notebook, and she couldn't find it. Some of her classmates were watching her, somewhat curious and somewhat mocking, while she dug urgently through her folders over and over. Lidia asked her: Did you lose something? The first time it occurred, she apologized to the teacher: I left my notebook at home. But when the event reoccurred on subsequent days, she didn't dare give the same excuse. The third time, the teacher reprimanded her. Two weeks later the teacher sent a note to the headmistress complaining about Julia's lack of interest in his class. During her free hour, Julia hid her books and notebooks, but when she returned from the headmistress's office, the Greek notebook would be gone. Then Lidia, or one of her friends, would say to her: I found this notebook, is it yours? That strange game drove her crazy. Why do you hide my notebook?, she reproached Lidia one day. You're her favorite, aren't you? —Julia presumed she was referring to Señorita Mabel—, well, deal with it.

Another day, at the beginning of religion class, the priest who taught the course took a piece of paper off the top of his desk, read it, shouted: Who wrote this? I want the person who wrote this filth to stand up. The students looked at each other, surprised; nobody stood up. I'm going to say this one more time, whoever wrote this note raise your hand, otherwise I'll punish the entire class. Lidia stood up: I didn't want to tell on her, but . . . I saw who did it. And she pointed at Julia. Julia, in a tiny voice, said: That's not true. But two girls and a boy, Lidia's friends, claimed that they had also seen her place the paper on the desk before the beginning of class. The priest expelled her from the room: And don't come back for two weeks, we'll discuss this then, he shouted. Julia thought she was going to die of shame and she stumbled out of the room; her legs were shaking and tears clouded her vision. The priest followed her out. Wait here, he demanded in the hallway. The priest, with the offensive paper in his hand, went into the headmistress's office. After a few minutes he came out and, without saying a word to her, went back to class.

Señorita Mabel called her from her office. Was it you? Julia shook her head. The Greek teacher gave me a note complaining about your behavior; it surprises me coming from you, said Señorita Mabel. What's going on? I thought that lately you were feeling more comfortable at school. Julia nodded her head. Is something going on now? Yes, she murmured, crying. Are you tired? Is there some problem? What is it? Señorita Mabel went to hug her. Julia threw her arms around the headmistress's neck and clung to her. I don't know, she said. Above Señorita Mabel's shoulders, Julia realized that Lidia was spying through the half-open door, she smiled mockingly and then disappeared. Fear took hold of Julia, she anticipated a strange and mysterious revenge. Someone was trying to take something from her that she hadn't even possessed yet, something she had only desired. Do you want me to talk to your mother?, asked the headmistress. No, shouted Julia; no. What's the matter? Can't you tell me? She was afraid, terribly afraid, but she couldn't explain why. I don't know, she repeated; I don't know.

She met Lidia in the hallway. Did she make you feel better? You're the old maid's favorite, but I can handle you; I'll always win if I want to, she said, staring at her and smiling in an odd way. Julia didn't respond. She went over to the sink. While Julia silently washed her face and hands, she saw that Lidia's expression, reflected in the mirror, changed suddenly. Lidia's transformations disconcerted her. One minute she would be glaring at her sarcastically, and the next, she would reward her with one of her best smiles and throw an arm around her shoulders, saying: You're as silly as a goose, but I love you. Lidia's unexpected changes disconcerted her, she didn't have time enough to react.

Lidia came up to her; she put one hand on Julia's shoulder and with the other one began to caress her hair. It's all messed up. Julia didn't respond. Lidia was just as likely to slap her as ask for permission to comb her hair. She didn't understand why Lidia seemed to want to hurt her at times, and at other times she showed her affection and admiration. Come on, don't hold a grudge, you're my friend, right? I won't play any more tricks on you, I promise. Julia screwed up enough courage to look at her, and she seemed sincere. Lidia was taller and heavier than she was. But sometimes you make me mad, Lidia continued, why does she fascinate you so much? Who? Don't play dumb. Lidia was much stronger than she was. She couldn't get free. It seemed, for a few moments, like the air wasn't getting to her lungs and she was going to suffocate. Let me go, she begged. The faucet was dripping, and the sound of water falling on porcelain resonated in her head. It seemed like the obscene words, scratched in the paint, were moving, running up and down the wall like ants escaping from a fire. She closed her eyes and had the sensation that the ants had jumped off the wall and were climbing up her legs, her back, her neck, her arms and face. Lidia's loud cackle of laughter brought her back to reality. Now do you understand that I'm going to win? You have to do what I want.

A wave of fury and indignation overwhelmed her. She slapped Lidia and ran out of the bathroom. She went into the classroom, gathered up her books, took off her white smock, put on her jacket, and left for home without asking permission.

She spent a week without going to school. The stomachaches came back. The doctor diagnosed nervous disorders again. He recommended that she be seen by a neurologist, and the neurologist insinuated to Mamá that it might be wise to have her see a psychologist. Mamá fought with the doctor. How is a seventeen-year-old girl going to be sick in the head if she doesn't have to do anything but study? She insisted on taking her to a stomach specialist. The specialist assured her that Julia's stomach was in perfect shape, but he prescribed a medicine that made the pain go away for a while.

She was terrified of going back to school and seeing Lidia, but after a week she had no choice but to resume classes. Lidia and her followers continued to harass her with even crueler jokes. Offensive notes frequently appeared on the teachers' desks and they would accuse her of it. There came a time when, if a teacher asked: Where's the scoundrel who wrote this?, Julia would simply take the blame and, without waiting for them to insist, leave class. The situation got worse when the literature teacher, who had never given anyone a grade higher than a seven, gave Julia an eight. Notes began to appear on the blackboards: Julia, teacher's pet. Julia pays twice.

Señorita Mabel no longer asked her to help fill out report cards and mail the monthly fees. Julia spent her free time in the classroom, without going outside; she wouldn't even peek out into the hallway for fear of running into Lidia. Lidia kept on bothering her as much as she could. In drawing class she and her friends would find any excuse to get up so they could walk by Julia's table and bump it, pretending they had tripped. The drawing papers would be splattered with india ink, and she would have to do them over and over. Lidia often came up to her table and said to her, sarcastically: I'm going to the bathroom; if you come along, I'll comb your hair. Or she would ask in a loud voice so that everyone could hear her: Aren't you helping the headmistress out anymore?

Julia took advantage of the slightest opportunity to avoid going to school. Every three or four days, when Aurelia woke her up in the morning, she pretended to have a stomachache so she could stay home. She would be in a bad mood all day, close to tears. If Ernesto suggested: Skip out this afternoon and come see a movie with me, she accepted. She didn't feel like studying, and her report card reflected it. Señorita Mabel hadn't asked for explanations for her absences or for the teachers' accusations, but as soon as her grades started to go down, she called her into the office.

Señorita Mabel appeared nervous, uncomfortable. Julia, I've

been forced to stop treating you with... the special deference I felt for you. I hope you understand. I know you aren't guilty of certain accusations, they won't be taken into account, but it would be better not to give your classmates the chance to accuse me of the affection I've shown you until now. That way they'll stop bothering you. They're wrong, but envy and jealousy are common at your age, do you understand? Yes, Julia responded. She was filled with resentment. The other students had everything: their games, their friends, the groups they formed, their secret conversations, the coded phrases that only they understood. They were capable of chatting away all day long and still having things to say. They had their parties on Sunday afternoons, group excursions; they were always happy and laughing about everything. And they, these very same students, had conspired to take away her half hour of free time in the headmistress's office. She felt powerless to fight that injustice, helpless to defend her one hint of well-being, the single compensation she awarded herself for attending that detestable school.

I wanted to tell you something else —continued Señorita Mabel—, about next year. I'm going to talk to your mother. I think you should leave this school and take classes at the Institute. Why?, Julia interrupted. One of the reasons is that if you did your college prep classes here, you would end up having the same classmates. You need to make an effort to change the way you are a little bit; you wouldn't be able to do it here. Even if you turned yourself inside out, everyone would still see you the same way. At a new school, it'll be different. They'll see whatever you show them. I'm very sorry to have to talk to you like this, but it's for your own good. And if you're going to change environments, it'd be best that you attend the Institute; there're more classes there. In two years you'll go to the university, and it'd be good for you to get used to classes...

Señorita Mabel smiled broadly at her, talking in a soft voice, trying to be as nice as possible. She was attempting to convince her that going to the Institute the following year was the best thing for her. Every time she asked: Do you understand what I'm saying?, Julia answered: Yes, of course.

When she left the office, Julia felt defeated. She didn't even feel like crying; her whole body ached, and the strange sensation of being dead softened the blow of what she had heard. She returned to class, sat next to the window. The freshman boys were playing in the recreation area. She noticed one of them sitting on the ground, alone, with his head between his knees. She told herself that she wasn't the only one. In almost every school in the whole world there must be boys like that one and girls like her. The thought didn't console her in the slightest. She felt humiliated. They had won, and she was certain she would never have enough courage to confront the perpetrators of that injustice, the malignant genius who governed the prison in which she found herself locked away forever. She observed her classmates. She felt the resentment which had accumulated inside her, but —and she was surprised— not against the other students, not even against Lidia. If, one day earlier, they would have placed in her hands a weapon capable of eliminating all of them, she would've gladly accepted it. Now she wouldn't. She didn't want to get revenge on Lidia or her friends. She was full of resentment, but not toward her classmates. She told herself she was weak and a coward: they would always win. She felt ashamed of herself. She remembered the walks along the port with Rafael and the hikes in the woods in Don Julio's company. Like her grandfather had predicted, the five years in the mountains had been wasted, five happy years that had slipped over her and hadn't left the slightest trace. She didn't feel pain, or sorrow, or the urge to cry, only resentment against herself for allowing them to defeat her and for a loneliness that promised to be eternal. She wished she could leave the classroom, run down the stairs into the street, and find someone waiting for her around the corner: Rafael or Aunt Elena. She would hug them hard. She wouldn't need to explain anything. They would understand, and their presence would erase the oppressive sensation of complete solitude.

Mamá found the headmistress's advice to be personally offensive. In other words —explained Mamá to Grandmother Lucía— she wanted to tell me she's expelling Julia from school. Who does she think she is? I'm not questioning the fact that Julia is antisocial and odd, but her responsibility is to prepare her to pass her classes, nothing else. She tried to convince me that I don't know my daughter. I don't have a problem with her studying at the Institute; but trying to tell me how to raise my own daughter, that's going too far.

The Institute only admitted girls, and some of them welcomed Julia's company. She soon acquired a reputation for being intelligent and —she didn't understand why— friendly and a good classmate. The classes each had fifty students. Julia got good grades but not the best in the class. She was among the top ten, but she didn't stand out as decisively as she had at her previous school. Also, the other six or seven girls who, with Julia, got the best grades had taken on the positions of class delegates for various activities: sports, study groups, theater, and so forth. They were the group organizers and made the decisions. Julia didn't take part in any organizational group. It was the other girls who, by making themselves seen and heard in class, became unpopular. For the same reason, Julia enjoyed an intermediate position: she seemed agreeable to the majority of the students, she got good grades (not the best), and at the same time she didn't act proud or dictatorial. Since she didn't belong to any specific group, she was spared the little quarrels that often took place between their members. Belonging to one group meant avoiding contact with the members of other groups, and Julia found herself free to talk with any of them. It didn't bother her to lend out her notes or to let them copy her Latin and Greek translations. She didn't like it or dislike it; it was simply that they asked a favor of her and consenting was the path of least resistance. When she went into class, some of them clamored for her to sit by their side: Julia, come sit with us; if they call on us, you can whisper the answer.

The Institute was in the city park, next to the zoo. The class was quite big, big enough so the teachers didn't read the entire attendance list every day. They calculated the day their name would be called depending on their last names and organized outings in the park. Julia, at times, went with her classmates. She liked to walk in the gardens, next to the water-lily pond where, with a certain arrogance, the swans would swim slowly by. The other girls talked about boys. Her classmates were between seventeen and nineteen years old. If one of them had a boyfriend, the others wouldn't stop bombarding her with questions. Some mentioned boyfriends they had had before, but that later: I stopped liking him all of a sudden. The rest of them had some boy they liked but "he doesn't pay any attention to me, he's so mean." The girls at the Institute weren't surprised, like the ones in her last school, that Julia didn't have a boyfriend and that no boys came to pick her up after class. They found it normal, and in a way they liked it because they had found a subject in which they had an edge on Julia, who paid attention when they talked about amorous themes. At the end of the day, there was always someone who went home the same direction as she did. They would catch the Balmes bus on Paseo Colón and get off at the corresponding stop with a See you later.

They were classmates, nothing else. They didn't see each other outside of the Institute. On Mondays, she would hear everyone else talking about the party they went to on Sunday afternoon, or about going up to the Tibidabo with boys. The events that the other students enjoyed didn't appeal to her at all. When she listened to them, she felt envious. She thought that there was something abnormal about her, something that made her different, but she didn't stop to dwell on it. At home she was bored to tears. When she returned home from the Institute, she would close herself in the library. She dedicated little time to her studies, just enough to keep passing her classes; and once she closed her textbooks, she would try to distract herself by reading some novel. The weekends when Papá didn't get her seemed boring and interminable. That's what you get for not having friends, Mamá said. If you weren't so antisocial . . .

Ernesto, some afternoons, would take her to see a movie. During her year of college preparatory classes she saw movies like *West Side Story*, *Splendor in the Grass*, *Breathless*, *To Kill a Mockingbird*, *Days of Wine and Roses* . . . On Saturday nights he also invited her to sessions of a film club where, after seeing a movie, there was a colloquium between the public and a critic who came to introduce the film. Ernesto seemed interested in the colloquium, but Julia would fall asleep from boredom. In her eyes, every audience member was entirely convinced of what he had seen, and if he stood up to say something or ask something, it wasn't so that some point could be clarified but to show off, publicly, his meager knowledge of cinema. In one of the sessions, Ernesto met up with an old schoolmate: Andrés. They had been in college together. Ernesto, back then, was in his first year of architecture and Andrés was finishing philosophy. I've heard you turned into an artist, said Andrés. Ernesto, proud, invited him to visit his studio: Any day that's convenient for you. Andrés didn't make much of an impression on her. She hardly paid any attention to him.

Sometimes on Saturday Papá would call her on the phone just after lunch. Get ready, Julia, I'll come by in half an hour to pick you up. And she would spend the weekend with him.

Papá had rented an apartment on a small, dark street close to the Borne Market and Santa María del Mar. The apartment had two bedrooms, a kitchen, and a bath. Julia thought it was dirty and disorganized. On the walls and ceiling there were damp stains; the little bit of furniture it contained was old. Maybe Papá was having money problems. At times she heard Grandmother Lucía grumble: I'd like to know what that man lives on, when he runs out of money he'll come crawling back on his knees. However, in spite of Grandmother Lucía's words and the miserable condition of the apartment Papá had rented, Julia figured he couldn't be hurting for money when he had a new car, took her out to eat, gave her presents, and traveled all the time.

On Saturday nights they would go out to dinner and then to a movie theater to see either a Jerry Lewis film, a Western, or a superproduction with a historical theme like *Ben Hur*, *Cleopatra*, *The Fall of the Roman Empire* . . . They would return home, walking along the Ramblas and then down a series of badly paved, short, narrow streets. They would come to the Santa María del Mar church, lit up at night. Papá would stop in the middle of the street. Look at how beautiful it is, Julia. They would enter the maze of narrow streets once again and arrive, after a moment, at Papá's apartment. Julia liked it. From the balcony you could see the illuminated church, the port, and the sea. The rooms were too cold in the winter, but Julia felt good in that place. In spite of the prevailing dirtiness and disorder, she felt calm, at peace. The next morning, Papá wouldn't wake her up until eleven or twelve. They would wash up and get dressed in a hurry and go down to have breakfast in a café in front of the house. The café was pretty dirty and damp too. The tables and stools sported wine stains that the waiter would try, unsuccessfully, to clean with a rag that was more than a little questionable. On the counter top there were *salchichones*, *longanizas*, ham, and other kinds of sausages that the clients pawed over before deciding what to order. In spite of everything, Julia liked having breakfast there. Papá would take the newspaper from the counter and read it while he ate. Afterward they would walk along the Ramblas and through the Barrio Gótico or go up to Montjuich or walk around the discount book market that was open on Sundays in the San Antonio Market. They would have a drink and then have lunch in a restaurant in Plaza de Cataluña. Around four in the afternoon Papá would take her home. I'll call you next Saturday, all right? Papá said good-bye: See you next Saturday. But Julia knew it wasn't true. Papá called her once a month.

Papá didn't talk much during their time together, and this pleased Julia. He only asked her about her studies and about Ernesto: if he was studying much and what type of friends he was spending his time with. He would promise: In a couple of years I'm going to move to a new apartment and you can come live with me. If he would have suggested it a few years earlier, Julia would have rebelled at the idea of being separated from Mamá. But now she didn't care which one of them she lived with. The only advantage that Papá offered was his lack of conversation, on the other hand she felt safer with Mamá.

They were having breakfast in the café when Papá told her: Today we're going to have lunch over at my friend's house. Who? You don't know her. But she knows you. She met you at Don Julio's house, but you won't remember; her name's Eva.

On the radio, which the owner of the café had on as loud as it would go, they were announcing the songs that had won the contest in San Remo that year: "I'm Not Old Enough" and "That Night at Luna Park."

Eva lived all the way on the other side of the city, almost at the foot of the Tibidabo and very close to Ernesto's studio. She had a penthouse from which you could see all of Barcelona, from Montjuich to the Tibidabo. Eva, when she talked, moved her hands and smiled constantly. Her eyes were very big and her hair was dark. She invited them in, acting very pleased, and recognized Julia on the spot. Papá said: She's already in college prep classes. Well, in that case, we'll be seeing each other next year at the university.

Papá and Eva chatted nonstop during lunch. The dining room opened onto the patio and sunlight flooded in. It was spacious, decorated tastefully. On the white walls there were paintings that didn't represent anything specific, but Julia liked them. The antique furniture was gleaming with wax; the black leather armchairs and sofa, very comfortable. Julia sank into one of them while she followed Eva and Papá's conversation attentively.

They talked about the years when they had studied together and about old classmates. They kept asking each other: And what do you know about So-and-so? Well, I haven't seen him for years, but What's-his-name told me that . . . It's too bad you gave up your career, said Fva. And then Papá began to talk about Grandmother Lucía, Mamá, how difficult it is to find your way in life: When you get caught up in things, you think you can get out of it whenever you want, but in reality you're already lost . . .

Julia had the sensation that Papá's words were expressing bitterness and resentment, as if in the past he had bet his entire future on a single card, knowing that he was going to lose but incapable of resisting the crazy odds. Eva started to explain her plans for the future, and Papá interrupted her to continue commemorating their years at the university, disrupted by the war, the return to a more or less normal life, and then, capitulation. Papá added: It's so easy to do stupid things, to make mistakes. Compared to Eva, sure of herself, cold but cordial, Papá seemed like a teenager with gray hair and a wrinkled face.

Julia turned over in bed. Facing the balcony, she saw that it was beginning to get light out. She would have liked to go outside in her nightgown, barefoot, and walk, walk hours and hours through the deserted city, until the exhaustion, the cold and dampness, turned her into a motionless being, frozen, without sensation, capable of looking without seeing, of being without feeling, of listening without hearing.

Soon a new day would dawn, identical to the last one, monotonous, boring; and she would try to get through it as quickly as possible, trying to make use of anything, no matter how foolish, to distract herself, to make it shorter, to lose sight of how the hours were creeping by, interminably. In the morning, she wanted to close her eyes and open them again when afternoon came; in the afternoon she would prowl anxiously around the library, kill time by going out with Andrés, or, with a little luck, go to Eva's house. Like every day, she would suffer the disappointment of going home; she would have dinner as fast as possible to be able to go to bed, she would want to sleep, sleep, only sleep. Surely she would manage to get some rest at night, the night of the day that was now breaking. The exhausting insomnia she was currently suffering would be unlikely to repeat itself the next day. She frequently spent one or two nights awake, but on the third she would fall into bed exhausted and sleep twelve hours straight.

During those last hours of insomnia, she made an effort to resist Eva's image. Thinking about Eva caused her unbearable pain. She would be filled with despair. She had an urge to rip her sheets, tear up her blankets, grab an axe and destroy her furniture, open her drawers and fling objects out onto the street, onto any passerby who dared to flaunt his perfect tranquility, taking it out for a stroll while she struggled against the terrible and eternal absence that had always dogged her. When she thought about Eva, the fury she had restrained during the day took hold of her. She longed for Eva's presence more than anything in the world; to hear her voice, see how she moved her hands when she talked. She realized how poor and insignificant her desires were: to see Eva, listen to nice words come from her lips, nothing else. She wondered once and then a thousand times why she had to suffer over something that was so simple, so easy for everyone else. Her sole desire, absurd at her age, drove her to despair. It made the solitude that naturally surrounded her more obvious. Why should Eva stay by her side? Eva had her life, her concerns, her work, her friends; she, Julia, was nothing more than one student among two hundred, a student whose father had been Eva's friend, and to whom Eva, for that reason, had offered some friendship. Eva had felt pity toward her, protectiveness, when she recognized her at the university at the beginning of Julia's freshman year, feeling like a lost cat, ownerless, running from one side to the other, possessed by the craziness of not knowing her way around, curling up suddenly in a corner to try to find a reference point, only to throw herself once again into the frenzied race toward an unknown goal. Julia came to the conclusion that she had inspired Eva's compassion.

On the first day of the semester, when Eva, tall, thin, self-assured, entered the room where her Spanish literature class was about to begin, Julia had the premonition that she would leash herself to Eva like a lapdog. When she was calling roll and read Julia's name out loud, she raised her eyes from the sheets of paper she held in her hands and fixed her with a gaze. She sent her a fleeting half smile that disappeared from her lips in mere seconds, but it was enough so that Julia knew she had recognized her. At the end of class, Eva spoke to her. She asked about Papá, about Mamá, and before saying good-bye insisted a few times: Come see me if you need anything, if you have any problems with classes or with anything at all . . .

Eva's personality attracted Julia and frightened her at the same time. She admired Eva's self-confidence, the severe and rigid tone that she imposed in class, the coldness with which she treated her students, who didn't dare open their mouths or make comments during class. A few days were enough for them to realize that Eva wouldn't waste time giving out warnings and that if they annoyed her, she had no problem expelling them. She seemed hard, implacable. When she bumped into her in the hallway, courtyard, or cafeteria, Julia, for a few moments, questioned whether she should greet her or not; the truth is she didn't dare to, and she waited for her to take the lead. Eva smiled openly at her. How're things going for you? Do you like your major? I'm glad. Say hi to your parents for me. Julia responded in monosyllables and said good-bye quickly. Eva looked directly at her, and Julia felt stunned when it occurred to her that, by simply searching her eyes, Eva was aware of everything she harbored in her mind.

Some afternoons, alone at home, when she didn't feel like picking up a book to study or a novel to distract herself, it would occur to her that she could make up some excuse to go visit Eva. She would walk around the library for half an hour, considering the pros and cons of the projected visit and what she should say to her. When she made up her mind to call her and ask if she could come over, she would start worrying that Eva would respond with the coldness that she showed in class, and her plans would come crashing down. But she still didn't give up on the idea of the visit. She reminded herself that it had been Eva, after all, who had said she could go to her house whenever she wanted, and being Papá's friend and Don Julio's ex-student, she wouldn't dare receive her badly. The excuse could be anything related to her classes. She took the phone book, looked up Eva's number, lifted the handset, and hung it up again before dialing. She didn't dare. She was clumsy and cowardly enough that she didn't know how to tell lies or pretend, and Eva, intelligent enough to realize that any question posed about class was nothing more than a stupid excuse. She was afraid of behaving ridiculously in front of Eva and then not being brave enough to return to her class. The next morning, when Eva walked into the lecture hall at the university, the air itself would resonate with coldness and rigidity. Julia congratulated herself then for not succumbing to the temptation of calling her on the phone and exposing herself to a huge disappointment. However, if she ran into her in the hallway and Eva acted friendly, she would think that she had been a fool for wasting the previous afternoon in absurd digressions.

During her freshman year at the university, she barely opened her books. She only studied Eva's subject, to avoid making a bad impression. She would study the other ones when she was very bored or the day before the test. She had no interest in them.

In the morning she got bored going from class to class, walking through the courtyard or garden during her free time. At the university she met up with some of her classmates from the Institute, scattered by the admissions process into groups that were different from the multitude of groups they had formed the year before, and their relationship was limited to saying hello and questions like: Where does such and such class meet today? Can you lend me your notes from art class? Did he take attendance in Greek? She also met up with Carlos, her brother Rafael's old friend. Sometimes he would accompany her on her walks in the garden or sit by her side on a bench in the courtyard, and then she wouldn't be able to shake him off all morning. At the beginning she was bothered by Carlos's presence and by the fact that he took the liberty of telling her: Let's go have breakfast in the cafeteria. Or: We have an hour free, we can take a walk to the Ramblas. He called her on the phone some afternoons to invite her out for a drink. They would meet on Diagonal, close to where Julia lived. Do you feel like walking?, we can get away from this area, it's so bourgeois. For Carlos, getting away from the bourgeois neighborhoods meant walking to the Fifth District and having a glass of wine in some grimy bar.

Carlos was of medium height, extremely thin, very tan, and he was constantly biting his lower lip. He wore a navy blue three-quarter coat, black pants, and a black sweater almost year-round. When they arrived at a bar after a long walk, Carlos would take some folded sheets of paper out of his coat pocket and start reading poetry. It was the moment that Julia feared the most. Of the two hundred and fifty students, two hundred and forty wrote poetry and spent their mornings passing verses back and forth. Carlos's poems were identical to the ones written by the other two hundred and thirty-nine poets in their class: they dealt with God (pay attention to my goal here, Carlos would say. I mention God, but I destroy him, and he reread his discourse with great pride), with love (because even though I'm a revolutionary, I'm a romantic and I'm always in love with somebody), and with themes that he called social. Carlos considered his poetry protest poetry and claimed that he "destroyed everything." Julia was sick of God, of love "in the most liberal sense of the word, of course," of Andalucía's dry and arid plains, of the farmers and their hands, hard and calloused from so much toil, of the farmers' wives who cried at night because their children were dying of hunger, of the Vietnam War, of United States imperialism, of declarations of universal peace, of young people dying in wars without having enjoyed the pleasures of life, of hunger in India, of racial battles, and other related themes that two hundred and forty of the students in her class wrote poetry about. The poetry recital was followed by Carlos's opinions on bourgeois decadence, the revolution, freedom, socialist countries, the economy, the agrarian problem, and: Capitalism is an outrage.

Carlos bored her to tears and, at times, when he acted so sure of himself, of his intelligence, of his brilliant future, and of his certainty that he knew exactly what the world needed so that everything would work out, he drove her absolutely crazy. But she was prevented from rejecting Carlos's company by inertia, the nervousness which overwhelmed her when she stayed at home, and a lack of the courage needed to snub him. In the end, although he was rather foolish, Carlos was nice, and since he talked and talked, she didn't have to worry about coming up with anything to say to him.

Before, staying at home bored her; now it infuriated her. Papá had returned, and the simple presence of any member of her family made her tense. Papá's return resulted in an increase in the amount of power Mamá and Grandmother Lucía wielded, to do and undo whatever they wanted. When Papá left home and stopped managing the shirt and underwear factory, it began to falter, and Papá, after a while, began to complain about a lack of funds. As both Papá's finances and the situation at the factory got worse, they overheard long telephone conversations, preceded by Uncle Ricardo's meetings with Grandmother Lucía and Mamá, Papá's short visits to Grandmother Lucía and Mamá, and arguments between Mamá and her friend Antonio. One night, Papá, Mamá, Grandmother Lucía, and Uncle Ricardo locked themselves into the living room after dinner, and they didn't come out until almost morning. The next day, Julia found Papá having breakfast in the dining room with Mamá, Grandmother Lucía, and Ernesto.

Julia remembered hearing Grandmother Lucía say: It's impossible to keep up appearances for very long, and family scandals are always bad for business. She didn't remember anything else. She was overcome with shame and refused to listen any further. Mamá, Grandmother Lucía, and Ernesto seemed content, not because Papá had returned home but because they had won. Papá didn't act happy or sad. Julia, full of indignation, thought that Papá didn't even realize he had been defeated. Either way, it was a disaster for Julia, a concession for which she would never forgive him.

He hadn't simply given up; by letting himself be enslaved again he had tightened the chains around Julia's neck and, in the end, around Ernesto's too. From now on, she would have to fight not only against the two women but also against Papá and Ernesto. She wasn't brave enough to spit on them or slap them, hurl insults at them, and then let them lock her in a convent (like Grandmother Lucía threatened). She sat down at the table for breakfast, without knowing what to say or what expression to wear on her face. You look very pretty, Julia, said Papá. I've seen your cat, it's huge.

Petunia, the cat, had indeed become enormous. She spent the day sleeping or licking herself, in an armchair or in Grandmother Lucía's lap. She wasn't even her cat anymore. She remembered Porky, jumping out of the basket and running toward the mountains, and Don Julio's smile as he contemplated the cat that had recovered its freedom. For a while, Julia had thought about Porky a lot. Maybe he had died of cold or had been devoured by a wolf. But ultimately the cat had chosen his own destiny. Maybe she needed to jump, scratch, and protest like Porky had to free herself from the tension that, at times, wouldn't even let her draw a breath; but she didn't know if she would ever have the guts to do it. On the inside, she did. She shouted with indignation and shame, but no sounds came out of her mouth; she didn't know what to say or how to act, the fury kept accumulating, gnawing away at her insides, at her own being, not at anyone else. The only external manifestation of her rage was refusing to answer certain questions Mamá asked, not going to mass or saying the rosary with Grandmother Lucía, not taking care of her personal appearance, returning home at nine fifteen instead of nine, but without ever stretching the delay out until nine thirty, acting as unfriendly as possible when they had guests over for dinner, studying philosophy instead of law, biting her nails to irritate Mamá, and becoming physically ill (Mamá and Grandmother Lucía, since Rafael's death, had a rough time of it whenever they had to call a doctor). Simply small displays of rebellion; she didn't dare do anything more. She was afraid of Mamá and Grandmother Lucía, she fell silent, her feet nailed to the floor, when Mamá, shouting, reproached her delay past nine o'clock and began to shower her with questions: Where have you been? With who? Why not at five o'clock instead of nine?

In the end, letting herself be beaten by the police at the university was nothing more than a small protest against Mamá, Grandmother Lucía, and Papá.

Every morning after one of their classes, the course delegates would climb onto the platform and lead assemblies. Sometimes Julia, because of inertia, stayed in class during the assemblies; at other times, when they were debating the same old things, she would go out for a walk in the garden. If they dealt with anything important she would find out from Carlos, who had been more annoying that ever lately, with his ideas about the reform of bourgeois structures, social justice, freedom, the havoc reaped by capitalist imperialism, and "look at what's going on in Vietnam." The meetings would take place one after another, and Carlos would spend the day talking with different people, asking their opinions, and arguing about the situation at the university. The walls were full of posters, signs, and announcements about protests. They hadn't agreed to strike yet, but when the professors began their lectures, the classrooms were nearly empty because the majority of the students would stay in the courtyard or the cafeteria, talking about what was going to happen.

The day before, a few groups had demonstrated in University Plaza. When she went out on the street, she saw a large group of male and female students go by, running and shouting. Suddenly someone grabbed her arm and forced her into a clothing store. It was Carlos: Careful, Julia, they're going to arrest as many as they can. University Plaza was full of onlookers who were observing the stampede of students being pursued by the police force. Julia saw three squad cars parked in front of the university building. It's starting, a clerk in the store said. What do they want now? Oh, the same as always, vacations, what do you think they're going to want besides parties?, answered a woman who was picking out a sweater. Another one added: This is all the Communists' doing; they always find a few simpletons who listen to them and get caught up in it; a disgrace for the parents, a disgrace for the poor parents, nothing more nor less. They just don't want to study, added the clerk, that's their problem, if they had to work ten hours a day they would stop . . .

I'm going to stay, Carlos told Julia, and then he advised her: You go on home, it's better, girls don't know how to run, but if they catch you, don't worry; the worst they'll do is take you to Layetana Street, take down your name, and let you out later in the day.

They didn't arrest her and she regretted it. She imagined the displeasure that Grandmother Lucía, Papá, and Mamá would suffer if she didn't come home at lunchtime and they found out she had been arrested by the police during a student protest. Ever since the beginning of the demonstrations at the university, Papá had done nothing but warn them, her and Ernesto, not to get involved in anything, and he advised them: As soon as you see that things are getting tense, you two should come home. You never know what's going to happen in this kind of situation; but it won't be anything good, that's for sure. You students don't even know what you want, they manipulate you and you follow along like sheep. Grandmother Lucía blamed the Communists, Anarchists, and Masons. They're always the ones who want war, godless men who simply want bad things to happen to decent folks. You two just study, that's it, what're you going to get out of all of this? What do you care about politics? Your duty is to go to classes and study; leave the politics for the politicians. Around that time the son of one of Mamá's friends was arrested, and, judging by the proclamations made by Grandmother Lucía, Mamá, and Papá, that was the worst thing that could happen to a decent, honest family. Ernesto was tense and in a bad mood all the time. He was the School of Architecture's sports delegate and was very nervous. He was constantly bragging about his position and, faced with this new situation, he didn't see any way out. Papá and Grandmother Lucía insisted: You keep your nose clean and that's the end of it. I'm not going to submit my resignation now, they'll think I'm a coward, Ernesto argued. After all, I haven't done anything. Innocent people always pay the price for sinners, said his grandmother. Stay out of everything as much as you can, and as soon as there's any commotion, you come on home.

Observing Grandmother Lucía's words and Ernesto's fear, Julia began to laugh. You're a Communist, her grandmother shouted. You'll get messed up in something and bring disgrace down on all of us. And she threatened to lock her in the house and not let her go anywhere near the university until the demonstrations were over. Ernesto, when he was alone with Julia, asked her: What's going on in your part of the university? Nothing. What do you mean nothing? Have they arrested anyone? Nonsense, what do you think this is, war? No, but . . . , I'm afraid, maybe . . . I don't know what to do, would you resign? You're a chicken, Ernesto. I know, Sis, but since I'm the delegate I have to participate in the demonstrations, otherwise I look like an idiot, and if they arrest me . . . Papá and Grandmother Lucía will kill me. Julia laughed. Do you think they're going to elect you victim of the week because of your good looks? It's not funny, but . . . well, I'll manage.

One morning, the walls were more plastered with paper than usual. Enormous posters that could be read from any part of the courtyard hung from the second-floor handrails. After the first class, a boy went up on the platform, alongside a group of district delegates, to announce both the strike and a special assembly at midmorning in the university courtyard. The news was greeted with applause and whistles.

Carlos looked happy and energized. Wonderful, the university needs to be reorganized. Everything's going to turn out just perfectly. Julia, be careful, the police will probably show up today. The special assembly isn't authorized, but it's going to be held anyway. Let's go up to the second floor, we'll be able to hear better. You can see how great it is to listen to the delegates on the loudspeakers and see more than a thousand people crammed into the courtyard.

They could barely walk through the courtyard. They had to elbow their way through. The second floor was also full; students were packed along the handrails from which you could see the first floor. The uproar was deafening, and Carlos, in order to make himself heard, was shouting at Julia: If the police come in, don't start running, just stand still, up against the wall as if you're not involved, that way they won't use their billy clubs on you.

A voice came through the speakers asking for silence, and the special assembly was opened. The delegate had scarcely begun to announce that the strike had been declared in the entire university district when a threatening noise was heard, as if a mountain range had collapsed. The policemen appeared, clubs in hand, through the two doors leading into the courtyard and through the hallway on the second story. The voice that could be heard through the loudspeakers yelled: Everybody down, sit down on the floor. But nobody paid any attention to him. The students started running in every direction, getting in one another's way. The classrooms were shut and guarded, so they couldn't find a way out. Julia tried to cling to the wall and stay still like Carlos had recommended, but she found herself dragged along by the mass of students who were running from one side to another. Suddenly she was caught by a hard, dry blow to her back, executed with such violence that she fell to the ground. In their frenzied flight some students didn't have time to jump over her body, stretched out on the floor, and they stepped on her. Others, racing along, tripped over her, and still others fell on top of her. Lying on the floor, she raised her head and saw a group of policemen running by. She rested her forehead on the floor again. She tried to stand up but couldn't. She felt like her chest had been split apart, as if they had snapped her in two. She heard a confused rumbling of voices, and it seemed like the columns that stretched from the handrail up to the arches of the vaulted ceiling were very small and very far away. She tried to get up again. Everything was spinning around her. She got on all fours. She was wounded from her knees to the palms of her hands, she couldn't catch her breath, and she thought she was going to faint. She noticed that her lips were wet, she raised her fingers to her mouth and when she pulled them away, they were bloody; she had hurt herself when she fell. The pain of the blow she had taken on her back was unbearable. She was thinking she would never be able to get up, when someone grabbed her arm and quickly dragged her into the literature seminar room. Once she was inside she recognized Carlos and another student. You're such a fool!, exclaimed Carlos. How could you let yourself be dragged into that mob of idiots? If they hadn't started running, nothing would have happened.

In the seminar room there were two professors, Eva, a girl with a bloody leg, the seminar secretary with a first-aid kit in her hands, and a couple of students, besides Carlos and his friend, who had taken refuge there when they saw the police. The secretary began to dress the girl's leg, and Eva approached Julia with a flask of alcohol and another one with Mercurochrome. Let's see, what happened to you?, she asked. They broke my . . . everything: my back, my ribs, a leg . . . Eva began to laugh. It can't be that bad, she said. She soaked a cotton ball in alcohol and applied it to Julia's lips, while she said: Pull down your nylons, let's take a look at those knees. When the liquid poured over the cuts, she thought she was going to kick Eva, and Carlos and his friend, who were holding her legs.

Thinking about going home and the reception she would get

from Papá, Mamá, and Grandmother Lucía made her shake from head to toe. On the one hand, she felt satisfied when she imagined the great displeasure they were going to feel; on the other, she was terrified. She told herself they wouldn't talk about anything else for weeks, they wouldn't let her out of the house for at least a month, until they were certain that the university had returned to normal, they would kill her with their screams and sermons, and they might slap her. She understood Ernesto's claim that he was much more frightened of Papá and Grandmother Lucía than of anything else that might happen to him. She was scared too, not because of the police or the blows, but because of thinking about her family's violent reaction when they saw her come home limping and covered in Mercurochrome.

Eva seemed to read her thoughts. What are your parents going to say? They're going to kill me. It won't be that bad. Oh!, it sure will, said Carlos. And then he explained in front of everyone what had happened years before, one day when he went to pick her up at her house to go to the beach and Grandmother Lucía was rude to him. These bourgeoisie, they're so rotten with money, they deserve to be given a good lesson; I wouldn't save a single one of them, added Carlos. Eva laughed, showing white, even teeth, throwing her head back. Don't worry, she said. I'll go with you. Carlos seemed very pleased about what had happened. He went from one side of the seminary to the other, with his eternal black sweater and pants and his messy hair, biting his lips. He would argue with the professors who were discussing what had happened at a distance from the wounded students and then return to the spot where Eva was dispensing treatment and say: This is great, just great. I'd like to see your old lady's temper tantrum, this is going to scare her to death. Your family is old-fashioned, they give you issues you're going to have to learn to deal with. You're not from our side of the tracks, but today you behaved wonderfully, you've redeemed yourself... Leave me alone, exclaimed Julia.

She understood what motivated Carlos, Carlos's followers, and the people whose orders Carlos obeyed, whether they were Communists, Anarchists, and Masons, as Grandmother Lucía claimed, or troublemakers looking for a vacation, as was the opinion of the onlookers who formed groups around University Plaza when there was a demonstration, or young people who still don't know what they want, but at least they're motivated by something, and I'll bet something good comes out of it, as one of Papá's friends commented, proud of his tolerance and understanding of the kids. She understood the order given to the police to prevent the unauthorized assembly in the university courtyard, Carlos's indignation, and the violent reaction of the two professors against the students when they saw their teaching posts, their social position, and their families' daily bread endangered.

Carlos was arguing heatedly with the two professors, who exclaimed: Yes, we agree, but everything takes time, and with this type of uproar you don't get anything except a bad reputation and bad press. The valid ideas that you could all bring to the table, if you have any valid ideas, will be buried by this kind of uproar, what do you want to achieve? —and interrupting Carlos's words, added—: nothing, nothing, nothing, you have no idea; studying, that's what you should all be doing, studying, studying, and studying, everything else will come to you in time —and then, addressing Julia—, what've you gotten out of it?

Julia didn't respond. She didn't care what the two professors thought, or Carlos either. The only thing that mattered to her at that time was the beating she had received; the displeasure her family would feel, which she both anticipated and feared; and the presence of Eva, treating her knees. After a few moments another boy came in with a large, bloody bump on his forehead. Damn Communists, exclaimed one of the professors. Carlos was pleased that more people were wounded. Do us a favor and shut your mouth, the professor shouted at him; you, sir, are a Communist . . . You better watch out, I could sue you for slander, Carlos responded, irate. The door opened and a functionary and a police officer announced that they should vacate the room and that the streets were now open. I'll take you home, repeated Eva. Where do you live?

The courtyard and hallways were completely deserted, but the policemen had surrounded the building, and University Plaza was crammed full of people who were wondering what had happened. Some of them condemned "the students' disgraceful behavior," and others excused them: They must have their reasons.

Julia could barely walk. Lean on me, Eva told her. She didn't dare hang on her arm. Eva placed one hand behind her back, holding her up by the waist, and Carlos accompanied them to Eva's car.

Once they were on the road, Eva asked her if she was involved in something she shouldn't be. It doesn't matter to me, I'll tell your father that you were leaving the classroom and ran into the clash between the police and the students, they can't punish you for that.

She rang the bell. She was shaking from head to toe. At any moment the door would open and she could anticipate the reactions she would get from Papá, Mamá, and Grandmother Lucía. Eva patted her head. Don't be afraid, I'll take care of it. She didn't care about anything anymore; the more they shouted at her, the better. Suddenly she felt happy that she had let herself be beaten, and safe in Eva's presence.

Aurelia opened the door and screamed: Good Lord, they tried to kill her. Bad news twice in one day. Julia, without thinking, clung to Eva's arm; Eva smiled and winked at her. Papá and Mamá came to the foyer. Confronted by the presence of Eva, Papá was dumbfounded and Mamá turned red. Once they were in the dining room, Eva explained what had happened according to the story she had invented. Grandmother Lucía was crying nonstop and muttering from time to time: Dear Lord, forgive them for they know not what they do. Papá, very upset, said that just ten minutes before, one of his son's friends had phoned to inform them that Ernesto had been arrested. And in the School of Philosophy, added Mamá. If he studies architecture, do you want to tell me what business he had over in Philosophy? Making war, making war, that's what he was doing, exclaimed Grandmother Lucía. That's how he's wasted time all these years, sticking his nose into things that don't concern him. A disgrace, a disgrace for his poor grandmother. They're going to kill me between the two of them.

Julia spent three days in bed. Ernesto, when he got home, pale and frightened, didn't know how to apologize enough. Papá lost his temper, calling him a bad son. From bed, Julia heard her grandmother: Good God in Heaven, a traitor to the family, you'll be the end of us. Then her grandmother retired to her sanctuary, and the next day she had to stay in bed. From time to time she would call Ernesto and make him kneel down, beg for her forgiveness, pray, and recite an act of contrition out loud.

The second day she was in bed, Eva phoned to ask about Julia's condition, and Carlos and his friend came to visit her. Grandmother

Lucía didn't let them in. Ernesto told Julia what Grandmother Lucía and Mamá were saying: They think you got caught up in some mess, and that it was Eva who got you involved in it; they say Eva is entirely to blame. Julia, enraged, called Mamá stupid. You're not little enough for me to hit you, but you're still young enough that I have to take care of you, and I don't like Eva.

As soon as she could get out of the house, Julia made her way to Eva's without giving it a second thought. The aversion and dislike that Mamá and Grandmother Lucía felt toward Eva increased her desire to go visit her. She had called first. She thought Eva sounded pleased when she said: I'll expect you at five.

She received her warmly. Eva wasn't usually excessively affectionate, but when she addressed Julia her typical coldness and reserve disappeared. I knew you'd come, Eva said, smiling. The truth is, I've been expecting you since the beginning of the semester. Why?, asked Julia, surprised. I just knew it, Eva responded, looking at her intently and smiling. They had tea in the living room, the most spacious and luminous room that Julia had ever seen. Eva remained silent for some time, and Julia felt inhibited, without knowing what to say. She looked at Eva out of the corner of her eye and saw that she was observing her with curiosity and smiling, amused. Eva broke the silence, heavy and overwhelming for Julia, by asking her about her classes, her family, and if Carlos was her boyfriend. No, responded Julia. The question bothered her, she decided to leave, but then she told herself that she didn't have any reason to get irritated; after all, it wasn't an insult to assume she had a boyfriend. Her teaspoon fell to the floor, and Eva picked it up. Don't get mad, she said in an amused tone. It wouldn't be so unusual. Eva, somewhat ironic and irritated, criticized Julia's family and the way Mamá and Grandmother Lucía had reacted three days earlier. Julia was pleased by the harsh words Eva used to ridicule the members of her family, and she felt at peace with her once again.

After a while, Eva showed her into the room where she worked: it was spacious and also looked out onto a patio. There were shelves full of books on the four walls; in the middle of the room, a worktable covered with books and papers. Eva explained to her that she had a lot of work: class preparations, grading, collaborations about linguistics and Latin American literature in national and foreign journals, and two voluminous essays in progress: one about Villamediana's poetry and the other about Arab Andalusian poetry. What do you do in the afternoon?, Eva asked her. Do you work?

No. Do you want to help me?, I need somebody two or three afternoons a week.

When she left, satisfied and happy, the streets seemed small to her, as if she didn't have enough space to walk. She went down Balmes, from Tibidabo Avenue to Diagonal. She tried to go slowly to prolong the time it took to get home, but unable to control herself, she began to almost run with joy. The winter cold, which bit her skin and penetrated her bones, felt like a caress. She walked easily, without hearing the deafening roar of the traffic or getting impatient when she had to stop for a red light. She was hungry and went into a café, without experiencing the uncomfortable and lonely feeling that would overcome her at other times.

She got home at around a quarter to ten. She didn't pay any attention to Mamá's and Grandmother Lucía's exclamations and reprimands. She didn't even hear them. She was thinking about Eva, about the afternoon they had shared, and about her promise to call her very soon. Where have you been?, Mamá asked her, approaching hysteria when she found out about the visit to Eva and the job she had proposed. I forbid you to visit that . . . , shouted Mamá. Papá interrupted the argument: Enough. Eva is an intelligent woman; Julia can learn a lot from her. Then Mamá and Papá began to fight and, like usual, Mamá interrupted him: In things concerning my children, I'm the boss.

Eva let twenty days go by without calling. Julia spent her afternoons at home in case Eva called, as she had promised. During those twenty days she was restless and in a bad mood. Sometimes she would tell herself that Eva must be busy and at other times that she wouldn't call, that she had been pulling her leg. She didn't go out with Carlos for fear of missing the call, and she wandered through the library and the hallway, biting her nails. Finally, one morning, at the end of class, Eva came up to her: I'll be expecting you this afternoon at four, is that okay with you? As soon as she heard those words, the resentment that had accumulated for twenty days disappeared, and she told herself that Eva was the nicest, the most intelligent, and the best person she had ever met.

Julia remembered those days as the most peaceful time of her life. In Eva's office, the afternoons went by quickly, too quickly for her to be able to absorb the calm and security that surrounded her.

During the five hours she spent at Eva's house she stayed alert, without thinking about anything. She sat at the worktable, and Eva dictated to her. At other times she would help her read the students' exercises. Throughout the afternoon, Eva insisted on taking two or three breaks so they could drink something or chat. They rarely found themselves in situations that were uncomfortable because they weren't sure what to say; Eva had a thousand anecdotes to tell, and when she didn't, she asked Julia about her family. Eva often told her about Don Julio: What a great man your grandfather was; he was a force of nature. When she talked about Don Julio, Eva did so with respect and admiration, and Julia was grateful for it. She also liked to answer the questions that Eva asked her about herself. Eva expressed interest in Julia; although the questions intimidated her, Julia, deep down, felt satisfied, aware of her own existence: somebody, in this case Eva, noticed her and presumed that she, Julia, in spite of being much younger, had thoughts, opinions, life experience. What do you think about this book?, about that movie? I don't know. What? She forced her to think, reason, about something outside herself; Julia had to make an effort. A book or a movie simply was or wasn't to her liking, without any more to it than that; she liked them when they amused her, made her sad, or filled her with an oppressive and profound weariness toward everything; otherwise, they bored her. She had never asked herself if a movie was good or bad, or why she did or didn't like it. Eva made her understand the reasons. She made an effort, then, to think about her opinions, and in the end she learned, almost without being aware of it. When Eva subjected her to that type of question, in spite of its difficulty, she was happy. Until then, living had meant remaining isolated from everyone else, at the margin, in another world. Elaborating thoughts, opinions, would be absurd. She lived inside her head and, in there, nobody asked her anything. The thoughts, words, and images that she formed inside herself and directed at herself were beliefs, demonstrated certainties, and she simply accepted them or didn't, without any possibility of an argument, since she didn't share them with anyone else.

During those five hours, she remained alert, without thinking about anything except the work and the conversation, following Eva's gestures, her words, attentively. At night, alone in her room, she would try to remember everything that had happened that afternoon detail by detail, record it in her mind, and, in that way, prolong in her memory the hours that had passed in a flash. The afternoons with Eva were the continuation of a walk in the mountains in Don Julio's company, around the port with Rafael, or on a brief morning outing with Mamá; they were the continuation of a party abruptly interrupted many years before; a crazy open-air party, decorated with Chinese lanterns, where frenzied laughter floated up to a star-studded blue sky. A party that promised to last a lifetime but suddenly began to die out. It seemed to Julia that this lavish banquet had barely occupied a few seconds of her life. Little by little the Chinese lanterns started going out, the colored balloons lost their air; someone turned on the lights and the guests, stripped of their masks, understood that the blue sky, radiant, starless, was nothing more than a decoration. She understood their disillusion: the murmur of laughter was lost toward who knows where. She imagined it flying through the air, above the houses, cities, mountains, valleys covered with snow, rivers, and oceans, moving off toward a mysterious place inhabited by desires, illusions, dreams, everything that was lost and that never returned.

The afternoons with Eva were the continuation of an ancient and happy banquet that might never have existed; a gift she took as compensation for the boredom of the rest of her day. When she went to bed, she pretended not to be in her house but in Eva's; in the morning she wouldn't be woken up by Aurelia but by Eva. Classes would go by quickly; in the afternoon she would work with Eva, and, after dinner, she would go to bed under her roof.

She didn't say anything at home about these afternoons. She was afraid that Mamá and her grandmother would object to them, depriving her of her only pleasure. After lunch, seeing that Julia would leave in such a hurry, Mamá would ask: Where are you going so soon? I have to take notes in the seminary. Or: I'm studying with some girls. Mamá always asked her: With who? She made up names. If she made the mistake of giving the name of some girl who was the daughter of one of Mamá's friends, and Mamá investigated and discovered the lie, Julia excused herself by saying she had met up with Carlos and gone for a walk. Mamá didn't like Carlos too much, but she liked him more than Eva.

The mornings in class seemed less boring to her than before. Carlos acted surprised and almost offended that Julia didn't pay more attention to him, and in the morning, she avoided him. Julia was bothered by Carlos's presence; Eva might see them together and believe they were dating. The supposition wasn't ridiculous, but it annoyed her. Besides, Carlos was boring and pedantic. Come on, Julia, let's go out this afternoon, what are you going to do stuck at home? You have fun when we're together, don't you?; I'll wait for you at six. Julia would tell him over and over: No. It's your loss, Girl . . . It ate her up inside when she heard him say: Let's go have breakfast in the cafeteria, sure that she would go, or when he saved her a seat in class, next to him, without asking her if she felt like sitting with him. She didn't know why, but she was certain that Carlos believed he could control her. As soon as she caught sight of him, happy, carefree, and sure of himself, she felt irritated. She couldn't stand any contact with Carlos's hand when it happened to brush against her while they were walking. She understood he didn't do it on purpose, but she felt like slapping him anyway.

Do you have a boyfriend?, asked Carlos. Me? Yes, you, why not? Carlos seemed uneasy. No, exclaimed Julia. Then . . . why don't you want to go out with me like before? I got a job, I told you. If you tell me where, I'll wait for you when you get off. I don't want to tell you where; I don't like to have people wait for me, I don't like to say where I'm going or what I'm doing. She looked at Carlos out of the corner of her eye and saw that he had turned red and was biting his lower lip. She felt bad for responding rudely. Okay, okay, don't be like that, Carlos said. But . . . are you in love with someone? The questions drove her crazy, but she controlled herself. What nonsense!, she muttered. It's not nonsense, said Carlos. She felt Carlos's arm around her shoulders, and then the moist lips on her cheek. Carlos was breathing heavily. She tried to stand up, but Carlos's embrace trapped her on the bench for a few seconds. Fear paralyzed her. She wanted to get up, but it was impossible. Carlos's lips slid down her cheek, searching for hers. She felt the moist contact of Carlos's mouth pressing against her mouth, and her stomach heaved. She shoved him and began to run.

For the rest of the day she couldn't think about anything else. When she remembered it, her legs shook, her head burned, and her heart beat wildly. Her own body disgusted her. She rubbed her lips over and over with a handkerchief soaked in cologne. She told herself that a kiss wasn't important, that even if she had made love with Carlos, none of that was remotely important. But she loathed Carlos. She should have slapped him, scratched his face, his eyes, wrung his throat until he suffocated. But even the thought of touching Carlos to hurt him repulsed her. She wanted to minimize the importance of what had happened and not hate Carlos. But when she remembered the contact of his moist lips on her skin, she felt like screaming, kicking everything within reach to pieces.

That night she woke up with a terrified scream. She felt like she was being shut into a wardrobe, or a coffin, and that she would never get out. She couldn't breathe. Her heart was beating hard, or maybe it was stopping. She thought she could hear heavy breathing next to her bed. She turned on the light. As usual, there wasn't anybody there. She had dreamed that she was in Eva's house, sitting on the sofa in the living room, next to Carlos. She, Julia, was naked and Carlos was kissing her, caressing her body. In the dream, she was overcome by profound disgust, but she couldn't move. Suddenly Carlos's mother appeared. Julia had never met her, but she knew she was Carlos's mother, without knowing why. With no transition, the dream moved to another place: the counter top in a café. No station was visible and no train whistles could be heard, but Julia was certain she was in a train-station café. The counter in the café was very long, metal. The feel of it disgusted her. At the end of the counter she spotted Carlos and Papá. She didn't talk with them, but Carlos seemed mad at her. Papá was taking him on a trip. She was certain that Carlos was waiting for her to say something to him. Papá and Carlos left the café, and she did too. She found herself on an escalator. The railing was metal and, just like the counter at the bar, it disgusted her. Someone put a hand on her shoulder. She turned around, and it was Carlos's mother again, smiling at her.

When she woke up and remembered the nightmare, she realized, terrified, that Carlos wasn't Carlos but rather her dead brother Rafael. She decided never to see Carlos again, while, at the same time, an image came back to her: a beach, rocks, a sea urchin, the paddle boat floating on the sea. She looked at the clock: three o'clock in the morning. And without making any noise, she went into the bathroom to take a shower.

When the school year and classes were over, there were more obstacles than ever to prevent Julia from going to Eva's house in the afternoon. Questioned by Mamá and Grandmother Lucía, she couldn't use the excuse of studying with a group of girls or going to the library to take notes. It was useless to tell them lies, like she was going to the movies or for a walk with her friends. Mamá knew she had absolutely no friends. She had no choice but to form an alliance with Ernesto. Ernesto accepted, obligated in some sense. He assumed that Julia was aware of certain rather unpleasant facts about him. Over the course of that year, Mamá had insisted on finding a girlfriend for Ernesto. A nice-looking girl, from a good family, good breeding, in short, with class. Every day, at lunchtime, the daughters of Mamá's friends were paraded by. Ernesto moaned: Mamá, I'm too young to get engaged. You're twenty-eight years old, you could be married by now. Mamá failed several times. Ernesto would make excuses: Mamá, that girl was an idiot. Or: She's vulgar. Or: I don't like her. But then Mamá, through the mother of the girl of the day, would find out that she had been the one who had dropped Ernesto. Mamá complained: I don't understand it, a handsome boy, intelligent, with a brilliant future . . . Mamá didn't understand it, but Julia did. And Ernesto knew it. That's why he accepted the deal his sister made. Three days a week, after lunch, he would invite her to a movie, or to go out with friends, or over to his studio to show her a new painting and some recently acquired books. They would leave the house at the same time and, once they were out on the street, separate.

During the summer, Andrés appeared at Eva's house. He was preparing for exams to become a teaching assistant in the Spanish Department, and Eva was helping him. Julia didn't particularly like or dislike him. I know your brother, said Andrés. He spoke quietly and very slowly. When they were both at Eva's house, Andrés would leave at the same time Julia did and invite her for a drink. The walk home would seem endless to her.

One afternoon, at the beginning of August, when they split up, Ernesto told her: When you come back, tell them I'm not having dinner at home, I'm going out with some friends. That night, when she returned, it was Mamá who opened the door for her instead of Aurelia. She didn't even have time to feel surprised. Where were you? I just left Ernesto, he's going out with . . . Mamá pinched her lips together. Julia, disconcerted, saw that Mamá's hands and nostrils were trembling. She felt two slaps across her face. Liar. Mamá grabbed her arm and dragged her into the dining room, where Ernesto was pacing nervously from one side to another. I'm sorry, Sis: I told you they'd find out. Ernesto and his friend had bumped into Mamá on the way out of the theater that afternoon, and they had to explain to her why Julia wasn't with them. You've been lying to me for almost a whole year now, Mamá shouted. But this is the end of it. You're not going to take one single step out of this house by yourself for as long as I live. And now you're going to give me the phone number of that woman, it was a shameful maneuver. Papá, who had remained silent, objected. You don't need to call anyone. You're the one who's guilty, you forced Julia to lie. Papá and Mamá began to argue. They brought up the way Papá had abandoned the family, Antonio, the shirt and underwear factory, money . . . Mamá complained about Julia, comparing her with Ernesto: She's strange, no one can stand her, if she lied to me about going to that woman's house, she's certainly done so about other things too, how am I ever going to trust her again? Next year we'll send her to school in Pamplona. The number of things she must have been up to without you two even being aware of it, said Grandmother Lucía. I always said you didn't educate her properly. It was wrong to ignore God's wishes and not send her to a religious school . . . and on top of that, the university, what's a girl going to learn at the university? To misbehave, to misbehave and nothing else.

Julia didn't respond. She staggered down the long hallway. Her legs were shaking and tears clouded her vision. She locked herself into the living room to call Eva, who had no idea that Mamá had been unaware of Julia's visits to her house. She had to warn her, otherwise she'd be dumbfounded, not knowing how to respond to Mamá's shouting and accusations. She needed to call her and tell her what had happened. Somebody had to be informed about this injustice, about the atmosphere of cruelty and misapprehension that surrounded her and would end up suffocating her. Eva's voice, on the phone, was dry, sharp. Hello, Julia. I can't talk to you now, I'm having dinner with a few friends. Call me tomorrow. And she hung up. She dialed the number again, with trembling fingers. She had to tell Eva what had happened, but Julia heard the cold, almost unpleasant voice again: I told you that I have work to do, is there some problem? Don't be a pest. I'll call you tomorrow. Good night.

She thought she would never be able to stand up again. She rested her head on the back of the chair. The ceiling became more and more distant; Julia was falling little by little into a profound and dark well whose sides, covered by filth and grease, were getting narrower and narrower. Her entire body was screaming Eva's name in a stifled sob that she struggled to restrain. Someone opened the door. She thought she saw Ernesto and heard something confusing. I'm sorry, Julia. The way these damn fools carry on. And she didn't understand anything else. She was sinking, the emptiness and darkness were swallowing her up by the second. She would get revenge, she needed to make them suffer. She hated Mamá, Grandmother Lucía, Papá, Ernesto, Eva, and she hated herself for not having the courage to go back to the dining room, where Mamá's screams were coming from, and slap them all, saying: I'll do whatever I want. I'm sick of all of you, sick of you sticking your noses into my business; I detest you and I won't put up with any more of your contemptible attempts to control me. She was running desperately toward an insurmountable wall that retreated as she advanced. She would never be able to knock it over or run in the other direction.

Ernesto continued hurling insults at the family, reproaching their cowardice. But she didn't listen to him. She got up, left the room. She walked slowly, her body was made of lead. When she passed in front of the mirror, she saw that she was pale, disheveled. She looked like a ghost. She felt like she was asleep and living a nightmare. If she could have managed to talk to Eva, to make herself heard... She went into Mamá's bedroom and picked up a bottle of pills; then she did the same thing in Grandmother Lucía's room. Her hands and legs were shaking. As she gulped down the water, the knot in her throat came undone.

She went into her room and, without turning on the light, lay on the bed. She wasn't afraid of the darkness, the blackness that often fooled her into seeing imaginary ghosts. She wasn't afraid of the darkness or of being alone in her room. Nothing mattered to her. She was only afraid of the stupid, absurd action that she had just committed. Something gnawed on her insides: even at that moment it horrified her to think about the reaction Mamá, Papá, and Grandmother Lucía would have. Now she wouldn't hear their screams, their accusations. She was taking revenge on them and at the same time on herself, on her cowardice. She had imagined that action many times, delighting in it. She was surprised: it was as simple, absurd, and contradictory as she had planned it. It even seemed less real than in her old thoughts. For some moments she doubted; maybe she had gotten carried away by her crazy imagination, and in reality nothing was going to happen to her. She wanted to go outside, walk silently, breathing very deeply, walk, walk, walk to the docks, inhale the fresh sea breeze and lie on a bench while losing herself in a calm, refreshing sleep.

Aurelia's voice came to her from very far away: Come on, Julia. It's after eleven. Everyone's had dinner already. She didn't respond. Someone took her by her shoulders, forcing her to her feet, but she collapsed back onto the bed.

The brightness hurt her eyes. The light flooded in through the window and intensified the whiteness of the tiles that covered the walls of her room. She closed her eyes. The pain of a needle prick in her arm startled her. Her pulse, pounding inside her head, prevented her from raising it. Her body ached, especially the nape of her neck, her jaw, her eyes, and her stomach. She had the vague sensation that her head had gotten monstrously large and that her stomach was full of holes. She could barely open her eyes. Papá was sitting next to the bed. She remembered, as if in a dream, that she had thrown Mamá out of the room, but she didn't have any idea of the amount of time that had elapsed since then. She felt sorry for Papá. She sank back into a profound sleep. When she woke up, Mamá was pacing through the room, and the clicking of the high heels startled her. Mamá stared at her, with a stern expression and red eyes. I'll never forgive you for the pain you've caused us, she said. Julia observed Mamá: she had been to the beauty parlor and was dressed as elegantly as ever. She didn't respond. Ernesto said: Look, Sis, you're in the paper, in the crime and accident reports. Grandmother Lucía ripped the newspaper out of Ernesto's hands: What shamelessness, you've committed the worst sin there is against God, you've condemned yourself forever. Julia began to scream. She was unable to restrain the insults that came flying out of her throat. A nurse came in and threw her grandmother and Ernesto out of the room. From now on you can do whatever you want, said Mamá. But if you get into trouble or have any problems, don't count on us. She fell asleep again. She slept restlessly, constantly rolling over in bed. She was hot and had an unbearable headache. Mamá was caressing her hair. Julia saw that her eyes were full of tears. When you were little, Julia, you loved me, you just wanted to be with me, you followed me around everywhere like a puppy dog, and when I left you at home, you waited on the balcony for me to come back . . . now you don't . . . I'm not a child anymore, Julia interrupted. She thought: I'd give my life to be able to be one again, to love you like I did, to follow you around everywhere like a lapdog . . . But she said: I'm tired. She was filled with an immense sorrow, she felt like crying, but she waited until Mamá left the room, until they had finally all left her alone.

She turned toward the window, and the light hit her eyes again; she closed them. She heard the continuous ticktock of her watch, abandoned on the nightstand. She thought that hours could go by, months, years, from that moment on, with no objection from her. She wouldn't even notice the passage of time. Something essential in her had fled. She felt empty. She tried to sit up to put her watch away in the drawer. She couldn't. She imagined she could get up, hide her watch, and approach the window. But in reality her body didn't obey. It didn't even occur to her to place the palms of her hands on her bed to sit up. She had forgotten that to walk to the window she had to move the blankets out of the way first, pull her feet out, put them on the floor, and stand up. She couldn't coordinate her movements. She was afraid she had become paralyzed from the neck down. She wanted to sleep, but confusing, suggestive images kept popping into her head, overwhelming her with anxiety. Dark fragmentary scenes, Mamá with red eyes and Papá pacing nervously. An unbearable pain in her skull prevented her from concentrating and remembering what had happened in the last hours. She pressed her face into the pillow. She tried to remember something, the reason for the strange sensation of emptiness, nonexistence. She breathed deeply, trying to relax. With her eyes closed, she let the images invade her mind little by little. First, she saw only darkness. Curled up against her pillow, she felt small, as if her body had shrunk in half. She noticed that her arms and legs were short, her head small. She tried to remember what had happened, the last events she had witnessed, the last image her eyes had contemplated, the last words heard, the last sensation felt before that absolute silence, the great void. She wasn't dead, but she was stretched out in a hospital bed, blind and paralyzed, without thoughts, without memories, without desires. She didn't exist, she had suffered a great defeat, and they had exiled her to a place with no name, unknown, outside of everyone else's time and space. She pressed her face against the pillow; thick blackness filled her memory. The day before, she just wanted to remember the day before. And then she saw herself the way she was, the way she had always felt. Little Julia appeared in her mind. Little Julia, with the eternal shorts and navy blue sweater with an anchor drawn on the chest. She didn't come to her through time, through her memory; little Julia came out of her insides, out of herself. She had always been there, crouched in the mysterious corners of her being, in the forgotten shadows of her mind, waiting for an opportune moment to attack and defeat her. Fifteen years hadn't gone by, nothing had transpired. Little Julia remained in the doorway of the summer house, waiting, patient, certain to continue waiting fifteen, twenty years more, her whole life. Julia —she knew it now— had never existed. It was little Julia who, at five years old, forced her to be bored all day long, to be afraid at night, to reject the presence of Andrés, Carlos, Papá, Víctor, to be uninterested in classes, to protect herself from the other students, to desire the presence of Eva, Aunt Elena, or Señorita Mabel with the hope of continuing an interrupted party that would never again be resumed. Only little Julia had existed during those fifteen years, of which nothing, absolutely nothing, remained. She, little Julia, small, thin, barefoot, and with her braids undone, was erasing it all with her presence. She was getting revenge by reappearing now, after so much time. Julia, in the end, understood the trap laid by little Julia, her revenge. Almost physically, she felt little Julia's fingers ripping off her mask, her twenty-year-old mask. She understood little Julia's intention immediately: from the doorway of their summer house little Julia would drive her down the narrow, sunny streets to a corner of a solitary beach. She would make her feel the sun beating down, sliding over her skin once again, and an ancient pain inside her body. She blamed her for abandoning her there; the ignorant arrogance of believing she could go on living without her. She would drag her down the length of the immense beach and then abandon her in a deserted house, whose inhabitants were elsewhere —at a place from which she had been permanently excluded— enjoying a beautiful and wild party that was over for her. Little Julia told her about a strange and unforgettable party that had lasted merely five years of her life and of which Julia could only remember the ending. A party for the others, celebrated in an immense garden, as immense as the world, decorated with Chinese lanterns, where some people challenged others with games, words, laughter, and dreams. A party that promised to last her whole life and from which little Julia had been excluded without knowing why. A lavish, never-ending party in which everyone, except Julia, participated.

She felt drained, defeated, tied to the hospital bed with a thousand cords. They had won. The wire netting that separated her from the world, from reality, was growing and growing. The ceiling seemed to rise up quickly, while she felt herself sink toward the dark depths, where little Julia was dragging her. She had tried to kill little Julia, and little Julia was the only one left. An oppressive drowsiness began to invade her. Before she fell asleep, she thought that maybe some day she would be able to win, and it would be her, Julia, who would drive once again to the beach's solitary rocky point, approach the sea, lie on the sand, and dream without fear, for the first time, about a beautiful party that awaited her somewhere. But she realized suddenly, with an absolute, relentless certainty: from that moment on, telling lies would be absurd, unnecessary. She had tried to kill little Julia, and little Julia was the only one left, she was the only one left anymore.

She turned toward the window; the light poured in and intensified the whiteness of the tiles that covered the walls of the room. An offensive brightness hurt her eyes. Little Julia had won, and she was there, small, alone, with the shorts and a navy blue sweater with an anchor drawn on the chest. She had lived for years in an unchangeable, motionless world, outside of time. And from there she would return, she would always return to remind her that she wasn't dead.

Dawn was breaking. Julia looked at the clock. It was almost six in the morning. In two hours she would hear Maruja's footsteps down the hallway. She would come in, without asking permission, and exclaim: Julia, it's eight fifteen, come on, get up, I had a terrible nightmare, I bet you anything I'm going to fight with my boyfriend today, I dreamed about cats, that's bad.

At a quarter to nine, Andrés would pick her up to take her to school. She would go to class. At ten Andrés would pretend to bump into her so they could have breakfast together. At eleven she would go to another class, at twelve she would take a walk. At two Andrés would wait for her to take her home again. In the afternoon, if Eva invited her, she would go to her house; otherwise, Andrés would call her on the phone at seven: I worked all afternoon, what do you think about me swinging by to pick you up so we can go for a walk? At ten she would eat and go to bed.

She only wanted to sleep, sleep, ten, twelve, as many hours as possible. Every day was the same for her, monotonous. The world that surrounded her, an unreal space where other people seemed to live an existence that was completely different from her own.

It was now daylight. Why should she get out of bed? Why not use the excuse of some illness and stay in bed all morning, all day, every day? The light began to come in through the balcony. The shadows seemed to move in the corners of the room. And there she was. Like every morning, little Julia had returned, little Julia, sitting in the doorway of a house, small, thin, barefoot, her braids undone, the shorts and navy blue sweater with an anchor drawn on the chest, looking down, staring at two stones that she was pounding together. She had spent so many years sitting in that doorway that she had gotten old there; she had had time to mature, to become conscious that she could twist Julia around her little finger. She had become a persecuting god, a god who demanded continuous sacrifices to calm her ancient pain. Julia knew that, like every morning, little Julia would order her no, today you're not getting up, you're not getting out of bed ever again, you're sick; or, yes, get up, start a new day, a monotonous day, boring, unreal. And she would obey, because little Julia would never forgive her for abandoning her in a motionless universe, outside of time, in whose shadows she would always struggle and from which Julia could never ever rescue her.

Barcelona, August–September 1968
Barcelona, 1991 (second version)

IN THE EUROPEAN WOMEN WRITERS SERIES

Artemisia
By Anna Banti
Translated by Shirley D'Ardia Caracciolo

Bitter Healing
German Women Writers, 1700–1830
An Anthology
Edited by Jeannine Blackwell and Susanne Zantop

The Edge of Europe
By Angela Bianchini
Translated by Angela M. Jeannet and David Castronuovo

The Maravillas District
By Rosa Chacel
Translated by d. a. démers

Memoirs of Leticia Valle
By Rosa Chacel
Translated by Carol Maier

There Are No Letters Like Yours: The Correspondence of Isabelle de Charrière and Constant d'Hermenches
By Isabelle de Charrière
Translated and with an introduction and annotations by Janet Whatley and Malcolm Whatley

The Book of Promethea
By Hélène Cixous
Translated by Betsy Wing

The Terrible but Unfinished Story of Norodom Sihanouk, King of Cambodia
By Hélène Cixous
Translated by Juliet Flower MacCannell, Judith Pike, and Lollie Groth

The Governor's Daughter
By Paule Constant
Translated by Betsy Wing

Trading Secrets
By Paule Constant
Translated by Betsy Wing
With an introduction by Margot Miller

Maria Zef
By Paola Drigo
Translated by Blossom Steinberg Kirschenbaum

Woman to Woman
By Marguerite Duras and Xavière Gauthier
Translated by Katharine A. Jensen

Hitchhiking
Twelve German Tales
By Gabriele Eckart
Translated by Wayne Kvam

The South and Bene
By Adelaida García Morales
Translated and with a preface by Thomas G. Deveny

The Tongue Snatchers
By Claudine Herrmann
Translated by Nancy Kline

The Queen's Mirror
Fairy Tales by German Women, 1780–1900
Edited and translated by Shawn C. Jarvis and Jeannine Blackwell

The Panther Woman
Five Tales from the Cassette Recorder
By Sarah Kirsch
Translated by Marion Faber

Concert
By Else Lasker-Schüler
Translated by Jean M. Snook

Slander
By Linda Lê
Translated by Esther Allen

Hot Chocolate at Hanselmann's
By Rosetta Loy
Translated and with an introduction by Gregory Conti

Daughters of Eve
Women's Writing from the German Democratic Republic
Translated and edited by Nancy Lukens and Dorothy Rosenberg

Animal Triste
By Monika Maron
Translated by Brigitte Goldstein

Celebration in the Northwest
By Ana María Matute
Translated by Phoebe Ann Porter

On Our Own Behalf
Women's Tales from Catalonia
Edited by Kathleen McNerney

Memoirs of a Courtesan in Nineteenth-Century Paris
By Céleste Mogador
Translated and with an introduction by Monique Fleury Nagem

Dangerous Virtues
By Ana María Moix
Translated and with an afterword by Margaret E. W. Jones

Julia
By Ana María Moix
Translated by Sandra Kingery

The Forbidden Woman
By Malika Mokeddem
Translated by K. Melissa Marcus

Absent Love
A Chronicle
By Rosa Montero
Translated by Cristina de la Torre and Diana Glad

The Delta Function
By Rosa Montero
Translated and with an afterword by Kari Easton and Yolanda Molina Gavilán

*The Life of High Countess
Gritta von Ratsinourhouse*
By Bettine von Arnim and
Gisela von Arnim Grimm
Translated and with an
introduction by Lisa Ohm

The Life and Adventures of Trobadora Beatrice as Chronicled by Her Minstrel Laura A Novel in Thirteen Books and Seven Intermezzos
By Irmtraud Morgner
Translated by Jeanette Clausen
With an introduction by Jeanette Clausen and Silke von der Emde

Nadirs
By Herta Müller
Translated and with an introduction by Sieglinde Lug

Rosie Carpe
By Marie NDiaye
Translated by Tamsi Black

Music from a Blue Well
By Torborg Nedreaas
Translated by Bibbi Lee

Nothing Grows by Moonlight
By Torborg Nedreaas
Translated by Bibbi Lee

The Museum of Useless Efforts
By Cristina Peri Rossi
Translated by Tobias Hecht

Bordeaux
By Soledad Puértolas
Translated by Francisca González-Arias

Candy Story
By Marie Redonnet
Translated by Alexandra Quinn

Forever Valley
By Marie Redonnet
Translated by Jordan Stump

Hôtel Splendid
By Marie Redonnet
Translated by Jordan Stump

Nevermore
By Marie Redonnet
Translated by Jordan Stump

Rose Mellie Rose
By Marie Redonnet
Translated by Jordan Stump

The Man in the Pulpit Questions for a Father
By Ruth Rehmann
Translated by Christoph Lohmann and Pamela Lohmann

Abelard's Love
By Luise Rinser
Translated by Jean M. Snook

Why Is There Salt in the Sea?
By Brigitte Schwaiger
Translated by Sieglinde Lug

The Same Sea As Every Summer
By Esther Tusquets
Translated and with an afterword by Margaret E. W. Jones

Never to Return
By Esther Tusquets
Translated and with an afterword by Barbara F. Ichiishi